FRAGILITY

MOSBY WOODS

MGC

Morris Gordon Cheats Press
"Raphèl mai amècche zabì almi."

ISBN: 9798770810417

MosbyWoods@pm.me

"We live between the fingers of a
giant graven image!"

Abram Tertz (Andrey Sinyavsky), quoting another
prisoner in a letter to his wife from the Soviet gulag
(1966-1971), *A Voice from the Chorus,* 1973

1.

Whenever discouraged, I'd shuffle past my stacks of dictionaries to the window. If that huge pile of books crushed me to death, I'd only have *my shelf* to blame. What word does the dictionary spell *wrong?* I don't know, but I schtupped your mother. I slid the window down, and pushed my head out the gap. Why did I have opinions? Why did I find things funny? The coronavirus pandemic had shut down the joke industry. Nobody had walked into a bar in months.

Some day the pandemic will end. And when that day comes, you'll smirk at the memory of how we behaved. You'll laugh about the

COVID-19 fears we had... Not every one of you, of course.

And so I breathed in the scent of leaves. I'd look past the branches of my fruitless pear tree, and cast my sense beyond. My dictionaries told me that our English word *opinion* rose from the ancient proto-Indo-European prefix *op,* which means, "to choose." Is truth a choice? Here's another opinion: the earth used to be flat... Until they buried yo' mama.

This night, down below, I heard the wet footfalls of two individuals. Their masks reduced the pair's breathing to a series of puffs.

I listened for the articulations of the city over my porch roof. To rid myself of feelings I sung, "ptum, ptum, ptum." The word "feel" comes from the Greek "psallein," to pluck a harp. I swallowed the wet air. I breathed in the truth and exhaled the lies. After I began to cough on some of the gray areas, I pulled back.

I hadn't heard my new guests knock. They introduced themselves, Zoë and Tom Archon, sister and brother.

They stood a pair in traditional gender conforming clothing, as I had learned to say, posed in the doorway. Who wishes to intrude on secrets of the flesh? Each carried an umbrella. They had modest, thoughtful faces – as much as

I could tell above the masks covering nose and mouth.

Zoë was a tall woman, with red lipstick, a pearl necklace, pleated skirt, and flower pin. With latex gloves, she took my smartphone. My smartphone's passcode she already knew.

As she searched through my phone, Tom, too, peered, over her shoulder. In a leather jacket, he was small and slight of frame. A long chain looped from his battered jeans. He had folded up the bottom hem to show his boot buckles. Tom looked up knowingly.

I trembled. The First Amendment called: It

told me I need to have my own opinions and stop agreeing to everything! I agreed.

The twins started to search my text messages. Fortunately, I knew better than to implicate my friends, to risk their jobs for what I said. I had been self-censoring for years.

One contact tried to escape…unbraided, it fell on the floor. It wriggled its letters like centipede legs. It righted itself and tried to scurry away. The woman crushed it with a twist of her stiletto heels.

Meanwhile, Tom took pictures of the pictures on my walls, the baubles of my travels on my kitchen windowsill, the titles of old paper books on my shelves, the half empty bottle of antibacterial gel, my nieces' artwork yellowing on my fridge.

Sharp-eyed, he ran his finger along my dictionaries. With a grunt, he called Zoë over. As they examined my dictionaries, me too, they judged — my body, my gestures, my behavior, my aptitudes, and my achievements.

I felt naked, exposed, and humiliated. It reminded me of when I invented the word "plagiarism." Shame warmed my ears and neck. I asked, "Are you cancelling me?"

The two breathed out slowly and looked down. With jokes that asserted a faith in fixed definitions, I increased the suffering in the world. What justice awaited someone like me? It surprised me to discover that I was glad my doom arrived. I felt relief.

2.

"Even in laughter the heart may ache," says the Proverb. I didn't like to hurt people's feelings, but if the joke was funny, didn't that signify? Was it futile to share a laugh at the nonsense, such as women didn't bear children, but "birthing persons" did?

Yo' *birthing person's* so poor, the ducks throw bread at her?

No. Ducks won't. It's not true.

When Joey Half-Pint writes to Santa that he wants a little brother for Christmas, will Santa write back, "Okay. Send me your *birthing person"*?

No, Santa will not. It's a lie.

It made me uncomfortable if my jokes sometimes felt rude. The definition of *mean* included both "sense, opinion" as well as "cruel, rude." Was it cruel when I wisecracked about a real problem? By definition, men don't have a womb. It's not an opinion, but a fact. Unfortunately, that fact was my opinion.

Finally, the woman officiated, "We consider you an ally, Mr. Ketman."

I can't even tell you how frustrated this made me. This was like the time I found out that *aarghh* is not a real word.

12

"We noted that you deleted your thought after expressing it," Tom explained. He held up an old dictionary from my shelf. A relic of civilization, it was ragged, its spine broken.

Zoë, accepting it from her brother, fingered through it.

Tom continued, "You doubted yourself. You listened to us."

His sister looked up from a page of Ls. "We can trust someone who capitulates to us more than anyone else." The dictionary suddenly split in two and fell left and right out of her hands to the floor.

13

I staggered. I felt their declaration scrub me. A large nubby towel of aggression, the statement of alliance scoured off the difference. It ideologically smoothed my public protuberance of discomfort. They soothed me. They affirmed that I was good. They knew I was kind and didn't mean it. I felt strangled with a strange emotion.

Zoë scrutinized me. "What's that hideous face he's making?"

"He won't let himself cry," Tom observed. "You're going to break, man."

Something flashed. A fissure appeared. The near wall faded, paled, disappeared. Through this transparent matter, I looked out and saw my city, Portland.

Churches and office buildings rose like mushrooms. Glass curtain walls, stucco, vinyl panels, brick, all connected by wires, looped, knotted, nested, coiled... They were the cables and fibers of an enormous brain. Restaurants wired to condominiums tied to offices, hair salons, gardens, and the art museum. The zoo and motley apartments slung loose to the antique towers of bridges, draw, lift, and arch. Synapses flickered and swayed.

A shape rose. A dome rose... slowly... a bald head... a thought-furrowed forehead... then rose two transparent circles... No, a pair of giant lenses... they moved upward. Each lens distorted the eye behind it. The glasses lifted and with it, a masked face. Was he real? Certainly, in a sense. He just formulated out of the atmosphere.

It was the face of the Masked One. I tried to take it all in: the bald head, so meaningfully hairless. The cold metal frame glasses, the intense eyes through the mask.

The Masked One's face was not unkind. Calmly he spoke, — with a French accent, slightly muffled: "The gaze that sees is the gaze that dominates." That was his introduction. He looked at me now. "My job is to make windows where there were once walls."

3.

Now, the Masked One raised his arms.

The face in the April sky parted the rain like an umbrella. The twelve bridges rippled across the Willamette River. The drops fell on the streets and houses. It softened them and made them permeable.

The city opened like a loaf of bread. You could see the crumb of the loaf, the slices of cozy row houses and people tossed in bed, alone or together. Heavy men puckered like babies. Their large wives smirked over a secret. They breathed evenly. Their bodies rose and fell toward the yellow-silver light of early dawn.

The light reflected on the Masked One's shaven head.

There were no crafts for sale at the downtown Saturday Market. It was closed.

The Masked One shook his head and pointed elsewhere.

One woman bent in the middle of her work. Now she stood at the window, and opened it. She looked out at the pandemic city.

My dictionary told me that the 'pan' of 'pandemic' meant 'all'. I replied, is that *pan?* The 'dem' part of *pandemic* comes from 'people'. So *pandemic* could be more clearly called *panpeoplic.*

She was one of the *panpeoplic*.

Into my ear the Masked One murmured.
"You must follow her. Basil DeKay." He
pronounced her name *duh-KAY-yuh*. "She is
your hero. Follow her through her work, her
family, her dreams. Defend her. Exalt her!"

The woman looked out at the world with
fluffy, professional hair. She stretched out to the
city. She reached to exhort, or perhaps to
strangle. "Man," she pronounced. Was she
perhaps about to say, *"Man was born free, and
he is everywhere in chains?"*

We listened. "Maaan," she drew out, and
"Man-n-n-nnn." It became evident that this, a
first utterance, would be profound. Would it be,

19

perhaps, *"Man is least himself when he shows his face. Give him a mask, and he will tell you the truth."*

What would the full thought be? Finally she shattered all speculation: *"Mandatory!"*

Against this blast we leaned back, then leaned forward again. For she had more to say.

"Galvanize," she pronounced carefully, relishing the consonants more than the vowels, in particular the Z. "Motivate. Propel. Pro-o-o... pell-ll-ll..."

It was not possible to hear everything. The city's night murmur rose and fell. A freight train woo-wooed. An airplane buzzed. A poor wretch cursed his phantoms. It was sometimes hard to know what phrases came from DeKay's mouth, and what came from the landscape:

Dentity… Onouns… On Inary…
Cuse – Oxic – Pology –
Anceled.

And then came another rush of DeKay: "Our vibrant community." She calmed herself, and, just for exercise, experimented changing the stress on an important word: *Mod*-ule. Mod-ule? … Mod-djuh-yule…" Soothed, she was ready to strike: *"Problematic!"*

A moment passed, as we took this in. The Masked One and I turned to each other again. He was about to speak. But then he stopped, and turned back to her, for yes, she had more to say:

"Uniqueness," she called. "Belongingness*ness.*"

Suddenly she jolted, and reached to pull on a KN95 mask. Thus she faded into the distance. The city drew back with her.

The Archon twins folded their umbrellas and began to collect my dictionaries. Tom piled them in Zoë's arms. Then he grabbed his own pile. Unsure of right and wrong, I said nothing.

The Masked One intoned a command:

"Power creates a hero. Don't make her the subject of your story. Give her power! Make

21

yourself her subject."

I shivered in my striped pajamas.

"To support DeKay," the Masked One told me, "you must disrupt the dominant discourse."

What did that mean?

4.

The Masked One looked out again. We watched the woman at the window.

Her aspirations seemed to increase. If only more people would think like her!

The night city wavered. With the rhythm of the waves came the sense of the Masked One's explanation. Words and power make something called *discourse.* Some forms of oppression do not require physical force. Discourses are the way power trickles down to everyday practices. What was the discourse of a pandemic?

The Masked One took my smartphone and showed me: on social media, a doctor moved his medical mask below his chin to make a statement: Yes, the big face said, the virus was real. We should take precautions. However, he claimed, the shutdown harmed more people than the disease ever would. Yes, we saw the daily graph of the infected, the graph of death. Where was the graph for economic suffering? In Yiddish he said something. Then he translated: *Love is good, but it's good with bread.* Where was the graph for psychological suffering? *When the crickets play, the bedbugs dance.*

Who posted this video, I wondered, the heretic himself? Or his enemies? Clips of his opinions continued — his opposition to the so-called "other ways of knowing" in science and decolonization of the scientific method. He called on its proponents to use healing feathers, instead of oppressive Western colonizer anesthetics, in their next surgical operation. Who was this doctor? Why didn't he know better than to say what he thought? I turned to the Masked One for answers.

Again we looked at the woman in the

window. Wafted gently by urban energies, she muttered into the darkness. "Pie chart." She warmed up before practicing a speech. "He, she, per, they, ve, xe, ze." Meanwhile, the shadow of the president reminded us that his giant form floated overhead.

The Masked One's face rose. His eyelids closed like the teeth of a vise. His glasses turned to mirrors and reflected Venus for a moment. Then the glorious dark of night burst forth from the Douglas firs over a hill park, a small extinct volcano, across the river and five miles east. On top that hill, a bronze pioneer patriarch scowled back.

"I will help you make windows

25

where there were once walls," the phantom told me.

His masked semblance gave way to a pink deepening to blue. The streetlamps stained the sky with yellow, the color for caution.

So he was a big talker, as befit a phantom. And yet, I felt different somehow. When I thought, "Port," or even just "ort," a slipper danged on my toes, then fell off. My feet searched, and found a new purchase. I looked down. Without asking my permission, my feet had risen off the floor, balanced on the word, "land". The meaning of a word is its use in the language.

My guests had left, each with an armful of my dictionaries. I hurried to the sink to wash

my hands with soap, hot water, and words. The
week had begun nicely.

5.

Discourse, I thought as the guests faded in the murk of dawn. It's a word that comes from the Latin: *discursus.* It means, "running to and from." Thus, it was my task as the Masked One's writer to run to and from. I would be a wooden shuttle that ran threads in the Fates' loom. As the Roman poet Catullus wrote:

"Receive the truthful oracle which on this happy day the Sisters reveal to thee; but run ye on, guide the woof-threads which the fates follow, ye spindles, run."

In my case, the Masked One bid me to disrupt — to run disobedient threads. How could I run any kind of threads, be they woof, cross or *discursus* knotted? I figured this out later: To undertake my mission, he had lent my feet spectral powers of tread. I could grip my soles on the warp and woof of the city's narrative. I could whoosh and whirl from citizen to citizen, from street to street, and, to a limited degree, dream and thought. I found windows where there was once walls.

Why? To disrupt the discourse? But which one? The dominant discourse? Did I want to? And which one was dominant? Subversively, I had found one dictionary they left behind — my portable one, hidden in my bathrobe pocket. I took it with me as I put on my mask and left my home.

29

I pushed my sentences to the right, passing the nine-foot tall bronze elk on Main Street downtown. Then, like a bull dancer of ancient Minos, I suddenly leapt back left over the antlers, much like I could leap over the discourse! Due to the pandemic, the city shut down all public fountains. Yet the elk's burbling fountain shot up a squirt to spritz my behind. Upsetting the dominant discourse was one thing, but how? The proper path of disruption was not as clear to me as the Masked One's exhortations lead me to expect.

The elk stood on its fountain plinth in the middle of the incline. I heard a bronze voice, incongruously tenor, call out to me. "My granddad used to perform as a statue. I remember him, *still.*"

Now, after the bronze elk spoke to me, what? With the knowledge of where I was and why, I retained my poise. The street climbed up from the river park. It climbed to courthouses of local and federal government, to the city hall, and onward. In 1900, amongst a carnival, the aged pioneer generation erected this bronze statue. It honored the Oregon Humane Society. Kindness to animals was just the beginning of the bronze elk's meaning.

It encoded in metal a memory. At its carnival unveiling, it remembered the beauty of the wild, the inhuman that abided. Where did this sublime abide? It was just beneath, just behind the city, somehow. The three thousand-pound bronze elk guarded the navel of the city.

D. P. THOMPSON'S GIFT TO PORTLAND

6.

A triumph in mind, Basil DeKay grimaced as she studied the report on Bomberger's offenses. Tired, she closed her laptop and set her reading glasses on top. Her living room was her home office. Dr. Bomberger was an odd man, physically and intellectually big, at the same institution as Basil (Basilica) DeKay. An obstetrician and tenured professor of medicine, he was a well-known curmudgeon and jokester.

He claimed the multicultural model of society had failed, and called for a return to the Melting Pot: from many, one.

Return to the Melting Pot, she recoiled? What of American Indians? What of *people of color?* Here she made an error, and corrected it. There was a new, more powerful term she could use to seize the airport and radio station of any conversation: *people of the global majority.*

She looked out her window. Mist covered the hills. Would the sun break through to lift it?

DeKay gave the doctor credit: arguably, he had saved some young women from suicide or self-mutilation, doing what he did for them. Like so many women, DeKay's eyes turned into Kung-Fu whirling cleavers when this topic arose. How the doctor, supposedly a religious conservative, could do it was a mystery. He accepted no pay for it, nor would the talkative man discuss it. DeKay guessed that there was a turbulence for him in there somewhere.

The clouds above brightened. Below, crows

33

walked in the middle of the street. Basil DeKay
prepared to sleep. When video meetings
permitted, she preferred to work at night. Night
subverted the ways bureaucrats slowed activists
among the ranks.

But she refused sleep. In her pajamas, she
studied this doctor's history. A history may be
right, perhaps, DeKay thought. Or, it might be
wrong. But one thing it may not be, from
yesterday to yesteryear, is offensive.

DeKay had met him once at a function to
celebrate a new grant for a medical research
laboratory. To her irritation, DeKay couldn't
help to feel respect for his strength.

For example, that one time she spoke with

him, the big, loud man told her this:

"A doctor, an engineer, and a social justice advocate were sitting in a pub arguing about whose job was the most important.

"The doctor said, 'It is we physicians who came first in the world. Look at the Bible: Who do you think created Eve from Adam's rib?'

"'Nonsense,' the engineer objected. 'We technicians came first. Who do you think created order out of chaos?'

"'You are both wrong,' the social justice advocate declared. 'Who do you think created chaos in the first place?'"

Irritated, DeKay resented this, but at least it didn't include incomprehensible Yiddish words or phrases. He quickly followed this joke with another:

"A straight white man walks down the street and says to himself: 'Gee whiz, I'm really tired of getting blamed for everything.'

"Two student activists with metallic pink hair come running with their smartphone cameras, and yell: 'Go ahead, Mr. Privilege, tell the whole world!'

"The man panics and says, 'No no no, oh golly gee… you misunderstood me... I said, I'm really tired of minorities getting blamed for everything.'

"The students reply, 'Shut up! We know who's getting blamed for everything.'"

The doctor's hair was white, but he did not ever seem tired. His eyebrows were thistles. On his shape, any clothes looked slovenly. Everything about him, even his genius and the cover of his good works, irritated her good taste. She wondered why anyone would want to be his friend, or even feel sympathy for him. Even if someone merely read about him, she wondered... Who might that *someone* be? Me, I have no idea. What if that someone were *you,* dear reader? What if your employer *somehow* found out that you were curious about Bomberger's opinions, opinions which turned out confusingly to mean the same thing as violence? Are you perhaps wealthy so don't need your job, nor need a new one in that same profession?

Or if payment processors ceased to provide service for you because you read Bomberberg's cruel statement on social media that the recent explosion of gender dysphoria was a social contagion among the young fed by social media, do you perhaps have a cabin in the woods where you could live? Do you mind gnawing on pine bark for sustenance?

Ridiculous! You dutifully update truths as fast as they tumble down the chute of progress. Of course you don't want to hear those bad old truths; I certainly do not, which is why I never did listen. We should vouch for each other, should a tribunal arise.

If Bomberger said something about socially parasitic American elites, about hubris and nemesis, about the folly of removing the foundations of the house you live in, and not expecting the walls to wobble and the roof to fall... If, as a result, a doubt nagged you, a doubt that later dulled your facial expression of enthusiasm for a cause, could you afford to loose one hundred points of your social credit score?

After the election of President Baboon, the doctor's wife Ginny threatened to leave him. It was around then that he volunteered to work at the clinic for young women.

7.

But no, Basil DeKay drowsily recalled as she lay in bed, Dr. Bomberger had not seemed to notice the prosecutorial way she listened to him. He continued to say the same things. Encouraged by her fixed smile, he told her a third joke:

"A man in a large corporation asked another, 'How do you feel about the diversity training?'

"The second man became nervous. He thought carefully, and declared, 'I feel the same way you do.'

"The first man replied, 'Then I'm going to have to report you.'"

Yes, she had thought as she listened with a

grim smile, we have to report you. Some journals were now embarrassed to include his name. Two had removed his publications from their archives. Would a mere investigation create enough pressure for him to resign? At least, could DeKay pressure him to withdraw from prominence, to be quiet? If only he would apologize! With an admission of guilt, she could dismantle him. She encouraged him to keep his big mouth going. He did:

"An American history professor addressed his university students: 'Regarding the final exam, I have good news and bad news. The good news is that all the questions are the same as last term. The bad news is that some of the answers are different."

He had smiled and worked his peepers appraisingly before she could register her annoyance. She resented the beak of his jokes, that she did not make the world a better place. But she could not let him win by taking offense.

And then, Bomberger followed with a motto in Yiddish. She had repressed the urge to shout, *speak English!* But he translated anyway: *"Do not worry about tomorrow, because you do not even know what may happen to you today."*

Then he had walked away to joke with a woman who was younger and more zaftig than DeKay.

Did the encounter exasperate? Gnaw?
Ruffle, irk, and chafe? It was difficult to
calculate sometimes the complex index of social
and historical disadvantage mixed with
advantage. One had to make sure the evidence
fit the theory, because the theory was correct.

The administrative binder of sleep flipped its
pages. Each bullet point was a memory. Each
clipart picture was an enigma. Suddenly, a
device beeped. DeKay sat up, and opened the
light-blocking curtains. The mist had darkened,
not lifted. She had means to take Bomberger
down — maybe. She wanted to talk

41

confidentially about it with her ally, colleague, and friend, Bezz Larsen. A video chat might not be secure. But when could they meet in person? Due to the pandemic stay-home order, she had not seen Larsen in person since the winter.

A flurry of clicks updated her correspondence with allies in administration. With regard to an official rebuke of Bomberger, the vice provost replied with a quotation of policy and a cryptic statement: "Satisfaction of these requirements must occur prior to approval of any such request and issuance of any such action."

However, with her experienced ability to parse the arrogance and terror that motivated the nomenklatura, DeKay deciphered the code: *To promote diversity, inclusion, and equity, we must expose, humiliate, silence, and remove anyone who disagrees.*

"You'll learn what restorative justice means all right," she told herself.

Rubbing one of her ribs, Basil DeKay looked out her window. On the street below, there was little traffic. So much had closed for the pandemic. Except for the usual vagabonds, few walked around.

Something was going on with her daughter. Mother sensed it. Now she had confirmation. She would to talk to Sammy, but this might be difficult. Fortunately, the vice provost gave *her* the tickets to the concert hall, not Contessa Finger, DeKay's colleague, adversary, collaborator, rival, envoy, deputy, scold, fellow knitting club member, and sometimes best friend.

You know how, when you're pouring a little milk in your coffee and your mind wanders, perhaps in daydream about life in an apartment with exposed brick... A wagon-wheel coffee table topped with a ceramic guacamole bowl shaped like an avocado... and so occupied, you put too much milk in the coffee, so it becomes more pale than dark, but still a little dark? That color somehow gave Contessa Finger's personhood validity that no one in DeKay's

43

circle could question. What was her mix of ancestry? Everyone was afraid to ask.

Robed, the diversity officer padded to the kitchen. Before me, the bronze elk arose. Poised on its plinth and fountain, it faced the court buildings. That meant its rump faced the one-way traffic. Its rump had to point somewhere! Then the elk changed directions, or perhaps I did. My rump had to turn somewhere, too.

8.

To and from I hastened, under erratic clouds. Basil DeKay murmured protests in her sleep. Malevolent forces grew and took form.

"The concealment itself is concealed," it seemed to say. Puzzled, she slept again.

Were dreams part of discourse? I closed my eyes to investigate. Tension grew. In elementary school, I stood in line. Someone had done something. Punishment lurked for all of us. Escape was possible if I woke up. As I subsided again, I stood in a rocky field with my father and brother. There were too many rocks. I wanted to go home, so I shook this off too. Here was my fireplace chair, and here an open book. What was the book? What did those sentences mean? Didn't those words carry some kind of authority, some kind of answer? Why couldn't I read them? But time had passed. I looked up. DeKay drank coffee as she reviewed her PowerPoint.

Late, I hurried by a metal antlered quadruped under heavy clouds. From DeKay I dashed along invisible scaffolds of discourse to a man, a man awake, named Lourdes. It was not that I had become an otherworldly being. It was that the Masked One leant me power. The clean air lifted me. I avoided the proximity of dog walkers and lolling lovers by wide looping paths in the street. The summer night was reluctant to turn dark. A few drops fell. It would be the last rain before the fire season.

I walked quickly on, transpiring on ballet tiptoe around the haphazard refuse that formed the perimeter of a line of homeless tents.

Hawthorne Boulevard shimmered. Under a narrow lip of a protected overhang, the rain rolled just past Lourdes' face. He peered over his lime-green mask at his smartphone. Noah Beardsmore had not yet replied to his text.

He repositioned his linen scarf. "I'll give him five more minutes," he decided, "then I'll go." But it was too much for him. He started to press his smartphone to hire a ride home.

Then he heard a shout. He turned.

46

"Didn't you see me waving, Lourdes? You didn't recognize me?" Standing on the wet sidewalk, Noah looked improbably dry. He pulled his black mask aside for a moment to show his face. "I'm your guest, you said. It's your duty to wait for me." He smiled, eyes dark and resentful. He pointed to a dry spot beneath his umbrella.

The sloping brow of Lourdes' narrow head threw the weight of his character on his slightly protruding eyes. His expression was not cynical but lightly sardonic. His gaze tentatively pierced with implied judgment. He denied the thinning of his hair.

His insomnia was the result of a weakness he had not located. Time held him and shook him, too. Now in his forties, he could not avoid seeing signs of the force that thickened. His linen jacket helped him trick himself to believe that its lines were his own.

"Good afternoon, Noah. Yes, I'd given you up. I never use an umbrella. And I never get wet, unless I want to."

Noah shook his head; maybe, under his mask, he smiled.

Lourdes pulled down his scarf. In his urbane manner, oblique, his mask seemed to grin. But no, it was not a grin. It was a practiced half-twist. It was crafty.

48

9.

Noah's contemporary soft male mode strained with the conflicted convulsions of masculinity. Some blamed polluted nature, the synthetic estrogen dumped into the environment, for young men's delicacy. Some blamed nurture for men's weakness. Were they shamed, confused and medicated, sons of single mothers?

Noah was undeniably beautiful. Lightly muscular, he was robustly dolphin in torso. His manner showed a willingness to please through active signals. There was something slightly servile in its implication, deeply reserved. This reserve held a hint of resentment and rebellion.

The umbrella fabric rattled. The rain beat down and ricocheted on the asphalt. The square was a sea of bubbles. The bus stop shelter was an outpost of linger against nature. Since it not occupied by a homeless citizen, they dashed toward it. They braved wind and water.

Lourdes did not like his first name, the name of a mathematician, Euler. He steered people to just call him Lourdes. Hidden by his violet scarf, he dried his hands on Noah's coat sleeve.

"Let's not let the rain stop us," Noah exclaimed. "It's refreshing. But we can sit inside if you prefer."

Noah was a man who noticed the scent of rain, Lourdes quickly registered with a suppressed smile. He tried to discern Noah's expression under the mask.

But now Noah clasped the phone to his head. "Is that you, Basil? The rain is screaming." It was awkward to operate the phone while wearing a mask. To hear better he moved closer to Lourdes. Lourdes could feel the warmth of Noah's cheek.

"What's that? What? No, no. Don't wait dinner for me. I'll be back late — I'm dining out with Lourdes."

The smartphone gurgled. Its radio waves filtered through the rain. Noah's wife the diversity officer remonstrated at the other end of the signal. Lourdes forgave him his damp shoes. He forgave the fact that for all Noah's acceptance of his attention, he still held himself aloof.

Noah continued, "Yes, take Sammy to the concert tonight. Don't say that. Thank you. What's that? Oh yes… I do too."

Thus the husband placated his silly, trusting wife.

How did you like that, poor old diversity officer! thought Lourdes. *Noah said, 'I do too,' instead of 'I love you.' That was because I stood next to him and touched his hand!*

Diversity, schmercity. Lourdes disrespected silently, *Do they ever tire of inquisition by PowerPoint? Why did they turn the rainbow into such a joyless, bureaucratic thing?*

He thought of Halloween in San Francisco, the freakish exuberance, the outsider creativity he witnessed on a youthful visit. *I don't want to be an ally, Basil DeKay,* Lourdes thought. *I will be my own thing. I will follow my own rules.*

10.

Discourses entered our host cells to make copies of itself. So many new assertions grew in there, that our old words burst open with new meanings. The Phase One restaurants opened their fresh air tables on the wide sidewalks under sleek condominiums. Masked people crept cautiously at first, then faster to the tables. The new outdoor spaces wobbled with giddiness and curiosity.

Noah clicked the disconnect and glanced at his companion. "And what are we so pleased about?" Lourdes behaved just as he knew he

53

would.

Masks in place, they walked into the bistro.

Lourdes shrugged. "Maybe I was smiling because you weren't smiling."

At the doorway, the masked hostess explained the rules: Customers could remove their masks when seated. Anywhere else, the state required them to put the mask back on. She seated them under the sidewalk canopy.

"How could you tell I was scowling under the mask?" Noah sighed as he took his seat. "Something Basil said about us having dinner together... Never mind." He pulled off his mask. It caught on his ear and fell on the table. He tried to laugh at himself, and failed.

Lourdes took off his mask and rubbed his face. He decided not to explain how Noah's eyes glittered when he smiled, how his forehead formed an arrowhead when he was irritated. He decided not to comment that Noah himself was sensitive enough to detect Lourdes' own smile under the mask.

Instead he mused, "What remains for us urban white men is... skinny jeans, hide in plain sight, and enjoy a quiet dinner with another man." He folded the mask and put it in his chest pocket.

"I shouldn't care. But I don't like when women call men 'bros' or call male friendship 'bromance,'" Noah grumbled. "They want to ruin it out of instinct. Why be so threatened by male friendship?"

"Exactly. Any male space they hate, covet, and fear, except that of gay men. Look at the Boy Scouts — gone. Colonized by females, renamed *sans* the 'Boy.' But Girl Scouts remain." He pointed downtown. "As the city remodels *our* Portland Building, *our* municipal historical landmark, property of all us taxpayers, they're removing its urinals. Why? Any male space is problematic."

He leaned forward to whisper, "It's trans architecture. The rainbow bureaucrats want to nullify the phallus and pretend it doesn't exist." He leaned back and complained, "Is that queer? Does that question norms to increase possibilities? No, sir. That's a gray shroud of blah. That's an administrative clampdown on the category of men."

Lourdes broke off to order wine. Then he went on, "We are what we are, as we are, with male bodies, and not gay." Aloud he chuckled, "You and I, we know the phallus exists." He thought, *please Noah don't call me buddy*.

The older man regarded the younger and

considered doubt. He considered himself queer but not gay. This confused many, but that confusion helped him professionally. He had relished the haiku and slot machine of romance with women, of courtship, of strained lingers with men that ended when he could no longer pretend they were forbidden. That suspension of the question seemed like enough.

11.

As she looked out the open window, the same window through which I now found myself hovering, Basil DeKay asked her phone, "Noah? Are you there?"

Exposed to the infectious air, unsure, she put on her mask as she looked. As the moment paused, she thought she saw, stapled to a telephone pole, a fist silhouette against a face silhouette. What was that? The upward channel of her exhalations fogged the bottom of her lenses. She squinted at her smartphone.

But Noah said nothing more.

"Lost the signal," she concluded. A news headline interrupted: The baboon of a president banged pots and pans together.

Words that promoted diversity were easy to say. There was a lifecycle to the Diversity

Officer's efforts, from hiring to development and teamwork to promotion of non-white-male employees into leadership. For each client, Basilica DeKay worked hard to foster Uniqueness and Belongingnessness. There were Uniqueness trainings and initiatives, and Belongingnessness webinars and conferences. She explained the burden of cultural code switches, a burden on marginalized people, to fit in workplaces. She tried to help administrations understand the need for holistic change. Other than words on an obligatory diversity click-through course online, that required radical change in the practice of administration itself.

It didn't happen. The institutionalization of the diversity ideology bogged down in conferences, processes, and presentations without the kind of change in personnel she intended. They agreed with her, but administration acted as if having a diversity officer removed any of their own responsibility to help achieve her goals.

A leaky bucket problem plagued her, too. DeKay took it personally when a diverse employee left the institution, double for a really diverse individual. There was also the awkward and unspeakable difficulty of fostering the right kind of diversity, not the wrong kind.

She built her career on diversity initiatives that, wherever she worked, successfully nurtured a working community of women who looked like her and who thought like her. But it was harder to cultivate other historically disadvantaged groups who didn't look like her. It never occurred to her to support anyone who disagreed with her. Why should she support someone she knew to be wrong? That was not her mission.

Complications confounded her work. Some historically marginalized groups were now doing better on average than white people. What did that mean? Don't worry, one principle clarified all... That's all I can say on this matter. I will just stand over here. I say nothing. So you have nothing to report, except, "He said nothing." Or, if you need to write something down, tell them I said, "Don't do favors for evildoers, and no evil will befall you."

This was DeKay's contract year. She wanted a triumph to bring to her summer negotiation.

What triumph? That's all I can say on this matter. I say nothing. I will just stand over here. What do you want from me? If I let out an occasional mumble, so what? *Schme schmanted schmo schmake schmraight schmite schmen schmeel schmess schmof schmeir schminsufferable schmuniqueness schmand schmelongingnessness.* What? That was just some Yiddish about a wise man who calls out, "The thief's hat is burning!" to see who makes a hair audit.

Just west of downtown, over the steep hills

of Forest Park, under the clouds, the sun had not yet decided to set. The sun was still a ball of fire that made silhouettes of the Douglas firs. DeKay and Beardsmore's condominium lay under its hills. For a moment, the sun's horizontal rays revealed cloudlets of virion, a rash on the city. Then they disappeared again.

Basil DeKay was a pale night beauty. The English word "complexion" came ultimately from the Proto-Indo-European *plek,* "to plait." *What is our weave?* Her weave was sable haired, competent, ambitious, maternal, undeniably aging. Her beauty endured the wrinkles and gray hairs, but not the exhortational weariness of her work.

Across the river, I heard, *"We are male…"*

12.

Water rolled down Hawthorne Boulevard. "The phallus exists, and by an amazing coincidence, we are male," Noah agreed.

"Have you noticed? The more women hate the category of men, the more empowered and authentic they feel." Lourdes could not stop himself as he whispered, "That means they don't feel authentic as they are." His voice grew even softer. "They can't win that way. I feel sorry for them."

"So where does that leave us?" Noah asked. "Hide in plain sight, and enjoy a quiet dinner?"

The older man shrugged agreeably. "Male or not, queer or not, bodies need to eat."

The masked waiter brought the wine, then rushed to fix the dripping canopy. Even with his glass still empty, Lourdes tasted almond notes of victory, that Noah did not call him a buddy.

Noah touched his cheeks: was this a smile? "My first time out since the winter. Such a joy to break quarantine with a friend."

"Here, here!" Lourdes pointed to his glass. "I would like some wine. The waiter forgot to pour it. Shocking, really."

Noah lifted the bottle next to him. After pouring, he lifted his wine glass and swirled it. "I suggest you roll the Pinot like this for proper aeration."

"Oh yes. Right." Lourdes smiled with secret amusement. As he rolled the wine, he looked at the rich red Noir jostling and thought, *The poor women think they've won, as they took the dreadful world from our shoulders. Oh, the complaining!* "*I hate all men and wish all men were dead.*" "*Why Can't We Hate Men?*"[1]

After they sipped, Lourdes leaned forward. "Dear Noah," he asked, "may I be indiscreet and ask you one thing that's been puzzling me for ages…"

"You may ask me two questions if your inquisitive drive commands you."

Lourdes took the time to consider. With a soft and deferential tone, he asked, "Do you believe that diversity is strength? And my second question, since you permit it: Do you *Louvre* your wife?" He enjoyed this mispronunciation.

The moment required tact. I glided away on a slippery understanding.

13.

DeKay took off her mask. It was still light.
The rain had paused. Portland's sky hovered
like a child's drawing: a line of blue on top,
fluffy clouds below, a lollypop tree or two with
a bird pushing off by its large feet. It was
stressful to work but more stressful not to work.

Resisting guilt, she put her empty coffee cup
on the kitchen counter. She turned, and turned
again. Everything would be ready for his
birthday party.

Steam rose from the refilled cup. The edges

of her chest hurt. Her shingles had returned with stress. There was now a remedy, but she was afraid to go to the doctor during the pandemic. She rubbed the area.

Stress was the wound of her daily struggles for justice. It meant no peace for her nerves. After her miscarriage last year, she grew depressed. Antidepressants killed what was left of her libido. She reached for a box of cookies. How could she lose twenty pounds? Or even five?

Mother masked her worry and knocked on her daughter's door, then entered. With unease and stealth she approached a big topic…

"Working hard, I see, on your Chinese culture class..."

Sammy met her gaze with a blank expression, then returned to her book. On a muted TV, Ophelia whirled and kicked Hamlet in the face. DeKay turned it off, then walked over and picked up a flash card. She looked at the shape. It suggested a tree, a star, or a face. She flipped it over to read the English: *wood*.

Mother asked, "Will you spend some time off with your old mum? So much is still closed, but the Schnitz' is open, and I have tickets! A woman composed music about a pandemic."

Daughter's lips tightened. "Is this old music?"

"I think so. But to make it safe and fun, they've put ferns between the occupied seats. How does that sound? Noah's out, so it would be just you and me."

Sammy nodded.

As a cellophane wrapper, shed of its cookie, scrunches, crimps and drops, then slowly relaxes, so DeKay's face relaxed. How to approach the topic?

DeKay knew well that her daughter was not invulnerable to influences. At age eleven, at the same time as her best friend Sophie, Sammy declared she was truly a boy in a girl's body. To deny it would be an act of violence against her. Obedient and frightened, Mother suffered the obligation to call her daughter a "he". Later, daughter forbid her mother even to mention that embarrassing episode.

By age twelve, at the same time as her friend, she was back to a girl in a girl's body but *genderqueer.* The mother paused to put her glasses back on. The new word *genderqueer* sounded strange to her. She could not shake the impression it was dubious and self-indulgent. No! She had to keep up with progressive theory. The old language carried a legacy of power systems. She fought her belief that *genderqueer* was an empty word of generational posturing.

So that was fine by DeKay, but when Sammy wanted everyone to refer to her as "they," because she was *complicated,* the mother just looked at her.

Then there was the period in her late teens of mood disorders. Mother had to take Daughter back to a doctor to remove the contraceptive implant from her arm. Hormones were troublesome; there was nothing good about them. Sometimes DeKay wanted the government to ban them.

According to DeKay's training, she reassured herself, the individual realized her full autonomy only once she demolished the structures that helped form identities in the past. She was not a bad mother. Her daughter's brain was still materially forming, she told herself.

"Even if the music is old style, I think you'll enjoy being out of the house," DeKay assured. Casually, she offered, "By the way, I had a chat with your Professor Valley about knitting. She mentioned something."

The daughter's head whirled. "Professor Valley said something to you about me?"

"Not really. She said I should ask you. Are you seeing anyone, Sammy?"

The conversation had begun. It was a trick, but the concern was real. I clutched my head. So many concerns whirled!

14.

As I shuttled to and fro, a crow swooped. It dashed from one tree to another for a better skepticism. Did stores even accept paper money, that flypaper of microbes, at this time? Apollo sent a white crow to spy on his lover. I, too, would spy. Bees objectified the pink-violet fuzzy cones of Douglas spirea. A wet bronze elk watched it all, poised on its plinth.

Delicately, I must report to you that I heard that metallic, tenor voice again. "One day as I stood right here, up high on my fountain, just like this," it said, "Whom did I see rolling their bronze wagon wheel around Chapman Square,

but Bronze Pioneer Father, Mother, and Lad! I
beckoned. They stopped, then rolled the wheel
over.

"'Tell me,' I asked, 'why do you roll that
wagon wheel around Chapman Square?'

"'Mister elk,' the bronze man replied, 'I
repaired my wagon and I had one wheel left
over. I couldn't figure out where it went. So, I
thought I'd ask a professor. I hired a horse and
hopped on it. He started out slowly, and worked
himself up to a trot. So far so good. But before I
knew it, he was galloping full speed. *Woah!* I
said and I pulled the reins. But that demon
horse only went faster.'"

The bronze elk went on, "I told Pioneer

72

Father, 'That horse doesn't sound too *stable.'*

"'Frankly,' the bronze man told me, 'my horse was out of control. I gathered my courage, and jumped off. Unfortunately, my foot caught in the stirrup. Now the horse was dragging me. I yelled and I yelled but the horse kept galloping! Thank goodness one of the store employees came out and unplugged the machine.'"

Disturbed, I let out a low *moo*. Scrutiny of the elk seemed to betray a bronze smirk. That was okay by me. If bronze statues did decide to talk, they had reasons. I was grateful if it was a bronzy quip, and not a copper grudge, not brassy grievance, nor aluminum spleen. Marble, on the other hand, would likely preach the Just, the True, the Beautiful, and the Good.

Through the pandemic sidewalks I shuttled.
A simple human proximity was a threat and
insult. I felt alone in the drizzle of lies, the
selective procession of partial truths intended to
mislead.

I avoided the resentful glances of passersby.
I stepped around the dog walker stooping to
bag. The rain would, I hoped, wash away the
unpleasantness, and not just the dream of a
harmonious epoch.

Just then the drops thinned to a drizzle, to a
mist, and stopped. The sun ripped through with
rays that burned.

Main Street rushed by me. To avoid my
fellow citizen on the sidewalk, I looped around.
From the sidewalk to the road I looped, to the
edge of the bronze elk's fountain. A mask hid

half of my face. We all wore masks together in our emphatic division. Under the haunt-face of the bronze elk, together we harvested the dark spirit of Otherness.

"You know what else?" the elk asked me. "I'm tired of all these forced gender neutral terms. The elk cow I'm going out with insists on calling me just *friend* instead of *boyfriend.*"

"How and when will the pandemic end?" I asked it. "Where are we going? What's going to happen to us?"

There was no response. I guess the discourse didn't work that way.

15.

"Turn away from mother and daughter!" I
told myself. Guided by the bugle of bronze
rage, I hurried through downtown. Sometimes I
walked. Sometimes I flew on lines of invisible
discourse. One way or another, I veered to the
Hawthorne Bridge. Across it, up and down the
Buckman neighborhood I hurried.

Over the low buildings of light industry and
artisan breweries I flew, over the trees guarded
by crows, over the homeless camps, the
building complex of Catholic charities, the
methadone clinic, the cafés and boutiques, over
the Craftsman style residences and modest two

story apartments with themed names mounted on stucco, over the recently built New Urbanist condominiums with shops and restaurants on the ground floor, most of them still closed due to the pandemic shutdown. I found my way back to Lourdes and Noah.

The masked waiter washed the plates. The soap molecule unlocked the atomic structure of the virus. The broken parts of the disease washed away as harmless carbon and oxygen atoms. Take that, virus!

On the topic of *Louvre*, Lourdes's sharp eyes lacked mercy. "You don't need to answer now. I think we're on the same path."

After he said it, a worry struck him. The

words sounded inadequate. He blamed his insomnia.

Noah smiled politely. His careful beard stubble suggested a cosmetic of toughness. "It means so much to get out of the house, to be in the open air."

A crow listened to this and stored it for mimicry: *Air! Air!*

"I feel the same way. I hope we can do this again."

"Yes." Noah nodded. "It's good to see someone else's face, someone out of the household."

The crow, distracted, flew off.

Noah's eyes searched upward. What did he want to say? He wasn't sure, so he tried this idea: "I'm almost thirty. Why do I feel old?"

Lourdes' face changed. His counsel mode had switched on. He tried to restrain himself.

Noah waved his hand. "I feel healthy. I just… I feel old. What does it all mean? Why don't I have more reason to live?"

Lourdes had sensed all this before. Noah's malaise was the reason the counselor sensed he was vulnerable to seduction.

"Maybe we all feel that way sometimes. Sometimes the world is a wasteland, and we are its lizards. We have to create our own paradise."

Noah scoffed at the word *paradise*. It came from ancient Iranian, *pairidaēza,* for an enclosed park. So precious it was, only royals had such a thing as a park.

"Objectively, my life is okay," Noah

admitted. "But nothing means anything."

Lourdes knew why. Noah did not have enough responsibility. But Lourdes did not want to turn the conversation in that direction. It was an issue that, in his own way, plagued him at night. It also led Noah away from him.

The two faces sifted. The difference between reality and representation had collapsed. Sense and signification disappeared. All claims were false, but rhetoric intoxicated. "Can our friendship help?" Lourdes asked.

Noah's face remained mild. He turned it slowly, unimpressed but interested. He showed his portrait features. Meanwhile, Noah still did not call him a buddy.

The dinner plates cooled. "Friendship between men is less complicated," Lourdes observed. "And we are friends, aren't we?" He suppressed a grin, because he knew his goal was to complicate it.

Noah's face emerged from thought and landed in sincerity. "Well, this moment is special."

Lourdes couldn't suppress his smile any longer. "Yes, it is."

He had somehow started to whisper.

16.

There was a beat of silence in the DeKay-Beardsmore home. Time lurked. It malingered. I had found myself back in Goose Hollow.

Sammy made no move to speak or otherwise volunteer further engagement. She seemed stoic, but it was something else that made her face so still.

Her mother held a box of small cookies. "Is there a boy in your life?"

Indeed, at DeKay's initiative, they sometimes talked things out. Through her childhood, Mother tried to enforce communication and family dinners. Mother tried to limit Daughter's screen time. Mother, in the hard years after Father left, tried to moderate lenience and discipline in some kind of middle ground. It never worked.

Mother added, "This fellow. Is he treating you well?"

Sammy's young childhood was a delight. It was the happiest time of DeKay's life. They moved from one joy to another. With adolescence this smooth system sputtered. In her early teens, monstrous forces inhabited her daughter. They moved from one crisis to another. It was the worst time of DeKay's life.

Was it the fault of a missing father? Was it the nature of growth? Something something society? In secret bad moments, when she hated her daughter, Mother counted down from ten (sometimes twenty) until it passed. And it did pass.

In her late teens, so long as DeKay recognized her autonomy, her daughter was nice. The hard years passed somehow. Now she was finishing her college degree in Global Communication. It was tough to imagine that she would probably move out next year.

"You've got it all wrong, Mom!" Sammy exclaimed. "Oh my god. That's not what Professor Valley and I discussed. Not boys! Not even girls!"

Her mother indicated light interest. "Oh, it was something different was it?"

DeKay knew this all along. She offered her daughter a cookie.

Sammy put it on her desk. "Yes," she conceded. "I was asking about problems of freedom."

DeKay took off her glasses again to consider. She had heard this in confidence from the professor.

What is freedom, that you should make such terror of it? That every day you tear at it and test its limits every hour? Why do you hide your agency, your responsibility? Why conceal your doubts, your disagreements and confusion?

DeKay replaced her glasses. This action helped her suppress a smile. She removed a cookie from the box. "What kind of problems of freedom?"

Sammy started, then stopped. She took a breath and plunged: "The idea, that people are free to make independent rational decisions that determine their own fate… is, like, *fake."* Her eyes grew wet with feeling.

This shocked the mother, that her daughter felt such intensity for a political idea. She was about to take a bite of her cookie but now held back.

Sammy continued, "And not just a fake. It is a harmful delusion that, like, serves some by suppressing others. Freedom is a function of privilege. Therefore, freedom as we practice it is harmful. It has been for a long time."

DeKay's daughter further explained that what people call a free society was a way to structure and maintain inequities. If there was any substance of time in the room, these words left a crease.

DeKay wanted to feel pride. However, it irritated her slightly.

Without shame, self-consciousness or hesitation, Sammy went on.

A cookie DeKay chewed became smaller and smaller as Sammy explained the agony of her understanding. As the cookie shrunk, so DeKay's feeling of Uniqueness and Belongingnessness became average and alienated.

17.

Rails of discourse directed me across the river again. A young man and woman sat at a table nearby. They took off their masks and spoke hesitantly. Now they didn't speak at all. They looked at each other and tasted their wine.

Lourdes thought to himself: *I know why you need me, Noah. You crave recognition. I recognize you.*

He was staring. When Noah looked up in confusion, Lourdes improvised an explanation. "I was lost in thought."

The counselor paused; he had lost not a thought but a moment. He did not yet know

Noah well enough. Trauma in childhood, he told himself, becomes attraction in adulthood. Where was Noah's trauma? "It wasn't for *Louvre* that you married your wife, am I right?"

He loved the queer shape and sound of the famous museum. The way it contorted his mouth, and made his lips protrude, seemed to help carry his mockery.

Noah frowned. He felt a responsibility to respond. He eyed the rim of his glass as he traced it with his finger.

He explained that his wife was the first woman he slept with, and therefore the only. He was a bartender when they met. He had given up women after too many episodes of mistaken cues, mild drama, no sex, and strained talk about friendship. He figured most of them wouldn't even consider him because he was five-foot seven. It seemed like a third of his women peers were LGBTQ, a third chose men who treated them like dirt, and another third married their careers. They all seemed riled up in one way or another and could articulate why: "Men need to step up." He knew Basil was a divorcée, an older woman who had liberated herself from her overbearing husband. Noah's life was quiet and easy now.

Lourdes noted the lack of passion. He

highlighted this in a sly way. "Young women these days are stressed, conflicted creatures. But the beauty of youth remains. It's god's handwriting."

Noah's face showed wariness. "Beauty isn't enough."

"I don't know if I agree." Lourdes paused his fork. "I'll need to think about that." His fork resumed its plunge.

He heard Noah say, "Don't hurt yourself."

Lourdes chuckled and felt the warmth of his gaze. Suddenly, doubt followed. Behind the doubt was a wave of exhaustion. It was a wasting diet of an anxious, ever-shifting ambivalence. Passion did not drain away merely because persons felt fluid, shifty, unreliable, and ambiguous. There was another reason for his exhaustion, which he could not yet locate.

But Noah pondered how the baboon of a president provoked his wife again and again. When Noah saw her face darken as she scrolled her smartphone, he knew she was reading the news. So he'd quietly left the room.

He'd rather have a shared private moment that was genuine, than any number of exchanges of canned phrases against President Baboon. Politics made their time together

inauthentic, he decided. This troubled him more
and more about their marriage.

18.

The bronze elk was silent. What was the meaning of its bronze companions? Bronze Pioneer Father, Mother, and Lad, with their bronze wagon wheel? Standing Bronze George Washington with his cane, seated Bronze Thomas Jefferson, sad Bronze Abraham Lincoln, and Bronze Teddy Roosevelt on a Horse, what could they say about individual rational decisions, about freedom and fate?

How about bronze Joan of Arc on her Horse? How could various Bronze Lewises, Clarks, Yorks and Sacajaweas answer? What did the little face that bronze Sacajawea carried, bronze baby Jean Baptiste, explain? What about

the cruel bronze face of pioneer patriarch
Harvey Scott, on top of Mount Tabor Park?
And the bronze soldier who stood guard at the
Lone Fir Cemetery, over the four-sided
monument that remembered four wars,
Mexican, Civil, Indian, and Spanish?

I stepped off the shuttle bus *Discursus*. The
ideal of individual autonomy that underlies
liberal humanism was, Sammy explained,
nothing more than a power mechanism. It kept
the marginalized down through the obscurity of
structural systems of inequality.

Basil DeKay looked around as she listened.
She did not see me. Perhaps the first thing I
noticed about the DeKay-Beardsmore

condominium was its handsome walnut-stained wardrobes. The couch was old-fashioned. It had a back that swooped twice like a mustache. The flat screen TV was discrete over the gas fireplace. The angles were crisp. In the hallway was a series of seashell photographs that Noah had taken.

Two women cut off a drunken man's head: this was a framed print of Artemisa Gentileschi's Biblical theme painting, *Judith Slaying Holofernes,* of 1620. Noah called it, *Basil Slaying Roger.*

Nearby hung a framed poster of a vibrant painting of watermelons by Freida Kalo. Its knife had cut open some of the watermelons. This revealed the sweet pulp inside the shell of the ones that were not open. A cut in the green revealed red. It was the last painting Kalo completed in 1954, right before she died. Noah called it, *Basil Slaying Roger Forever.*

There were pale mirrors, two large artificial rubber trees, a dish of pebbles picked on coastal trips, soothing wall colors, and matched pillows on the couches. But after the lockdown and quarantine, the soothing aesthetic itself made DeKay want to break things.

Rightly, the home should fall ever deeper into a state of neglect. Sammy left her books and laptop on the kitchen table. DeKay had made the couch her workspace. It would be a dirty and disordered mess, if not for Noah's efforts toward order.

To express support, and feel it too, DeKay tried to compose her face. Despite her disagreements of intensity, she was proud of her daughter's passion for justice. "Yes, we have a long way to go… But working within institutions, private and public, we really are addressing harms..."

Sammy cringed. She shook her head emphatically. "Everything that facilitates the pyramid of inequality, sustains the pyramid of inequality."

"Everything?" DeKay exclaimed with alarm. But she couldn't continue the line of thought. She couldn't bring herself to praise the current system. She knew better than that. "The

corona virus is making us all a little batty,"
DeKay ruminated aloud, averting her eyes.

"Anyone who isn't mentally ill in an unjust
world," Sammy argued, "must be, like, blind or
evil — "

"You stop this catastrophizing," the mother
interrupted. "It isn't good for your mental
health. I'm glad you have taken to heart so
much American history. Your passion for
justice is the same as my own. But don't
discount how far we've come! Think of the
increasing justice and equality we push forward
every day! I've seen it across my lifetime. Your
own mother is a part of that."

Her mother had a point, Sammy felt, if you

granted her assumptions that were, in fact, false. She felt sorry for her mom, who grew up in a world of benighted standards, and was unwilling — or unable — to acknowledge it. And here, rather than go through it all, Daughter thought the shortcut expression, ...*boom-shaka-laka.*

Sammy picked up her smartphone and started scrolling. It was a sign that she wanted the conversation to conclude.

But Mother asked Daughter to put down her phone. The conversation was not over.

19.

Urban narrative wiggled its toes. As I bobbed upon those toes, I crossed the river again. I noticed that Lourdes hesitated, suddenly conscious that he wiggled his toes in his shoes. He worried that he had gone too far about beauty. He nodded to the young couple seated nearby.

This man and woman marveled: they were out of the home, their faces free. Before coming here, they had sat side-by-side and read a kid's book on the natural history of Earth. Life went on, beautiful and funny, as the book showed. With what tenderness they cited facts!

This young man, named Simon Rush, with a long narrow face, was beautifully obstinate.

"The book said, trees have been around three-hundred fifty million years. Sharks four-hundred million. It's our three month anniversary." He smiled. "Three months of hiding in my studio like fungus."

The woman, Tejashree Pandey, made praying hands. This included her fork. "I think we can do another month. The book said, four hundred million years ago, there were giant mushrooms everywhere, twenty-five feet tall. We're doing fine with our twelve weeks, I think."

Simon would rather die than be the one who did not communicate by a list of facts.

99

Tejashree's cropped metallic red hair showed off the shape of her skull. Last year she quit her job and started a micro restaurant in Old Town, with just two small tables and a takeout counter, to learn the trade; his apartment was above. That's where he worked for now, like so many office people, over the Internet.

The shutdown regulations grieved her. Her micro restaurant made micro profits, too little to pay her bills, but she learned. She had planned to expand just when COVID-19 hit. She had just met Simon, too. The isolation of the shutdown had, over spring, accelerated their winter romance as well as her debts.

"Let's buy another bottle," Lourdes offered. "What principles shall we drink to? What keeps the darkness away?"

Little jaw set, Noah proclaimed his certainty. "What keeps the darkness away is exercise. We aren't just minds that float in a glass jar. We have bodies too. Our nervous system isn't just in our head." He held out his hand and looked at it. "Our nerves extend to every limb, every finger and toe. Strong body, strong mind."

Noah pulled back his hand. "The first step is to stop talking and start doing."

Lourdes was beginning to bore of this topic. He grew intense. "I wish I understood you."

"What's the big mystery about me?"

This discourse had developed a pattern. In response to Lourdes' moodiness, Noah grew blunt.

"Why would someone as… the whole way you are…" Lourdes strung out his yearning into trite nothingness.

Noah rescued him. "Do I *Louvre* my wife?"

Lourdes didn't breathe, didn't move his eyes, he just stared and waited. But Noah didn't say more. Yes, yes. Lourdes appreciated Noah the more for his multilayers, including the blunt, resentful core. He was too young to be sardonic, but the seed of that self-distance grew.

The pair of young lovers at the nearby table pressed their foreheads together. Again, they pared off with facts. The man said, "Scientists resurrected an extinct flower using seeds found

in a 32,000 year-old Siberian squirrel's den.
You, Tejashree, are the last, best seed in my
heart's 32,000 year-old Siberian squirrel's den."

"Octopuses have three hearts. How they
must love!" Tejashree declared. "Thanks to the
pandemic, we fell for each other. I'll never hurt
you, Simon."

"If you need to," he declared back, "Do it!
I'll sleep for 32,000 years, until some scientist
finds me and gives my shriveled heart new
water."

"No," she replied. "No, I won't do it!"

20.

Whirling across the city, strange faces
amazed me. Who was not wearing a mask? The
kind mask hid our expressions as we hunched
over our Internet screens. We absorbed
informative microbes of anxiety. Everyone
washed hands in soap and water. Our hands
dried out and hurt. We were masked, fickle in
judgment, and therefore we glared.

Behold the mask-grimace of the pandemic.
The threat had placed upon its followers one
and the same mask — the mask of frightened
humanity. Now government's rhetoric of shame
withdrew one unit of measure. It released the
public from quarantine to a low level of

openness. We began to wait in drive-thrus. We waited in attenuated queues in front of food trucks.

And all who stalked along the streets gave each other wide arcs of shun. Those who walked inevitably met one another, at some distance yet face to face, on the dueling ground of sidewalk. They needed to settle without words which one must move to the road and which one may stay on the sidewalk.

Old men and women, youths and couples, children and adults, all exchanged frightened greeting-glances. We passed silently with faces expressionless and covered, except for the eyes. The mask blanked half the face. It half dehumanized us. We greeted each other with the face of the censor.

The word *mask* comes from mixed sources, the medieval Latin *masca* for "witch" or "specter," and the Arabic *maskara* for "buffoon." We who clung to hopes of health wore the clown mask of a death cult.

Discourse corkscrewed me. I found myself in Goose Hollow again. Mother explained to Daughter how professional women who looked like DeKay succeeded as working class creatures withered. Bam! Bam on the nose! Administration served DeKay and the women who looked and thought just like her. Sammy could be such an administrator. She already was a woman. The future was hers. Basil DeKay spoke and, as her daughter, Sammy had to listen.

She continued, "We're changing the language to suit the newest direction progress takes us. We accomplished all this unfolding process, and you want to throw it away?"

Discourse gripped me. Invisibly, small clouds of exhaled virus swirled or maybe they didn't. Irrational processes seemed to rule by emotion. On devices, graphs of the infected rose steeply, moderated, rose more steeply, and moderated. Other graphs showed more twisted lines. Dogs and their walkers became tangled in the leash. Leadership flailed in confusion. Leadership flailed again, to argue and cover up that confusion. The global economy recoiled, twisted. In the park, children swung each other.

Arms on each other's elbows, they swung their saddled feet. I flinched from their germs.

Sammy said nothing. She waited, expressionless. Face-to-face communication risked exhausting her, so she marshaled her reaction. It also kept her from making mistakes.

Mother and daughter looked at each other. Across the gulf of generation, the mother's expression offered Belonging.

DeKay strode with her coffee cup and looked out the window to look at the hydroxychloroquine sky. "So, you want to become a fierce administrative advocate for social justice, like your mother?"

Sammy shrugged. Her mother's words left her unmoved, but she wanted to be polite so this conversation would end faster. Her mother

seemed to say inequities were improving.
Clearly, however, everything was worse, worse
than it had been in a long time. Her mother
meant well but was a sophisticated enabler of
injustice.

The daughter curated her facial expression
for pleasant reserve even as she silently
resolved, *No. I don't want to advocate reform
through, like, human resource departments. I
want to destroy injustice at the root. The rest
follows, as sure as* laka *follows* boom-shaka.

21.

O that old home sweet feeling! Where can I find you again? What agony is this? What tickles my nose? The sneezy force is the absence of something.

A realization struck: The Masked One stood next to me. It was sudden, but it was also natural. I repeated my understanding: "Basil DeKay is the subject of my story."

"No." The Masked One was stern, precise, but not angry. "What is the etymology of 'subject?'"

This question startled me.

As I answered, I still puzzled over the objection that DeKay was not the subject of the story. "The word 'subject' comes from the Latin *subiectus,* which means 'lying under, below.'"

The Masked One slowly closed his eyes and opened them. This gave the impression of agreement.

"…It described feudal relationships," I added.

His mask writhed as he told me, "It wasn't until the fifteen nineties that the word *subject* began to refer to the foundation of a proposition, as your sense of *a subject of a story.* The fifteen nineties was the decade that the East India Company sent its first fleet to

110

India, led by a pirate. It was the decade that the queen commissioned maps of all England. Power needed new tools of explanation for its expansion. Feudal relationships became imperial. The meaning of *subject* changed as power flowed through it. What does that mean?"

I closed one eye and tried to answer. "You are advising me to found the subject of my story in relationships."

From his reaction, I judged this was not the worst answer, but not what he wanted. "Just as the meaning of words is never absolute," the Masked One explained, "the meaning of *self* is not absolute. Power creates it. Write her truth."

I tried to understand. "You mean, write her role in the greater truth?"

The walls of the Masked One's face loomed over me as he asked, "The etymology of *truth* is what?"

How did he know that I knew such things? Most laughs come from incongruity, which comes from expectations, which comes from a common understanding of truth. This requires definitions. "Proto-Germanic *treuwaz*, or 'good faith.'"

"Good faith doesn't go far without trust in honest outcomes. But outcomes reflect power."

The head of the Masked One hovered on a dark mount, a shoulder of darkness clothed with a turtleneck sweater of celestial expanse much darker than the Portland night ever was.

"There is no objective truth, no shared mythology," he confided, "no institution you can rely on. What makes an outcome honest? Your hero knows that the real political task is to unmask the neutral appearance of institutions. She wants to criticize and attack them to unmask their hidden violence, so that one can fight against them. Therein lies good faith. Let your hero have a turn. Join her myth. Let it be yours. You must become *her* subject."

22.

Portland, Oregon calls itself the Rose City.
Maybe this Portland is a rose, an experiment
from our test garden in Washington Park.
Maybe the ancient Persian word *urda* migrated
into the English language with the plant itself.
Cities, like words, drift and change. Maintained,
sniffed with nostrils of gratitude, the little city
grew, a close-budded miniature miracle of
amber, silver, and russet. But there was mold.
Beetles clambered, doctrinaire. *O! how much*
more *doth beauty beauteous seem, by that sweet*
ornament which ***truth*** *doth give.*

I hurtled through the microbic streets. I felt
sad for the distance. The sidewalk held the

113

silhouette of a bent elder in mask who shuffled with walker and grocery sack. A masked skateboard kid clappered in and out of view with no visible sense of the risk. A dog nosed a tree as his owner looked at her smartphone. Neither wore a mask.

I paused, leaning against the brick wall, and looked. There was too much pepper on the broccoli trees. The black birds roosted, raucous with the social media of caw-caw. The number of crows had increased each year to date. No one knew why. The trees drooped under the weight of crows.

Below, in a Hawthorne Boulevard bistro, I saw two figures gesture in an arguably human manner. They tinked the sinuous glasses... and spoke of the search for meaning in life...

Under red eyebrows, the masked waiter was slender. He wore women's pants. Under his mask, did he have a fresh shaved face? A snub nose? Bo Peep lips?

Lourdes leaned back from his plate. "I don't think I can make you happy."

"It's not your job... Why did you say that?"

Why did he? Was it guilt? Was he warning Noah, or himself? Lourdes was careful not to appear too intent, or too shrewd.

"You said you feel old. It's a consequence of your choices. You have to make yourself happy." This last point was manipulation.

Noah tossed a hand and half-laughed at himself. "Okay, yeah. I was dumb. Turning thirty is not a big deal. I'm still me. I'm always me."

Lourdes' expression turned severe.

"We're always me," he retorted in a tone of agitated profundity. "What does that mean?"

What a question! Noah thought, then declared, "Who are we, inside? My thoughts, my feelings …"

The counselor stopped himself from saying something.

"What?" asked Noah. He saw Lourdes' continued self-resistance. "Say it."

Lourdes hesitated, then burst out, "We're always me, I agree. But there is no *me.*"

He wondered if he had again gone too far.

On the side-street curb strip, the line of tents of homeless men appeared in the mist and faded again. The homeless tents encroached. Nice, pretty, law-abiding people crossed the street to avoid the junkies and the disturbed along the kind New Urbanist streets. But sometimes there was a lunatic waiting on the other side.

23.

Noah held up his hands in perplexity. What Lourdes said made no sense to him, and he didn't understand the fever behind it.

"What does it mean, you're 'always me'?" Lourdes asked. "Where does your 'me' come from? I believe there is no self, only our absorbed social norms, and our resistance to those norms."

Noah tried to understand. "Deny the validity of old restrictions, certainly. But deny that human nature exists? You don't deny the body."

The other man nodded, eyes burning. "The body is real. But human nature? The voice inside the head? People don't think it through, and I don't blame them. But since you asked: if you believe in a firm human nature, you don't believe that queer human nature is real."

"Oh…" Noah leaned back, realizing this was a Q thing of LGBTQ (more properly, LGBTQQIP2SAA). Now that he placed it, he calmed his expression, and set his tone to acceptance.

"That's why," Lourdes continued, "I don't believe in progress in the same way as other people. How can there be progress without a firm human nature to stand on?"

"You don't believe in progress?" Noah lifted his smartphone.

119

The counselor waved the device away. "Is technology progress, if it is useful, but increases mental illness? Decreases attention span? Et cetera? Is it progress, if increases in one area lead to decline in another? Everything has unintended consequences. There are no solutions, only tradeoffs. Have I shocked you?"

Indeed surprised, Noah twisted his head one way, then the other. "So you think progress requires a firm sense of human nature? It all depends on the voice inside the head?"

"How could there be a human society to improve," Lourdes asked, with a fraught lurch of his chair as he roused and restrained his vehemence, "without a human nature to build

upon? I wish there were a human nature!
Without a human nature, all we have left is
individual natures, nothing but a mass of egos."

"I don't know, maybe," Noah grudged.
"Are you thinking of social media?"

"If technology changes human nature, how
firm is that human nature?"

Noah couldn't reply, but his face showed
that he wasn't convinced.

"When there is no 'me', human nature itself
becomes a power struggle," Lourdes explained.
Then he smiled. He calmed himself. "Please
don't stop eating."

Dutifully, Noah ate. They both were quiet
for a moment.

"Maybe," Noah announced.

"Maybe I'm right?"

121

"Maybe the reason I lift weights is to try to build my sense of self. The body exists, right? Can one kind of strength become another?"

Lourdes considered and calculated. "Freud tells us that the ego ultimately derives from bodily sensations. You make your body strong, so yes. You're building your sense of self. Ego rises from pleasure. Pleasure comes from health, and other things…"

They were both quiet again. Lourdes wondered if he had expressed himself too fervently.

"It's your right to be the kind of sexual you want," Noah affirmed bluntly. "But it's your duty to your existence to maintain your health, which requires discipline. I'm trying to use exercise to assert my sense of 'me'. Increase your heart rate. Maintain the right form. Watch your heart rate. Count your reps."

Lourdes felt a moment of rapture. He felt dislocated for a moment in his happiness. Joy is unspeakable.

Red eyebrows with masked face reappeared to further the tapas: candied frustration, anxiety brazed with disquiet, a small skewer of grilled despair.

"I could not agree more. You assert form, proportion and… muscular self-recognition!" Lourdes found that he had closed his eyes and now opened them. "Maybe that's how, for you and me, beauty can overcome ego. Nothing is stronger than beauty, not even ego."

Unfortunately, as he said this a homeless old man approached their table's fence. Something essential had been forgotten. What is a human being, that you should make so much of him? That every day you examine him and test him every hour? Maskless, human, he approached and retreated from the diners.

The waiter appeared. He called the homeless man by name, Mayor Smoke 'Em. The waiter tossed a paper mask with casino dealer precision. That flick of the mask was the hidden agenda of bourgeois rationality.

Mayor Smoke 'Em, now masked, gave the waiter a thumbs-up.

The wet streets drained. The sunset hissed into silence. Finally, so late as to bring incredulity to the fact, it was dark. A summer bee flew, tardy and confused. Three stars and a planet appeared. A bee flew in starlight.

123

24.

Stone buttocks greeted mother and daughter. Images of the DeKay women flickered and warbled across the glittering leaves of the mirror wall. These images wore masks that matched their dark dresses. In a thousand silver scallops, the sinuous marble nude transpired. Turned left, turned right, the statue showed the rocky vocabulary of her buttocks: *callipygous*. The Greek origins of that word referred to the buttocks of a statue of Aphrodite.

At the proper archway, an elder woman stood bent. She sunk behind her black mask. Nonetheless, she cheerfully took their tickets. Another woman led them into the hall.

A jungle grew in the auditorium. Basil and Sammy DeKay were rare guests. Potted ferns filled most of the seats. A Spanish artist had worked with the orchestra to make this cautious event celebratory, with life in every seat.

The DeKay women felt safe together in a green nook. There were seats of ferns to their left, ferns to their right, ferns behind, and ferns in front.

On stage, black gowns, trousers, sleeves emerged with instruments. Space between each musician's chairs made it seem as if they did not like each other. The small orchestra fell into place on stage. And as they fell, DeKay too fell.

Beyond the fronds, below the spores, down on the stage, DeKay saw white scores on black music stands. Violin strings twanged. Horns breathed.

She sensed something wrong. She heard someone, somewhere, comment with a tone of frustration as if the observation didn't need her to say it: "The lack of fairness."

There are plenty of women in the orchestra. I didn't count. Maybe even more than fifty percent. There are plenty of Asian Americans, probably some Jews. The symphony does blind auditions. Thus the diversity officer replied to the voice in her head. She toyed with her necklace.

Down on the stage, there was a chorus as well. They stood in a gap-toothed arc around the twenty musicians.

Mother glanced at her daughter. She sat quietly, face impassive, head lifted slightly.

DeKay's head surprised her with a slight shake. *Ha*, the inner voice burst, in a gotcha tone, in argument with herself. *I thought you knew this. Musicians should be chosen based on disadvantage, disability, disqualification, and so on. Blind auditions support systemic oppressions. The symphony should do deaf auditions, then pick by equity ratios.*

DeKay sighed. She was *doing the work.* This made her aware, as well as irritated.

The singers assembled from each side. Each wore a mask around the neck. The conductor's long black gown swept the stage. Even this luminary wore a mask.

25.

A spotlight found the gray-haired conductor. Ostentatiously, she removed her mask. The audience, mostly women, let out high-pitched whoops. Victorious clapping shook the frond tips. The conductor greeted the audience and then, comically, the ferns. Ferns were mute, she observed, suddenly serious, and that used to be the rule for too many women.

The conductor articulated the houseplant silence, the silence of women composers, of individuals denied the opportunity of their brethren. Fanny Hensel Mendelssohn abided the dullness of stifled spirits, the missing honorific.

She lived in drawing rooms suffocated with graces and responsibilities. She felt the pressure, even scorn, to compose in a demure scale.

The brothers whirled, the husbands levitated, their voices rose and fell with opposition, with ambivalence, with moments of allied collusion. Royalty offered benefits or held them back. Hensel whispered with fellow composer Clara Schumann. The children raised their dimpled arms and whined. Regretful its relevance to us today, Fanny Hensel Mendelssohn wrote the *Cantata after the Cessation of the Cholera in Berlin,* 1831. For one hundred and fifty years we didn't know about this cantata. For one hundred and fifty years, no ear could hear it. Ears began to do so only in the last few decades.

"And now," the conductress proclaimed, "you and your ears will as well. But first, for the lost music of Maria Ann Mozart, let us tune our ears to the dirge of her silence."

The moment eased. The conductor took her position. And then the *Cessation of Cholera* began.

Four singers began with bright praise and joy for spring! Then came remembrances of the pain of childbirth. Enchanted agony! The solos seized a clasped posture. The choir's mouths moved in Os. The orchestra's many pages turned. Trombones slid in trio! The chorale returned to the praise of God. The evening

128

breezes praised Him in the trees. Trees gave
shelter — for a while. The shadows grew long.
Obscurity gathered.

Came then a procession of suffering, the
trials of Job. The singers lamented. The chorale
was plaintive. Relentless, the orchestra crashed.
And yet, Job continued to praise the Creator.
Job bent under suffering but continued to praise.

There was more. The choral expanded under
stress. The arc of music formed a dark archer's
bow for the dead. Its string trembled in tension
for sinners. It shot the dart, a three-headed
arrow of three trombones, into the light of the
Saved! Thank the Creator who made the world

and all of us from nothingness!

The dead ones called to Judgment. The living lament the dead. Reconcile with the Creator! The choral called for penance. We live! Praise the Creator who made us, who made the world. *Alles was Odem hat, preiset den Herrn:* "Let all that breathes praise the Lord."

26.

At home, Noah closed the door and stifled a
yawn. I turned the other direction: Basil DeKay
sensed her daughter stifling a yawn.
Intermission fell. Sammy's face lit up. Mother
knew she had flicked on her phone.

A few moments later, theatrical dark
returned. Next, the orchestra presented Hensel's
"String Quartet in E-flat Major." The fugue
compressed sweet motions and layers. Quiet
glances crossed a glade. They stood under a sky
with rapid moving clouds. It signified a whole
world. This world included DeKay and her
daughter! The power of that feeling
transcended. However, the music had odd
wrinkles. Was that a real sky or painted fabric?
A riverine sequence of scenes followed, with a
tender third movement, loving-kindness.

DeKay felt her mood slide. The shape of her
mind wobbled and reformed. The churn and
clamp of moral administration had hardened her
mind. She was not prepared for these emotions.
It was not the style of music she enjoyed. Yet,
the substantial artistry of it, she could not
withstand.

Her emotions whirled and subsided — and
whirled again. There was a whole world within
it, a mirage she could only sense. DeKay
listened and let the emotional notes form and
dissipate. She found herself resisting the artistic
argument of the string quartet. This scared her
for a moment. She felt the ghost of an empty

space.

Oddly, some of the young audience members left while the rest still were clapping. Maybe DeKay misheard, but one of these women who climbed the stairs seemed to scoff back and forth with another.

The mean spirit confused DeKay. But she also felt anxious. Had she missed an offense? "What did she say?" she asked her daughter.

With a wooden face, Sammy explained, "Too long."

"And what did the other woman say?"

"Too German, and too much bible."

"And what did you think? Honestly."

Sammy shrugged. "Too whatever."

This shocked DeKay. What had happened to the new generation of young women? They seemed so numb and yet so strident. Between her daughter and the love she felt for her, Mother felt less space to breathe.

As it departed, the sparse crowd in masks let out its plaintiff murmurs.

Tired, DeKay let out her own plaintive murmur. It sounded like "Xe," or possibly "Ze," but what she thought was, "I have raised a daughter devoid of charm or joy."

27.

Noah didn't hear his wife murmur in her sleep. She left traces of herself everywhere in the form of brushed-out hair, administrative binders, knitting project and skein, lost power cords, and snack wrappers.

As his wife slept, Noah picked them up. As he put them away, he stepped in his study. What did he study? He had a small desk with a laptop. There was a large screen, a chair before it with game console. By a mirrored corner sat an elliptical cycle, yoga mat, and medium-sized dumbbells color coded in pairs.

Around the corner was the kitchen. Smartphones made grocery delivery easy. On the stove, he simmered this, he stewed that. In a dish nearby sat the toppings in readiness. Decorative bowls and platters awaited presentation to the guests.

Noah had demanded to be the host of his own birthday party that night. Now he prepared a roasting tray with segments, wedges, and halves. Then he stretched. Thirty today! His turbulent twenties were gone. This was a forlorn thought.

He liked his physical fitness, but it did not satisfy his self-esteem. He used an electric razor with a setting to preserve a stubble around his chin. His hips were lithe, like those of a ballet dancer. What could he do about that? He could exercise some more.

He grated carrots, added raisins and cumin. He snipped some fresh parsley from the pots on the windowsill. Dice, mix, grate, sprinkle. Red onion? Tomato and cucumber. Seeds? Spices. He was ready for his first set.

Feet on the floor, Noah put the back of his left upper arm on his thigh. His right hand was on his right knee. Bicep curled with dumbbell, up, down, up, down.

Life, when free from threat, seeks abundance, seeks luxury, excess and waste. The weightlifter sought pain and responsibility. Up, down, up, down.

To lift iron, to press it upward, to manufacture constructive pain, to make one's muscles tough and hard... This is to sing a bawd at one's own wake. Even with his dolphin face and porpoise wrists, Noah could glimpse that glory. He grunted in constructive pain. Up, down, up, down.

Almost nude before the gifts on his birthday table, he bent to stretch. Not a young form, but still mostly lithe, he stretched. He squatted and slanted, up, down, up, down.

The floorboards creaked. He sensed his wife watching.

"Did I wake you?"

"Here I am."

"I'm eager to receive your feedback."
"Like."

He spoke with her without turning around.
Why shouldn't his wife admire him, see him
whole? He knew she had no desire for him, not
what he called desire. But he knew she didn't
want to admit it to herself.

Basil was eleven years older, but dedicated
and dutiful to their scheduled sex once a month.
They both wanted a child, but nature didn't
comply. They gave up. Since there was no
passion — and no pregnancy — he wasn't sure
what they were doing. Still, it seemed like the
right thing to do.

He didn't like to think about it. Not for his

wife, for himself now, he turned every which way. He let her look. For what else would he use his toned measure of strength? What else did his lean portion of power contribute? What did this expression of male physical confidence accomplish?

28.

Noah had enough of that and hurried to the shower. Soon he appeared again dry and dressed in a sports jacket. He rolled sleeves slightly back to reveal the wine red cotton dress shirt's cuffs. Perfect pleats cut his trousers. His rear end moved in its skinny elastic wool through elastic time and ever expanding space. He moved barefoot in flip-flops.

"Happy birthday, dear Noah." DeKay kissed his cheek.

He smiled. "Thank you for the gifts — so thoughtful. I love them all. There is one thing, though, that framed Obama 'HOPE' poster better go in your own area. It doesn't really belong in my space. It's the wrong style, too PC. Yes, I am excited about my dinner party!"

DeKay held the framed Obama poster with some chagrin at her poor choice. Shepard Fairey's Obama stared with a head tilted up, above the horizon, past the sky. Why that head tilt? Why that human kilter?

The scene unfolded before me from my hidden vantage.

In order to exalt young candidate Obama, maybe Fairey wanted to associate him with a far off hope that was religious, not legislative, not historical, nor in any way specific, except a better face for authority.

Anyone who offered authority now her daughter would call fascist. The English word *fasces* arose in the 1590s from the Latin, a staff of office, a bundle of rods around an axe with the blade projecting…

This is when the Masked One stood up from an empty chair in the bedroom to interrupt me. "And long before Latin, from the Proto-Indo-European, *bhasko*, for band or bundle… Continue."

While I watched with stoic reserve, my brain closed my mouth and tried to find my words. *"Bhasko,* for band or bundle… Continue… yes. The sticks represent the authority to whip…" Before I could explain the axe, he interrupted me.

"And how are the rods held to the axe?" the Masked One eagerly demanded.

"How are the… With straps," I croaked.

"With straps, tightly. As *bhasko,* the origin of the word suggests, the kernel of the word is the confinement of the *straps*, not the sticks or the axe, nor the punishments they represent," he corrected me. "The straps wrap the bundle tight around that instrument of the state's sole right to violence. The severity of obedience in a coercive collective, the straps are the key element of fascism."

Into my ear he whispered, "Disrupt this discourse!"

Before I could ask him how or why I should do that, he disappeared. Did he mean, cut the straps? Which straps? The stay-home order to suppress the pandemic by the suppression of citizens and livelihoods...?

The governor instructed residents to inform the police if their neighbors violated the State's pandemic protocols, such as an indoor gathering of more than six people.[2]

Fairey's candidate Obama made people feel hope because they had lost it. The painting's hope was an emotion and nothing more, but emotion was real. Obama's head had to tilt.

Hope now revealed itself as memory and waste. Things were so much worse now.

"Ptum, ptum, ptum!"

29.

"Ptum, ptum, ptum!" Time was shaky. Time in the city suffered. It crippled, mordant. Time required constant vigilance. Who could guard that long? I didn't know Time's scent, because a mask covered my nose and mouth. Time accumulated, like crows, in the thousands.

There were more than ten thousand crows in Portland. Perhaps there were fifteen thousand timekeeper crows in one blocks-spanning roost. An inhuman intelligence croaked and clicked in every tree and ledge. So many black feathers stirred. So much ink filled the trees' newspapers. *Caw-caw,* the ink yelled;

objectivity is for gulls.

Tejashree Pandey and Simon Rush sat together watching their streaming smart television. A husband tried to hide from his wife the fact that he could not remember how to tie his shoes. He improvised a peculiar lumpy knot left and right. Proud, he lifted each foot and declared his skill, strength, courage, and honor. He made a defiant resolution, then turned, only to walk into a wall. Tejashree started to laugh. And then she continued to laugh.

Simon paused the TV and looked at her. He smiled now, enjoying her fun. A problem arose: Tejashree could not stop laughing. Her convulsions of antic grew deeper. Simon leaned toward her with concern.

Tejashree continued to laugh until, gasping for air, the suffocation of it slowed her. She caught some of her breath, glanced at the frozen scene on the TV and started to giggle again.

"What's happening to me?" Tejashree laughed. "What's wrong with me? I'm losing it!" What was it? Simon knew. They all felt it.

Without supervision, time curled around warmth like uninvited belladonna. The trees themselves commanded a crescendo of heat. The heat cooked the city like a pot of lentils.

April evaporated. Was it ever really April? Who could prove there ever had been an April, for it was clearly May, was it not? It was May somehow. The month of May brought no spring. It was already summer. Through the fiery broom of a Portland early summer, the passionate were lush and unreasonable. Fantastical vegetation burst up inconveniently on no soil. Incubated chlorophyll revolted. The biome of secret self, an unrelenting insurgent, fought to restore its forest memory. Ferns unfurled in bark furrows.

For one, two, three months of pandemic stay-home, we ate as something to do while isolated at home in front of a smart television. Deceitful matter aligned inexact with desires and behaviors. Matter gave itself to exhaustion. It gave every shadow and reflection an odor of dread.

Dread of what? Was it suspicion? Suspicion of what? Once our civilization became literate, our memories weakened.

30.

Within the lush hilly nook of the Goose
Hollow apartment, human mouths opened and
closed. The green was the green of Douglas fir.
Here, city cuddled in an elbow of forest. The
lightrail train swooshed into the tunnel.

It was a trick to not hear the writhe of a
nation that chose to unevenly radicalize and
reshape itself. And yet, somehow, Noah's
birthday party gathered. They all wore masks at
first.

Noah offered a wooden plate. Carved in
Poland, a riot of bird and flowers rejoiced with
wooden vibrato.

A shared feeling of Uniqueness and
Belongingnessness grew. The small group of
intimates dipped down their masks and drank a
toast to Noah. Then, they sat. Awkward and
unsure of the new rite, they slipped their masks
back on.

How soon they drank the first bottle of Bezz
and Bumper's case of Preseco! They wished
Noah health and happiness! Somewhere along
the way, the guests pushed the masks below
their chins and ambushed their food.

Amidst the clink of utensils, among the up,
down movement of forks, Lourdes muttered
aside to Noah: "The bubbly Preseco has half the
pounds-per-square-inch than Champagne, much
as Bumper has half the PSI of Bezz. The Missus
offers us a self perception of luxury, whereas
the Mister is a mere value sparkler."

In such manner of cultivar-gangster wit,
Lourdes focused on Noah, seated to right, next
to him. DeKay sat on his left. Lourdes' quips
curled and crackled, entertaining Noah. The
women grew annoyed and envious of his
attention on the slender, fit, quiet man.

Bumper half-hid his smile under his hand.
He had the gaunt face of a long distance runner.
The tall, stringy resilience in his character
showed itself in a glib conspiratorial sociability
that was abrasive just enough to feel sincere.
They had all forbade him to quote the wisdom
of the old pop songs he revered. He thought
Portlanders were adorable; for example, it was
cute that they fawned over BMWs, which were

obviously a baseline standard.

Larsen was DeKay's graduate school friend, colleague, and a sort of lifelong aunt to Sammy, who was not present.

Confidence, poise, proportion, presence, and even a smile — Noah demonstrated all these host virtues. When Lourdes joked, he laughed. He delicately ladled food on the guests' plates. He even ate some samples himself here and there.

Noah did not neglect his wife. He clasped her thigh under the table. By subtle chin directions he orchestrated the passing of dishes, the exchange of condiments. He removed wine bottles. He passed soups. He handed the platter again. He even offered the sanitizer dispenser.

Certainly, the counselor knew, Noah was superior to Roger, DeKay's ex-husband. Noah lacked the arrogance, the aggression, the self-focus of Roger the ram, that freight and petroleum industry lawyer, years departed. Lourdes had loathed Roger. He had helped untrouble DeKay after the divorce.

Outside the building, a filthy man gesticulated.

31.

Bezz Larsen was in the process of finding a job for Dylan, the wife of her son (also named Dylan), when they announced her pregnancy. Life insisted on going on.

Larsen did not object to offer a smile for no reason or to make a tense situation easier. Her eye kept its own agenda, of course. One believed that for every challenge, it was one's moral and legal duty to identify the proper procedure to resolve it, to regulate and to prosecute. When Larsen lifted her arm at the elbow, her bangles rolled down. When she then lowered her arm, the bangles also descended.

She asked, "Where is Sammy?"

Basil DeKay answered: "She's in Tacoma. It's a demonstration to support justice for immigrants."

That was what Sammy had told them.

DeKay could not stop herself: "Sammy doesn't just talk. She acts! Unlike me."

Lourdes wiped his hands with sanitizer. It was a ruse to cover his bend to whisper in Noah's ear. "How much humble-bragging must we hear?"

Noah tried to change the subject: The government's message of warning and shame shifted! Federal authority, through the director of the National Institute of Allergy and Infectious Diseases, admitted he *lied* to the public about mask effectiveness last winter. He had announced, "I do not recommend that you wear a mask." He justified it, burning trust in authority to stall frightened citizens. This trick gave hospitals time to acquire the limited supply of masks. *Ha!*

But now, Noah went on, some people said the director was honest *then,* and lying *now* that he wanted us to wear masks, and here the table erupted. Plates argued with forks and spoons, while the bowls stayed mute.

Did Lourdes listen to this discussion on the decay of authority and national institutions? No. He noticed how, when Noah talked, the tip of his nose moved. Was the dolphin disturbed by the discussion of pregnancy, of family? DeKay had announced, indirectly, that he could have no child of his own, not with her.

Yes, Noah felt pain. Resentment surprised him. His patrimony was dust. He hadn't been certain he needed heirs. All the while, she had Sammy. What was the problem? He was not sure where he erred to let in his resentment.

As the conversation swept on, he thought of Sammy's secret. While he held the hand sanitizer dispenser, his face changed.

32.

Larsen and Bumper's daughter-in-law's due date, the inept preparations for the baby, was their next topic.

Lourdes whispered, "No more talk about babies. Let the birth rate decline. Heterosexuals had a nice run. Now, pansexual is the only true sexual, that and asexual, of course. The nuclear family is nearly kaput."

Noah muffled his response behind his cloth napkin: "Quiet, you. Have some lentils." The guests were not eating them at the proper rate.

DeKay came back from washing her hands under the kitchen faucet with soap and hot water: "To Noah! And let's raise our glasses to our children, our grandchildren, and to family life!" *Despite what Lourdes whispered about the nuclear family,* she thought.

Larsen admired Noah. "How lucky Basil is to have you!"

Lourdes whispered, "…Kaput."

"Two hearts that beat as one… our lives have just begun," Bumper, in song, quoted to his wife. He was a dreaded Californian expatriate. Worse, he was from Los Angeles. Still worse, he was a former music label executive. Somehow he hadn't spent all his money on cocaine. Was that how he acquired his nickname, or was it his passion for expensive cars? No one knew how he had money left, not even Larsen.

Larsen mock-sung, *"Forever…"* to her

154

husband, then they both leaned together and crooned, *"Ohhhhhh."*

There was no rush, but dessert waited: tropical fruits, banana cream pie, with cheese rind aromas.

But the friends laughed and cheered. "For Noah! Whoop, whoop!"

DeKay's face closed, opened again, then closed. Mask up, mask down, what was proper?

"I come from a line of large families," she declared with pride and aggression.

"It's too late for me and Noah to have more, but that's okay." Her open face showed that it wasn't okay, so she closed her face. Mask up, mask down, what was proper? Noah sighed.

More quietly DeKay told them, "Noah and I were hoping... I don't want to try again."

She smiled, self-conscious of her tears. "I delayed too long to have another child. I'll have to wait for Sammy. I'm allowed to want a grandchild, someday..."

Bezz Larsen was there for her. She caught the mournful tone. "You waited because of hard choices... If you paused your career, who would have taken your place?" She turned it toward anger. "Contessa said she does not want kids." The tone carried the epithet: back-stabber.

The women locked gazes. The three men shrunk aside, like bubbles caught in the sluggish gel of hand sanitizer.

Bumper hunched over the empty chair

between Lourdes and Noah. He had the gift of schmooze and natural ease at parties. He nodded at the two women. "Here it comes. Watch their eyes."

DeKay was drunk and fervid. She learned over to talk to Larsen: "Of course it's not a coincidence that it's my contract year when Contessa chose to say that thing about me…"

"What did she say?" Bumper egged on, not able to suppress a smile.

"Oh, she said that I know how to promote women," DeKay scowled.

The men didn't understand, so Larsen burst out, "Contessa means, Basil knows know how to create a welcoming environment for women, but she doesn't actually create a truly diverse community."

DeKay's eyes were hot, in part for Larsen's ready articulation of the offense, her use of the word *truly*. "I train people to create a welcome environment for diverse individuals! I don't have the power to hire anyone. It's so unfair for Contessa to judge me like that."

Bumper leaned into Lourdes. They watched the women complain. "Look how wide their eyes are, how round. As if outrage fulfills them in a way positive feeling never can!"

Lourdes leaned forward, relishing this confidence. "They crave it."

Bumper nodded eagerly as he spied.

Her lips purple, DeKay flung out an arm. Thus she threw out her words like incendiaries.

This pitch of air did not help her, as her flaming words landed astray. Words hit the ceiling and split. Fragments ricocheted. "Equal! Standards! Outcomes! But Outcomes? Standards? Equal?" A final piece fell on the floor: "Equity."

The men did not track the sense but felt the energy. Between the two other men, Bumper had given up his mask now. "Do you hear that?" he whispered as if to conspirators. "It's indignation and outrages that make our wives hot and bothered. It's not a man with a vacuum, am I right, Noah?"

Noah made himself chuckle.

33.

It was late, but the summer sun refused to set. Its nearly horizontal rays burned. Bumper and Lourdes had slunk into their drinks. Noah waited. He looked from one to the other and waited.

Drunken confusion brought Basil DeKay doubts. With Bezz Larsen she marinaded in Contessa Finger-flavored indignation. The women's conversation grew wild. It was not clear to the men if they were on the same side or not. Noah stared at his plate as Basil uncovered a Blue Willow bowl of marijuana cigarettes. These were now several years legal in Oregon, after drugs won the War on Drugs.

"What do we mean, (puff, puff, puff) by success, Bezz?" DeKay demanded passionately. "Is success by means of lower standards success at all?"

The male guests sat restlessly. They were comfortably digesting, and yet, why did the moment feel unsettled? Even Bumper had withdrawn his interest. He had to abjure drugs after those happy years of excess in Los Angeles.

DeKay wavered. "Right, right, the old standards are part of the problem. Except," she drunkenly added, "(Puff, puff, pu, pu, pu... u... u... ff.) Isn't it patronizing to lower standards? How is that justice? Where am I wrong?"

Larsen eyed her friend with concern, but she had disappeared in the smoke. So Larsen told the smoke, "It's not lower standards. It's different standards."

The smoke subsided. DeKay nodded and affirmed, as if memorizing, but the cannabis did *not* help: "The only standards are outcomes. It's equity. It's justice. It's revenge."

Larsen looked DeKay in the eyes. "I know you believe in (puff, puff, puff). So the only reason results aren't (puff), is, (puff), because (puff, puff, pu... u... u... ff). You know that (puff), means giving those (puff) who (puff), need (puff) the (puff) they need, whatever that (puff) is, to make them (puff, puff, pu... u...

u… ff).”

"Yeah, (puff-ff-ff), I (puff-ff-ff)." DeKay
stubbed out the last of the marijuana.

Noah was still looking down at his plate.
Bumper had his elbow on the table, his face in
his shoulder like a bird. He had felt a shadow
and a twinge in his side.

Now the women saw Noah, and grew self-
conscious. Lourdes suppressed his grin.

In the moment's sudden quiet, with masks at
this moment down, each scanned each face.

Which individual hid a secret that would
explode the evening?

34.

Phonograph records, obsolete and quaint,
were somehow popular again. Noah's collection
was unusual. His old albums survived many
apartment moves before marriage. He found
some titles in dingy stores; his policy was never
to pay more than a dollar. The young
generation's obsession with the old technology
made that more difficult. Still, old Top Forty
hits tended to gather in the $1 bins.

DeKay, Noah, and Larsen stood and held
each other. They swayed to Richard Harris'
"MacArthur's Park". Such nostalgia and pain it
expressed at the end of a love affair! Bumper

lip-synched:

We were pressed
In love's hot, fevered iron
Like a striped pair of pants

The tempo rose and fell in the long, agonized song, so camp... The sentiment was, however, forever human. It offered dramatic pain, fluid pain, pain that bent and twisted. How much we need our pain!

I will drink the wine while it is warm
And never let you catch me looking at the sun

Larsen complained, "It is impossible to

dance to!" and added, "What imbecile is in danger of looking at the sun?" Later she exclaimed, "That cake in the rain metaphor, what madness!"

It was as rich a metaphor as Homer's shield of Achilles. Larsen and Lourdes danced too, masked. Then Larsen and Noah danced, masked. Ms. and Mr. Larsen danced, unmasked. Then Bumper fell back on the couch with his eyes closed. Needles pricked the sides of DeKay's chest.

It was gently nostalgic or perhaps historic. They broke the quarantine together. All felt permission to let go the stays of their ideological corsets and wiggle a little. It was a safe space to colonize the roaring male heterosexuality of the songs.

Everywhere the wine warmed itself. The icing in the rain dripped down the walls. Love pleated pants with its electric iron. In fact, love even striped the pants; that's how much love there was.

Wife and birthday husband danced unmasked. They indicated their intimacy with their bare faces so close. Then Noah danced masked with the other people in turn, Lourdes first, then Larsen again. There was such vulgar charm of the old style of popular music. Outside the window, only now the parasitical fungus of twilight filled the sky. A faint dusting of forest fire ash stained the streetlamp.

35.

Masked, Lourdes and Noah danced to
another album rescue from the one dollar bin:

Lonely night, I cry myself to sleep
Tell me, what am I gonna do

Above his mask, Noah's tragic eyes
glittered. Under his mask, Noah's face was
numb. He absorbed the energy of attention.
Noah held Lourdes tightly, needy and
deferential. In that moment, perhaps a romantic
colonization of Lonely Nights on planet
Teardrops, Lourdes felt that Noah wanted no
one but him. Lourdes held out his arm, and

Noah spun under it.

What did this mean? Had Noah made his choice? And yet, that was the moment that Noah let go and embraced Larsen again. With the new record, Lourdes stepped aside and considered.

Put your man in the can, honey
Get him while you can

Meanwhile DeKay pressed her thumb against the chest needle. Oh yes, she spied Lourdes's sardonic expression.

The suspect turned away too late to look at the new album. He helped himself to another

CBD cookie. Meanwhile, with mask off, Bumper turned to face the couch's back cushions.

Doom doom doom doom doom— Bah!
R-r-rata tata tata tata
R-r-rata tata da dada doom

DeKay scrutinized Lourdes. She thought she received signals that suggested, in incomplete dotted line form, how pointedly he did not watch Noah.

Lourdes saw this and just smiled quietly eye-to-eye with DeKay.

Meanwhile, Larsen whooped and shook her chest back and forth. She threw her head back — and happened to give DeKay a reassuring look. DeKay knew just what she meant: *What was sisterhood? Stick together and don't sabotage.*

Noah smiled his little smile, steady. Through the rock and roll, DeKay remained calm even as Larsen wiggled. She seized the fully liberated privilege of her turn to wriggle shamelessly. Noah's spirit seemed to float away somewhere else.

In the mountains of the Cascades, wild goats crashed horn to horn. In the Redwoods to the south on the foggy California border, elks bugled and rammed antlers. Here in Portland, Lourdes danced his way in front of Larsen. As she backed away to Bumper's couch, Lourdes and Noah bobbed and writhed to the rhythmic honk of...

> *Lordy mama, light my fuse*
> *Rock and roll, hoochie koo*
> *Truck on out and spread the news*

DeKay's eyes narrowed at the two men dancing. Noah moved back and forth to spread the news, but what news? Lourdes' hands trucked onto her husband's back. One hand rocked down to roll against his waist, sliding over his posterior hoochie koo.

Eying this drunkenly, Larsen stood. DeKay saw her, impatient for another turn. Now Lourdes and Noah physically separated. Still they danced together. Under stress of colonization and disease, spirit dancing became more extravagant and evocative. DeKay absorbed it all with eyes remote and cold.

She spied over her cotton mask. DeKay did

not feel this was a domestic violation. She did
not feel jealous. She felt embarrassment. Horror
peered around the corner. Something went
awry, to the point of violation. It was
shameless.

She wanted to restore Noah's humanity. She
wanted to liberate him from the sinister
Lourdes. She wanted to stand next to the old
style high fidelity vinyl record player. And now,
with her powerful hips, she wanted to bump it.
There was a moment of horrible high-pitched
scratching, then a crash.

36.

I froze, only eyes moving. My eyes traced a cloud of virus as it fluttered — then I ran — I walked, ducked under a virion, caught my breath. Another virion bounced along the curb and I kicked it viciously. Then frightened, I ran. Tired, I walked, in my to-and-fro process under the sundial of the bronze elk.

Due to the rate of infection, the State cancelled plan 1 for Multnomah County. On the streets of Portland, people explained the word *Multnomah* this way…

When Lewis, Clark and company arrived here in 1805, they asked the natives for the name of the river that flowed strangely north into the Columbia.

The natives pointed: *Multnomah.* Later, settlers found out this meant, "You mean that river over there?" So they quietly crossed it on the map and penciled in *Willamette.*

But now, everything had to close for another two weeks. So, the State relabeled Plan 1 as New Plan 1 with an a, b, c, and d, each attributed to counties as the measurements qualified them. Legislators were the pandemics' unknown true poets.

What about the task the Masked One gave me? It made me nervous. The point of progress had become an urge to make words unsteady. I

171

shuttled back and forth and around the bronze elk in search of the narrative. The thought process assembled itself contagiously! *Disrupt the dominant discourse? How?*

It's easy in daylight to make one disbelieve the hidden city spaces. If hidden spaces existed, who controlled them? Something *wrong* lifted one shoulder in disrespect. This force disrespected the shining condominiums that rewarded hard work. It disrespected the humanely windowed café that offered a bento bowl. It disrespected the spicy kimchee option. It disrespected the chalkboard of one hundred kinds of hard cider. It disrespected the humane architecture, the two stories of residences above the street level business. It disrespected the New Urbanist promise of good people filling structures designed to promote a human flourish.

Asserting its rights, the Steller's jay let out its last gruesome shriek for the reluctantly departed day.

At night, a boxy vehicle whirred and whooshed. It washed the streets and sidewalks clean of crow drops. It washed the spilled drinks. It washed the urine, cigarettes, and discarded paper masks. Beneath the eggplant sky, there was a problem.

The problem showed here as a no-man's land stapled to isolation, just beyond a weathered old flier stapled to a telephone pole: the one read, *paint-and-sip,* the other read, *heroin-and-burglary.* Arrogant representatives of organized crime stood by the permanent makeup clinic. Perverts and the violently insane waited in slots and shadows, in riverbanks and rafters. No squirts of hand sanitizer seemed to help.

37.

Things were happening. In Hong Kong, at that moment, masked police batted their truncheons on the arms and heads of masked protestors. Some protestors carried umbrellas to shield their faces from the eye of security cameras and to ward off pepper spray. Digital cameras connected to computer networks added face data to the communist social credit system. Masks made it more difficult, but not impossible. The human gait registered as data.

Too many espressos! Too much wine, not enough bread, not enough consecration! Too much news! Too many citizens tested positive for COVID-19! Too many untested citizens had it and did not know it!

Sleepless rumination followed Lourdes' night gaze. It was too hot for leafy compost to decompose, so it just hid spiders.

COVID-19 tests sometimes gave false negatives, the laboratory email told him; but on the other hand, they sometimes gave false positives. Regardless, his reported negative. His thermometer reported no fever. But insomnia remained a riderless death-unicorn of his nightly apocalypse.

The unicorn, deep in the forest, sometimes must dine on nettles. Its horn could kill, but it was vegetarian. What drove the hunger of the urban unicorn? It dined on the shame of insomniacs. The more the pandemic lurked, the more the baboon of a president provoked.

The word "baboon" came from an old French *baboin* for "simpleton." Older than that, the word meant, "gargoyle."

True, dread seemed unwarranted. Lourdes' job seemed secure. Students suffered more

stress than ever. Whether they showed up for
their displaced virtual classes or not, they
signed up for his counseling. He could treat
them by video without pause. And he made sure
the administration knew about his queerness.
Frankly, he thrived professionally under the
pandemic.

And yet, the pandemic's reductions of
enrolled students led the administration to
wiggle early retirement packages in the air.

Did anything matter? He might cough, grow
feverish. He might find himself unable to secure
a sufficient breath. Would he suffocate, fenced
in a hospital's clear plastic? The threat was
unclear because of all the panic. It didn't kill
many who weren't elders or already ill. Likely
he would not die, but it was possible. And then
what would happen? He would die anyway.

Lourdes recalled how Freud observed that
death-related fears reflect unresolved childhood
conflicts. But it was socially dangerous now to
perceive childhood causes behind adult
behavior. All causes of suffering had to have an
ultimate root in injustice. This meant people had
a moral and practical obligation to respond to
suffering with an angry, accusatory expression.

Desire refutes annihilation. The unicorn of
death lifted its multicolored hoofs up and
stamped down. It march-stepped closer. How
could people possibly be free to make
independent rational decisions? How could
angry people determine their own destiny?

"Beware," he thought through his drowse,
"lest the cheerful death unicorn cheat me
through wise sounding words of *neigh-neigh.*"

38.

What was the gift of unexpected consequences? It was the inability of modern fluid ideology to replace fear of death, to replace faith. But there was no faith left to replace. What it had to replace was void. And that didn't seem to work. Time was fluid: past, present, future united in a way that was incomprehensible to flesh.

Lourdes then would sacrifice Noah to the unicorn of his insomnia. Yes, sooner or later, Noah might bend under the Lourdes' rainbow. And what would happen next? Lourdes trusted that the answer would arrive on clip-clops. Perhaps the unicorn's horn would deliver a pierced missive.

Noah needed something. Lourdes would offer his own directive to distract Noah's lack

— and Noah's lack grew. The porpoise man needed purpose.

Lourdes couldn't offer that, he knew. He would earn the right in time. Noah would give himself to Lourdes out of duty. The counselor was sure of it. And then what? Lourdes turned his thought aside.

How could a thinking person have any purpose other than his own selfhood? Queerness needed a fringe or it died. Only in a fringe could it see the virtue of its transgressions. Why did gender revolutionaries replace elastic, creative possibility with orthodoxy? Freedom could only be fugitive and subversive, never doctrinaire. Unyielding magisterial sermons and rainbow-hued castigations were more *smear-the-queer* than any adolescent ball game, if queer really meant anything anymore.

Everything was unknown. Everything was gray. Everything was queer or did not signify. Shrouded forms whirred in a mist, with the faint scent of marijuana. How did this not perpetuate dread? What became of discomfort? How could a disconnect resolve? It jutted. It made harmony with fate impossible.

Lourdes shut his laptop, spreading darkness again: no pornography could kindle him tonight. Annoyed with himself as the bright spots in his eyes faded, he smiled slyly.

He grew mirthful in the dark and eager again. "What humiliation awaits you, my Adonis, when I bring you down. My passion for everything will show you what a man could be. And now the unicorn, too, hunts maiden knights." With the laptop closed, he felt his superiority rise.

Lourdes rose out of bed and dropped a cannabis gummy bear down his throat. He was certain with all the power of his medium strong mind. So powerful abided the animal instincts, the urge coded in biology to defy time forward, that his obsession with Noah could push back fate. It could set aside and humiliate the darkness. By dominating Noah, he could humiliate the unsatisfiable force that created him. He knew he did not create himself. Lourdes gored sleep.

39.

With my hands against my temples, I hummed a *brzzdzzd* sound. Thus I hastened to keep up to events back in the Goose Hollow neighborhood. I saw that the record player still lay on its side, trailing wires. The vinyl record had snapped and thrown a chunk somewhere.

The odors of alcohol, food, and argument grew strong. Noah, naturally moderate and self-restrained, lost his forbearance. The last guest had departed. This left broken shadows. He plucked off his mask, wiped his face, and shut the door. This shut was a noise composite of three complicit sounds. He closed his eyes and opened them again, hot with sparkles of hostility.

Outside, on the curb strip, golden stubble screamed in the hot eggplant of night. Sunflowers wooed. Seedpods exploded. A car

182

alarm wailed and then cut off. Thistles began to disintegrate and lift. Inside, Noah navigated chairs, a bench, and a fold-down table.

Basil DeKay perceived Noah's saffron heat. With clipped phrases, she offered an observation. A husband should not let a person, man or woman, or any other gender, stroke him like that, other than his wife. It was obvious to him now, she hoped.

"Hope?" Noah demanded, "Like that framed poster of Obama you tried to give me?"

He let loose his complaint. Must everything always be political? Even at his own dinner party she complained with Larsen about politics. How telling of her priorities, how humiliating. Why did she seek such negativity? No wonder she felt stress. When President Baboon made her most angry, she wouldn't even look at Noah, as if he were to blame: he didn't hate the executive primate *enough*.

"I can't change who is president. I choose not to let him ruin my day," he explained.

No wonder! You can choose that because you're a man, she thought. *I don't have that luxury.* The varicella zoster virus seethed in her chest nerves.

Aloud, DeKay replied, "Yes, politics calls my attention. It's important. Yes, my job is demanding. Sorry, but I can't change my nature. I can't pretend that all the problems out there don't exist just because you have a birthday."

The Communist tear gas rolled down Hong Kong boulevards. Billions wondered, could there be a vaccine? When, when?

40.

Time walked on hind legs. The number of infected grew. Silence chattered. Had love's striped pants lost their pleat? A song promised the sweet, sweet hoochie-koo of lovers, but there was none.

"What of your family responsibilities?" Noah demanded. He turned away and changed his tone. "You don't even know that your own daughter had an — " He didn't say the word. He wrenched himself away from saying it.

Basil DeKay shrunk. She had intuited this but had not accepted her intuition.

She already knew that Sammy faced temptations unknown to previous generations.

Young women tread among these traps at the peak of their fertile power before they were fully adult. And everyone worked hard to tell them that nothing could stop them. No one told them that things stopped everyone.

Did Sammy's best friend Sophie pay for her yearlong trip around the world by working a minimum wage job? By waitress service, long shifts, and a smile for tips? No, she offered a naked show on live Internet video. Young Sophie earned a lot of money that year, more than DeKay did.

Why wouldn't this tempt her daughter? What was the principle against it? Not chastity. Not modesty. Not virtue. Not restraint before marriage. There was no principle.

There was Eros made algorithmic by smartphone software. The mother resisted the provocation to blame sexual freedom for Sammy's weeping. Sammy had cried that young men would only sleep with her, not be her boyfriend, and not love her. Her mother thought about it later and recalled several nice boys who seemed to want to date her, whom the daughter had rejected. She had called them schlubs and had thrown her body after the same few elite men and bad boys that most of the other women wanted and also cried over.

Relationships, thought the mother, are for those who can relate. Still, she could understand her daughter this far: Yes, all those nice boys were schlubs. What was the solution? How did parents guide kids in the old days? Arranged marriage?

It didn't matter. Some months after those tears, Sammy said she no longer felt that way. She had a term of identity for it: *demisexual.* That meant she didn't want to have casual sex anymore, only sex with love.

It mattered less and less. She no longer wanted to find a worthy man to court her. She said it was a waste of time. Also, she asserted she was *genderfluid* because she didn't want to wear makeup.

What to make of it? It was DeKay who encouraged her to put her attention into goals. Mother encouraged daughter to better herself and, along the way, just maybe make the world better. Sammy believed the first part followed the second.

41.

And somehow this happened. Sammy had an abortion. How did this compute? She had confided in whom? Not the mother. Sammy chose Noah, to whom mother and daughter never applied the role of stepfather. Maybe daughter still rebelled against maternal oversight.

With terror, DeKay realized she had nothing genuine and little of substance left of her family. She had not much husband, little of home, and no song of hearth. What would become of Sammy? If Mother held her tight, she'd flee.

Mother looked into Sammy's present to forecast her daughter's future. Now the girl was stubborn, extreme, and ill dressed, unwilling to accept real love. She might finish her degree, but meanwhile she made her left arm ugly with the tattoos of a hoodlum. Unrealistic notions captivated her. She lacked close friends and easy laughter. She lacked joy and curiosity. She lacked hope. No, DeKay told herself. Sammy failed to thrive.

DeKay did not cry, but her throat and inner ears ached. Tired, she looked below at the night prospect of May. The air seethed over the residential complex's garden. It was hidden from the street, a private repose. Among the leaves sat colored glass balls mounted on poles. These were a hysterical command of frivolity. Dim and blind, the garden desiccated until the rains would come again in late September.

"Why didn't you tell me?" she demanded, her voice muffled by emotion. Her face showed the mask marks of her evening as pink lines.

Wife and Husband stood in the darkness of their fate. They did not defend themselves against it. Her gestures were the sulk of unsated domestication.

"Why don't you ask Dr. Bomberger why I didn't tell you," Noah replied, his face cold.

This shouldn't have been a surprise. Alert, DeKay scowled. *Why does Noah want to hurt me?* she thought. If she asked her daughter about this, would it push her away?

DeKay, with a face drained of temper, sat in her domestic double-mortgage. She was proud, emitting not light but the shade of the boundless disappointment. She was sure that she did not deserve this pain.

She snapped, "As long as we're sharing forbidden secrets, why don't you ask Lourdes about how he helped me get past the pain of my divorce?"

Occasionally, Noah would attempt to register a reservation with a weak motion. He wanted to put up resistance.

But no, her wave of self-sufficiency thrust that meaningless gesture aside. DeKay moved triumphantly past his resolve. Her force flooded with its broad stream the feeble convulsions of his diluted masculinity.

His eyes remained hot. "Your daughter has problems that go back to your divorce. You

191

should have been paying attention to her, maybe, and not Lourdes."

This was bad enough. But her expression rejected this as an answer. So he added his interpretation: "You don't want to admit it. The truth is, you regret divorcing that jackass Roger. You need a jerk to feel like a real woman. I bet you never needed to schedule sex with *him*. Your mind is feminist, but your body is not."

Time had cracks. There was a fissure in the moment. Through it, a hot light flashed. The elastic of her scrunchy loosened. *"You should have told me!"* She slapped Noah.

42.

Afterward, Noah blinked and frowned. The light dulled to normal. Quizzically he gandered. If his wife divorced him and then she screwed ten guys, then she was an *empowered woman.* But if he did, he was *gay.*

She wouldn't soften, so she glared. She tried to hide her emotions. But her face grew darker and darker. A magical chant helped her: He, she, per, they, ve, xe, ze. He, she, per, they, ve, xe, ze! Ve-xe-ze, ve-xe-ze!

Noah retreated to his room. He shut the door and slowly sat. His face in his home gym mirror stared back. Before his eyes, his cheek reddened in a hand-shaped blotch. It amazed him. How horrible it all was!

In the jellied substance of the ghost that was Noah's self, the outrage sought resolution. He touched his face and considered reprisals. He knew he was a twenty-first century man. He had somehow let himself become an invention for the convenience of women by women.

That meant he listened and did not suggest solutions. He was more gentle, more respectful, more trim and fit but not threateningly muscular. As a condition for their engagement, he took a few months of therapy. He listened and he listened. Before the pandemic, he went to a hair stylist every four weeks. All that was okay. He was willing to watch videos that explained how to fix things around the home, but nothing broke. He drifted, he listened, but did not feel oppressed. He didn't mind his domestic duties. What was there to complain about? Nothing.

Noah winced as he heard DeKay smash something in her room. He realized, recently with horror, how his wife wrestled with herself. She wrestled with her remorseless and ugly animal need for him to snarl back at her. But the idea of that exhausted him. He just didn't have that mental brutality.

He wasn't like Roger. He didn't have the mass of personality that pushed a defiant fist through time and space. The best he could do to defy her was be her daughter's secret confident

when she chose. And now Lourdes offered
another way to be more of something,
somehow.

DeKay sat in her outrage, loneliness, and
humiliation. Red wine dripped down the wall.
Shards of her broken glass lay where they fell.
The pie wedges did not add up to a circle. She
sat in the bedroom by her dressing table. In the
mirror, wrinkles grew around her eyes. A print
butterfly mask hung from her coral jewelry tree.
The Obama HOPE poster leaned on the table.

The poster radiated, but was its outward
motion true? Maybe that outward motion had
stalled. Now it was passive in concentration. Its
simple lines manifested a hope for hope.

Stalled, was it poised now to draw inward?

The image tingled, ready to distend, to disintegrate, to discharge into a family. It required no female animality. It beckoned, an almost self-generating fecundity, a politicized femaleness deprived of brakes and pathologically rampant.

Noah should have told her, she thought. He was wrong about everything, but she dismissed that easily. Why was she so angry? Did Mother, for all her dedication and sacrifices, deserve to have Daughter choose *Noah* as her confidant? About something so private? Why did Sammy choose Noah?

Noah was cute and gentle, not a lover, but an ally. Roger was different — forceful, a challenger. DeKay's body had been hungry then for a man in a way that was no longer true. Her body had hungered for Roger. Somehow they started a family. Maybe it was a bad deal for Noah, but what about her? Why didn't things work out for her?

She closed her eyes. It hurt her, a remembrance of the scent of masculinity. The smell of her ex-husband's tobacco smoke, his firefighter mustache bristle, the rasp of his cheek stubble against her face, the mismeasure of his laughing eye... Any of that musky sensuality could stimulate this inflamed female administrator to a depraved parthenogenesis. But there was none. There was just the four-colored Obama HOPE poster.

She could have had a grandchild in her arms right now. She had lost her grandchild. Her daughter was not strong. Her future was uncertain. No, no, that was not right. Her future was error, error and pain.

She stabbed her chest with her fist. "What have you done, Sammy?"

And you, masked reader, can you remember the mad songs from yesteryear? The peaceful easy time of boredom? The spoiled times of mad rush? The pantry cartons full of blue sky?

Luxury of peaceful times passed! The songs of youth awake again in the heated night. I hear them sometimes, only sometimes. Sometimes in the alleyways I understand a loneliness that echoes on old bricks.

The dreaming crows half-listened. The sky turned sour, yellow-white with a burnt scent from Cascade forest fires. The freight trains rolled and shook their way up from California to course along the Willamette. The trains reached the city and let out bellow after bellow.

The bronze elk's neck swiveled on a hinge. Its old nostrils drew in the scent of no bronze ewes, just the orange poppies of seaside ranges.

Some time later, DeKay slept. In her dream, she tried to concentrate over slides of a PowerPoint presentation. "Vibrant," she considered. "Inclusive." It was difficult to concentrate without waking herself up.

Through this tension, a shape of sensation

showed itself in dream as worth and meaning…
"The concealment itself is concealed," it
seemed to suggest. "So great is this
concealment, that one is not even aware of the
concealment. One may even come to think of
the darkness as light."

Even in her dream, she remembered she had
dreamed this before. But now it was already
gone. Half lucid, she struggled back to work in
her dream. "Holistic," she thought. "Positively
impact…"

43.

Summer resounded everywhere tricky!
Masks flew off, as long as we stood measured
six feet apart. Freed, I flailed my arms, tossed
my head like the bronze elk, and pursed my
lips. The bronze elk did not kiss me. And then
someone yelled, "Put your mask back on!"

And so I did. I closed my eyes as I looped it
around my ears. When I opened my eyes again,
Zoë and Tom stood nearby, both masked. They
made sure I noticed them. They each nodded
politely and turned away.

There was an information exchange of
croaks and crooau-aucks. Of course, the

American crow, *corvus brachyrhynchos,*
offered this. They bundled the exchange in
family feathers. Last year's young blue-eyed
noisemakers helped their parents raise new
siblings in the park trees and neighborhoods.

Six hundred feet up the old cinder cone
volcano, now Mount Tabor Park, bronze
Harvey Scott scowled. With his bronze finger
he pointed, as if to scold, "East side workers,
obey the west side mansions!" He had no idea
that a crow perched on his head. Its pronouns
were caw, caw, caw!

Would the people receive another
government relief check? How would citizens
pay their rent? How would landlords pay their
mortgage?

Summer brought its special kill-light and
blue to the spaces between the sprouting tree

branches. Adolescent squirrels chased each other one way and the other. But the civilization of the inky feather walked on roofs, cynically croaking their arguments. They had their own opinions.

A crow soared over row houses in the Pearl District. In Bezz Larsen's back patio, the two women seated apart by a smart television.

DeKay apologized for her drunken doubts at the party. There was no time to discuss Noah, and anyway why should she reward him that way?

Motion burst! Thorns slashed against the Reign! 4-3-3 smashed into 4-4-2 with simulated fan sound. It was sometimes ghostly, for the televised seats lay empty. The forward Sinclair stole the ball.

Her ponytail flew! It jibed and jabbed along with its owner's chopping forelegs. It insinuated and lashed. It juggled and thrust. Suddenly Sinclair darted through the athletes representing Seattle. Tough, undaunted, she blasted toward the goal. The ball danced on her knee, her shin, and her foot.

How she intimidated with her Canadian swagger! How terrible, her ruthless Canadian glare, her go-to-the-devil expression, the basilisk blasts that everyone associates with the cruel, flinty face of a Canadian.

Seattle's goalie bent low, face stoic. She extended long yellow sleeves. She grimaced. She shifted right and left, crablike.

White socks flashed! Headbands flew! Black socks chopped! Ponytails whirled like propellers! The stands, full of emptiness, roared in silence. The goalie held the ball.

Soccer is a bunch of people running away from their *goals*. These women roared over the field and kicked. They jumped, twisted, shouted. And then one fell on her back.

"Yellow card! Yellow card!"

"But Bomberger has tenure," DeKay objected.

"Go around his tenure. Hurt him through the medical board. His support will unravel." Larsen pointed, "Look at that pass, right between them…"

An athlete slid across the grass on her side toward the white sideline. The ball shot like a cannonball from right to left. Run! Run!

What were the right themes DeKay should strike? How could she avoid the controversies and legal trouble without missing the necessary points? What did she want to happen?

Larsen continued, "His public advice for activists to abjure modern medicine?"

"Yes and he suggested we go through surgery without anesthesia. That's a violation of his Hippocratic Oath."

"Aside the hateful disrespect to Amerindian culture…"

"I see that, but it might not be enough. I don't want to go after his license. I want him to admit him he was wrong and then shut up."

DeKay eyed the array of athletes as they dispersed into formation. Footie filled all meaning. Lines of force manifested purpose by kicks.

"Shoot! No *pass,* she's open! Oh-h-h!" Larsen cried in disappointment as the goalie stole the ball. "Mmm. I think your best attack is to quote Bomberger's mockery of indigenous ways of knowing science — Oh, come on referee, did you see that? She's flopping! Get up, no one believes you!"

They waited for the injury to resolve. The young woman walked off with a limp. The juices of indignation helped stiffen her short, spiky hair. Red panting faces exchanged glances. The athletes on the bench clapped together. And the substitute hustled on the field.

"Still no score!"

"If you nail Bomberger, Contessa won't be

able to do anything but support your contract renewal."

"Hey see that? That? That was a trip. That right there's 'Defender commits a foul in the penalty box!' Seattle should have had a penalty shot on goalie."

As the forwards tired out, the coach replaced and subbed the four. He yelled for them to hustle, run, and be aggressive.

In every contest there must be a winner and a loser, except in soccer of course. Today's struggle ended in a tie. Such draws shamed all.

The women cursed social distancing rules and drunkenly hugged. How good it was release some of the pent-up plague-driven frustration! Life filled them! If only it could last.

44.

From Union Station, Sammy walked to the streetcar. It was a hot day. She passed the shabby line of tents on the sidewalk. She passed the blue plastic box with a slot for needles.

She crossed the street to avoid the garbage, broken bits of time, and stolen grocery carts heaped with the junk of street ration. Then she rode the streetcar with her bag on her lap. The city slid with a metal song. The triangular junctures of the bridge quivered. Sammy's expression was flat, even under her black bandana mask.

It was hard for me not to worry about my hero, Basilica DeKay. The Masked One had tasked me with her story — to put myself into her story. How could I do that? How could I not

207

let my opinions, ever poised on my nose like a bug, lead me my own direction?

My eyes followed Sammy's gaze. On the sidewalk, a young woman tried to catch the attention of all the traffic held at the light. Masked, she strode along the stopped cars. She held up a sign in black marker on brown cardboard torn from a box: *"RAISING FUNDS FOR MY PARTNER'S TOP SURGERY."*

"Ptum, ptum, ptum," I sang quietly. On the other side of the river now, Sammy stepped off the streetcar. I rushed to follow. I trailed Sammy into the leafy, well-kept Irvington neighborhood full of stately Edwardian homes. Yards were full of color.

Inside her apartment home, Grandma, maskless, did not get up. "You've grown, and you have a sunburn. Vitamin D. Good for you." Grandma did not leave her seat. She was her biological father's mother. If she had his blunt manner, she also had the same confidence. Sammy saw that the windows were open. She didn't have to open them to let any virus out.

Sammy paused. Still Grandma disdained to put on her mask. She never did like to hug in greeting. She kept her white hair cropped short. She had sagging cheeks yet steady vigor. She wore overalls, of all things. Grandma still thought of herself as a *tomboy*. That was an antiquated term for a human role that had no place in the new hegemony.

208

She typed at her computer, whacking the keys to make website words somehow steal the power bananas from President Baboon. Everything about Grandma showed unconscious competency. She also showed conscious discipline and lack of compromise.

Grandma half-turned her head away and barked, "Any arrests? What's your bail funding mechanism?"

Sammy explained that the protest was perfunctory. There were no arrests. "Mostly it was a memorial. A guy died trying to set ICE busses on fire."

The Immigration and Customs Enforcement deported illegal immigrants. To Sammy and many others, it was an instrument of the president's excesses. Grandma looked up from the computer screen. She looked at the wall right ahead of her, then looked over at her granddaughter. "He died?"

"Yes, some months ago. The cops, like... they shot him. This was his memorial."

But Grandma was already back at her typing. She cursed; she had hit the wrong thing somehow and lost all she had typed. She asked Sammy for help.

The granddaughter bent over and looked for the lost missive. Sammy found it in a minimized window, which she enlarged again. It was a commentary on women candidates scorned.

The granddaughter perceived the web platform; she restrained herself. Then she burst out, "You're arguing about women candidates in a Facebook group."

"Yes, Sammy. Is that a new tattoo on your arm?"

Sammy shrugged, for Grandma would never understand any *boom-shaka-laka,* then flopped on the sofa. She scoffed, "Well you know young people don't really use Facebook anymore, right?"

Grandma's head swiveled and she looked at Sammy. She asserted herself in how she sat: upright, firm. "Young people ain't got any dough, right? And dough is the sea that politics swims in. We've already raised fifty grand and we're only just getting started."

Lounging on the sofa, Sammy was prepared to resist the blast from grandmother's pride and self-respect. "Sounds very middle class. Sounds very bougie," she muttered with more insolence than she intended.

Grandma didn't listen — or didn't care. She whacked on the keyboard for awhile and then suddenly stopped. She twisted.

"The police shot your guy, you say? For setting busses on fire? Why busses? Oh, those cage busses for deporting immigrants?"

"Yes." Sammy raised her legs over the arm of the sofa and rubbed her shins together. In the back of her mind, she pondered a big change. "And I think he shot at the cops."

Grandma looked back at her work. "Idiot." Then she stilled and looked over to add, "What, did he have cancer or something?"

It shocked Sammy that Grandma guessed this accurately. "He was a hero. What do you think, like, typing on a website is going to change things?"

Grandma pushed her chair back and finally faced her granddaughter. "Does the officers' humanity count? You need a haircut, by the way. Salons are open now. You'll feel better."

Sammy didn't say anything. Her blank face drooped in sulk. *How was Grandma so strong and tough?* she wondered. *How could she* boom *without any* shaka-laka?

211

The older woman was looking for her mask now, cursing. She could not find it, so she wrapped a scarf around the lower part of her head, around and around.

With the palm of her hand, Sammy rubbed one eye, then the other. "People can't determine their own fate. They aren't free. What appears to some as freedom, is, like, the options that privilege gives some. With freedom comes responsibility, the responsibility to help others."

"That's a leap," yelled Grandma through the wrappings. "That's an unsupported claim. Get a haircut, child. Hair's in your eyes. Blocking your thought process. I'll pay."

Confused, unable to respond, Sammy

212

continued with stress, "That is why, to be ethical, we must use the privileges of our freedom to attack privilege itself."

Grandma's visible, upper part of her face looked scornful or perhaps curious.

But now Sammy's train of thought found its place. Her tone grew more satisfied: "This will seem to some like attacking freedom, but it's not. It's promoting equality. Only when we're all equal can we experience real freedom."

"Ha! You're more right and wrong than you know," barked Grandma through the scarf windings. "Of course freedom is an illusion, but not because of injustice. We're nature's marionettes. Reason doesn't make us free.

We're puppets that rationalize nature's choice as our choice. Anything else is error."

This puzzled Sammy. As she thought about it, she grew shocked.

45.

The microwave beeped. Grandma pulled out the spinach pie and inspected it. She motioned that they had to let it sit for a while. Then she pulled her chair ten feet away. Steam curled out of the open corner of the waxed cardboard packaging.

"What do you mean," Sammy asked, "we're nature's marionettes? I can think. I have will."

Grandma shouted through her scarves. "We are aware, sure, more than marionettes are. Awareness leads us to fool ourselves with a rebellious attitude toward our puppet performance. That's when we perform badly."

"I don't fool myself," Sammy objected, tears

215

in her eyes.

"We all do. You included. Me too. It's part of our nature. You're human, aren't you? We want to rise to a state of being that allows us to defy our limits. The modern way to do this is with knowledge. We assume the truth will make us free. However, it doesn't work like that."

"People should be equal," Sammy insisted. She became small again, young, childlike.

Grandma laughed. "'Should be equal!' That sounds like baby talk to me. Define your terms, girl! People are different. What do you mean by equal? Is an apple equal to an orange? One person to another? Equal in height? Equal in smarts, in beauty, in talent, in muscle?

216

Obviously false."

"Obviously true," argued Sammy.

"Look at you, crying. Your mother coddled you. You can't stand an argument without tears." Grandma demanded, "You need to toughen up."

The youth's hair fell over her face as she cried harder.

Grandma snorted, unmoved. "Pull yourself together."

Why was Grandma so hard on her? Sammy did not know how to respond. Her tears continued to fall.

"You're old enough to know from experience," Grandma continued. "We all learn the hard way that biological impulses bog us down. Unconscious forces botch our efforts and confuse us."

This confused Sammy. "But our privilege means we're responsible for…" Then she broke from that and cried. Neither *boom* nor *shaka* nor even the *laka* could help her.

"Listen, girl," Grandma almost shouted, "we can't control these unconscious forces. Your father left you and your mother. Do you think that was his original plan? You need me to show you how to be strong, or at least, resilient. Life is hard."

She broke off a moment as Sammy cried.

Grandma continued in a calmer tone. "It's worse for women, maybe, because we bear the children. Good god, the hormones. The animalistic experience of giving birth. Not to mention raising children. Thank god that's done for me. You, you must know. Rather than trying to impose meaning in your life, you're better off finding contentment. Let the sense of things come and go."

Sammy gestured at the computer. "But that's not what you do."

"I know that!" Grandma snapped. "This pandemic brings out my vices! Good thing I'm old. My life is behind me. I didn't waste it in politics. I had tickets to visit Morocco. Any time I go out that door," she pointed, "that germ might kill me. So I'm angry. I still can't believe the nation elected a baboon."

Grandma didn't make sense to Sammy. Grandma was always angry, or at least, vehement. The youth lay back on the sofa now. She clutched the afghan around her.

"Don't cry, girl." Grandma sat on the edge of the couch. She held Sammy's shoulder for a moment, and adjusted the afghan. In a gentler tone, she observed, "You look like your father."

Sammy touched her hair. "My dad?"

"You have his forehead, eyes and chin. That nose, that's not ours." Grandma stood up: the comforting was over. "Your mother has almost ruined you with indulgence. But I can see you have the unruly part of your father's personality."

Roger pounded holes. He found fulfillment in argument against the trend. He liked to argue the wonder of fossil fuels. Mostly, he needed to smash his antlers against another brute's antlers.

"Where is Dad now?"

"He's doing legal work with a petrochemical plant in Ukraine."

To Sammy she forced herself to ask brightly, "Would you like to see a picture of his new girlfriend?"

"No," Sammy declared. She was still crying. She knew she should feel shame but still did not. She asked if she and Grandma were alike.

Grandma advised her that she was young yet. "Time will tell. Do you want to be like me?"

The granddaughter didn't answer. They both were quiet.

Sammy lay on the couch, head back, eyes open. Above her was an old spider web. The ventilation made it gently flutter. She was now relieved. There were still a few tears on her cheek. She had come to a resolution. "The present regime is, like, fascist," she proclaimed. "Business as usual must end."

There was a hum of memories and ambitions. Grandma misunderstood as she proclaimed, "Of course it will end. Help me with the microwave controls…"

Grandma warned, "Best not to go home quite yet. Your mom and Noah are fighting. I'll send your mom an email. No, I don't need your help."

Sammy let her shoulders rest against her knees. She resolved that she wouldn't give up her principles. She resolved that there was a way to make all people equal. *If it requires us to, like, start over, so be it.*

46.

It had been about a hundred years since renowned East Coast park artisans trained all the way west and brought their urban green philosophy for citizens' industrial relief. The design fulfilled an implied need. That need came from a theory that civilization meant strife, that its stress, artifice and right-angle regulation crippled the human.

One hundred years later, taxpayer cleanup of the rows of sanctioned homeless tents couldn't keep up with the filth, crime, and litter that gathered under branches of yew, under hickory, under redwood and sequoia, along the sanctioned curbs of the old Olmstead park.

Under the balanced, branching sky-weave of Chinese dogwood, two men strolled through Laurelhurst Park. By one coyly articulated branch on which hung a tuft of coyote fur, Lourdes wooed Noah. However, the dolphin-faced man still refused to visit Lourdes in his home.

They stopped for a moment to view the layers of leaf and white flower spray. On they stepped, by crayon frolics of hellebore, waxy and robust, evergreen winter's cheer, freshened by spring. It held onto some of that freshness with summer. Some Susans already on their second bloom of piratical yellow. The sensual joy it gave arrived unpredicted and true.

A dark purple imbued what truth? Japanese maple posed in purpled contemplation, with no trace of the artist. North America's flowering dogwood wanted something with its fraternal republic of leaves, responsibly sized and spaced. On special days, it expressed that something with white buds and tiny flower explosions inside. That something was to fill your heart and then break it!

An invisible vehemence hid behind the beauty of the garden. Nothing could be more hierarchical, more dependent on cycles of energy and nutrients. In secret chemical exchanges, each sought something from its neighbor. Lourdes made sure that Noah harkened to the dark, fibrous heart of the black mondo. And yet it punctuated so sweetly!

How fortunate Lourdes knew he was to have Noah's company. Flattery was not the key to seduce him. He knew he couldn't rely on narcissism, because that was not Noah's motivation.

Lourdes reconsidered Noah. He didn't want Lourdes to recognize him as superior or even equal. Noah had an emotional need for others to recognize his existence as human.

It was by the duck pond that Lourdes confessed alleged feelings for Noah, according to calculation and experience. He pretended to be unhappy as the garden path turned. The men navigated it together.

Lourdes also confessed his insomnia. COVID-19 lurked, but he did imply that Noah was the reason why. It wasn't a homosexual thing. All that followed from Lourdes' self-assertions. Noah listened.

It was hard for Lourdes not to feel appreciation for Noah's heartbroken attention. The next steps were Noah's gratitude, and something like an obligation to demonstrate it.

Coveys of indigo and violet, a geranium hybrid writhed over the stately rocks. Purple sage proudly pursed its two lower green lips and, with its three upper lips quivering, said little. And it was there that Lourdes pulled Noah's mask down, then his own, and kissed the dolphin face.

Noah permitted it. Yes, he had permitted it. He permitted it, but did not kiss back so much as offer some weak lip reaction, his teeth closed. It was not much. But Lourdes seized the moment with the dolphin's kiss of consent! It was consent despite the taboo, the taboo of social distance, or alienation, and no contact.

But Noah shook his head and pushed him away. He refused to follow Lourdes to his downtown condominium.

"It's early." Lourdes waved his leaves. "Why would you want to rush home?"

He asked this with insinuation, for he had no special regard for Basil DeKay, no recognition

226

that she was even a rival.

"I always have things to do," Noah asserted with a lift of his chin. "I should be able to do them. I am married. You will have to step back and accept that."

The older man suspected that Noah, flustered, did not know what he was saying exactly. Still, he noted it with respect.

"My wife is not an administrative hector and bully," Noah continued, "not an American commissar, as you sometimes imply. She is a shepherd in a time of confusion. She *protects* employees when she explains the evolved new values that personnel needs to accept."

"The new definitions of new truths," Lourdes suggested.

"Yes. Newly recognized truths."

Lourdes stopped them. "Noah, my friend. All that is anti Queer. Queer doesn't reject old definitions in favor of new ones. Queer rejects *all* definitions. Queer rejects claims on truth. Maybe what some call confusion is fear of liberation."

Noah looked away. Lourdes remained calm. They resumed their walk in silence.

The two men came upon an elder and his grandchild. They both wore cotton homemade masks over their mouth and nose. The boy asked, "What do plants eat?"

The grandfather fondly explained, "To grow, plants need sunlight, soil, water and air."

The boy thought about this and tugged on his grandfather's hand. "Where does sunlight come from?"

The grandfather pointed upward. "The sun, a star. The planet goes around it." He smiled. "I think you know that."

"Where does soil come from?" the boy persisted.

"Soil comes from tiny pieces of rock mixed with decaying dead plants and animals. But mostly decaying plants."

"Soil comes from dead plants, rotting?"

"Yes," said the elder.

"Where does air come from?"

Grandfather gestured around. "From photosynthesis in plants, on land, but oxygen comes mostly from bacteria in the oceans."

The boy recoiled. "Germs make our air?"

The grandfather hesitated. "Well, yes."

Tears fell from the little boy's eyes. "But germs are bad!"

47.

Topple the emergency-powered government suppression of hair care!

The masked greeter led masked Sammy to an empty salon chair between the next young women. One of them wore a shirt that exposed the tattoos covering both arms.

A bottle of hand sanitizer stood sentinel beside each chair.

Behind a fashion magazine, still masked, I watched and waited. The stylist approached, also masked.

The masked stylist's name was Briana. Speaking in tones she designed to be likable, she admired Sammy's hair strength and fullness. "What are we thinking today?"

"Something drastic and powerful. I want change."

"Right on! Metallic pink, maybe faded purple?"

"More radical. More peace, more justice. But I also want *boom-shaka-laka.*"

"Like this?"

"Hmm."

"The sides are like totally shaved high, the top is left long and combed to the front. See?"

"I think so."

"We'd leave enough length to fall over the forehead. This makes unordinary bangs, merely vandalized ATMs, and an isolated case of a limousine on fire. What say you?"

The stylist discerned that Sammy had only

just begun to explore her sexuality as a schizophrenic warlord. Sammy wanted to see all the options. Briana tilted her head with a handhold firm on comb and brush. With confidence, she pinched a plume of Sammy's hair. The manipulations began.

   "How about the side-swept top? Outrageous for your video meetings, right? Why to the side, against the law of hair? Laws are just constructs. They have no value in and of themselves. They often serve to, like, legitimize injustice against different styling options." Briana grabbed a different ruff. "If you wake up and want it straight and let down, it looks more like a lob, like you just smashed a window in your sleep."

She moved the ruff to the side. "But you comb it and sweep it to the sides, it gives a unique look, very direct democracy and mutual aid." Now Brianna let go and pulled Sammy's side locks flat. "I'd shave the sides and give you a discreet cross-part that divides the shaved part from the top sweep. This would form local, voluntary associations of scalp."

Sammy eyed the mirror.

Stylist and client spoke with many disclaimers and hedges. The discourse was gentle and then choppy, back and forth. They trimmed off an inch of each other's sentence hair. There were offerings and withdrawals, trial ideas, assurances and check-in questions.

Briana found a picture and showed it. "How about this punk hairstyle?"

They both looked at it, in the mirror, next to Sammy's face. "Short," Briana continued, "but the hair is styled to the side, sleek and straight. One side I'd shave low, and then as we go up, the cut like gradually becomes short. The top is long, and falls on the other side to the ear. The back I cut violently. It allows you explore the different parts of your gender expression, the rage, resentment and self-doubt you feel as a woman."

Sammy pursed her face, considering.

Briana put the punk picture away.

She found a picture, and gave it for Sammy to hold. As Sammy looked at it, Briana manipulated her client's hair. "Long hair with a short side is a hairstyle for girls who are half feminine, and half masculine, to fight fascist hooligans. Flood your social feeds to change public perceptions."

"Hmm," Sammy said in a different tone.

Briana continued, "If you defy obedience to the law as a good in itself, try this half shaved head hairstyle!"

As they plotted alternative stratagems in the use of the motte and bailey of fertility, the ornament and function of women's hair, were they conscious of the landscape? How the aesthetics of the soft and hard, of contrasts between strong and weak, how hair did something profound to that landscape?

It was just as absurd to ask strength not to express itself as strength, as weakness not to express itself as strength.

Sammy and the stylist collaborated on a combination of shaved sides, swept top, longer other-side. Sammy hoped this would make her feel powerful. She hoped it would honor the part of herself she chose to validate.

A Portland woman's salon dedicates itself to a truth that is entirely provisional. With style and verve and a little gel, any woman can problematize her own meaning.

48.

It was late. The sun had finally set. I could only make out the glint on the elk's bronze knees. The rest was a silhouette among shadow. The shadows were libertine. The shade refused sanitizer. The dark refused Uniqueness. The night scorned Belongingnessness. The dark echoes appeared unsteady with reaching tendrils of appetite. They were not refined with choices of murk and gray, but riotous. The dim cheered with obscurity. There, a man lurked with a shiv made from a spoon of time's bones.

Afraid of germs and hoodlums in the lightrail car, Basil DeKay drove the short distance across the highway bridges into downtown. An NPR broadcast soothed her with its smooth certainty. The COVID crisis caused women to suffer more than men. More women than men lost jobs. In addition, infected men were more likely to die of the disease, so their suffering then ceased. On a bright note, during the pandemic, Americans adopted a record number of pets.

At a stop, again she saw, stapled to a telephone pole, a fist silhouette against a face silhouette. She made the effort to read it: DEFEND PORTLAND! NO FASCISTS ON OUR STREETS! JOIN ANTIFA.

The light turned green. Unhappy about her estrangement with Noah, she rolled by the old buildings with a distinct stone structure of pedestal, column, and capital on top. With less pandemic traffic than usual, she eased through the blocks. She burbled through the canyon of older architecture mixed with modern. Sometimes it lacked rhyme and reason, but the streets formed an easy grid of order. She accelerated past the lumpy modern sculptures. She braked to pause before red lights on the humanely half-sized blocks with fewer office-working people. Skateboarders, shoppers, tourists were absent. But there were more runaways, more felons released from infected jails, more psychotics, more alcoholics, and more junkies. Most of them wore masks now. She accelerated again, following the streets down into the underground parking lot.

The lone guard, Amon Parker, was a late middle-aged man with a long square beard. He had the copper-plus-a-little-tin alloy complexion of an Old Testament king. He greeted her as he found his mask and scraped it over his ears. "Working late again? I'm glad I'm not the only one in the building." He was used to her vampiric hours of labor.

His hatred of the pandemic incised fine lines on his mettle. Not only was his cousin in Fort Wayne sick at that moment, but the virus bled his dreams and hurt his marriage. Anxious, Amon Parker watched sports videos on his computer to distract from his troubles.

Yes, his troubles carved intricate but folksy designs on the whalebone of his temperament. His wife Alice was mad at him after he spoke to her severely for overspending, even after their budget talk. Alice claimed she was buying necessities for their adult daughter Ava, that this was an exception. But Amon knew that, bored and depressed, Alice shopped online as a form of self-therapy. And she never bought herself the Dremel tool like he'd suggested. Why couldn't she seek satisfaction in the inscription of wholesome designs, fish, ships and whales? She had lost her job with an airline due to the pandemic. She needed scrimshaw more than ever. Every time he saw the delivery truck park in front of their north Portland house, he cringed. He wanted her to take up something reasonable, like scrimshaw.

Due to the pandemic, the building was

mostly empty all the time. At night, unsanctioned by eggplant silence, the committee meeting room was even emptier. As a vessel of power and drama, the empty meeting room offered its highest potential. Empty, it was at its most safe, too, from the germs that wait.

Basil DeKay liked to practice and work through her presentations in private, in the actual conference room. Each of the fourteen chairs was empty. The janitor had pushed aside the podium and folded away the video mechanisms. They'd use that camera soon, with Contessa Finger's help, to assist a laboratory with its problematics.

She felt the solemnity grow.

49.

DeKay began with her usual words of sympathy about COVID-19 and stress. As she continued, she began to discover the deepest essence of that night's swelter, its tear down and restructure.

DeKay raised her hand. She pointed upward, as if at higher authority. *Yes Bomberger has tenure. But the faculty handbook permits suspension or abolition of it for reasons that include insubordination.*

Loosely controlled in concentration, she waved her hand instead of speaking, looking at her notes.

In her imagination, the prisoner (he was not a prisoner; this was a rhetorical flourish), Dr. Bomberger, poised for disintegration.

She ran through the objections silently. He claimed that the administration must be naive or worse to deny that there is an ideological basis to the training. That chronicled his ignorance and insult. She just might include that.

To DeKay, this was self-evident as a non-issue. Would the committee see it the same way?

The chairs remained silent and still. The chairs, in their neutral grays, listened, unimpressed.

How might Bomberger respond? She welcomed the phantom of her opponent to enter and make his demand. But no demand came.

With one arm behind her back, DeKay declaimed, "Ladies and gentlemen of the jury," (not that there was a jury — it was a rhetorical indulgence), "assigning diversity and bias management training is not coercive. If a mere assignment is coercive," she wound the rhetorical spring and paused... She imagined the spring of discourse creaking as it tightened, as it compressed...

She let it leap:

"Then every single professor on any campus is guilty of coercion! Then Dr. Bomberger, through his own assignments to students, is guilty of coercion!"

Never present, the phantom opponent

242

refused disintegration. She adopted a mild tone.

"The diversity and inclusion training," she offered with an expression of moderation and compromise, "simply poses questions and asks for the participant's best response. We offered Dr. Bomberger the chance to select answers by random method. Still, he refused!"

Was that sufficient counter-argument to close this point? She wasn't sure. She marked it on her yellow pad for further work.

Now, the slander against marginalized peoples, the harm and the threat behind it… DeKay gathered her lightning and thundered: "Dr. Bomberger publicly declared that 'other ways of knowing' in science, such as native myth, was, and I quote, 'Poppycock.' We cannot permit this to stand. Our silence on this matter would be violence."

She made a note. DeKay tried several ways to explain the facts. She tried both with "tone" and "cold." Because the facts were on her side, she thought cold first, cold again, then tone.

The shadows stretched, cold first, then colder. They grew with perfect horizontality of justice. As they merged with tone, they had no regard of their own identities.

She didn't like to articulate the thing the doctor said about feathers. But she had to do it. The disobedient thought arose: What if he had used a healing feather when performing that operation on her daughter?

A form struggled on the border between

243

nothing and something.

50.

Something floated near, repulsive, loud, and oblong. This phantom asked, "If I'm going to be like you, as you demand, then who will be like me?" He said a phrase in Yiddish, then translated: *When a shlimazl goes dancing, the musicians' strings break.*

DeKay remembered what Larsen said. All she needed was the Board's agreement to look at the matter. The administration would take that as a point against him. That alone would have him on the defensive.

Some facts disturbed DeKay. Some facts remained in Bomberger's favor. Noah had danced vulgar with Lourdes. Sammy had confided in Noah. Noah had taken Sammy to this doctor for her abortion.

In a sense, briefly, her grandchild had a fragile claim on existence. Now, her grandchild no longer existed in any sense. The problem of freedom was the freedom to make bad choices and then blame others. The problem of freedom was that she almost had a grandchild.

She rattled her legal pad, upon which she had drawn several exact circles with radial slices, each with a label. Dr. Bomberger's hateful offenses required appropriate corrective action.

She would not add that she had, unofficially, in her head, the names of three women candidates penciled as potential replacements. She'd forward the names to the appropriate committee.

Again, the oblong phantom of Bomberger rose out of the shadows. "You should love your neighbor, even if he plays the trombone."

Of the phantom she demanded, "How can you claim to be traditional and religious, yet perform abortions?"

The Phantom did not respond. It faded.

Oh dear, she reacted with a flinch. She felt a single pinprick in the side of her chest.

He reappeared at a distance. The tricks and care with which she and her colleagues had to navigate the conundrums of the successful minorities! (Sometimes she resented them. She pushed that resentment down deep. *Pie chart, pie chart. Bar chart? No, pie chart.*) Why were some historically oppressed minorities successful and others not? (She pushed that thought down too. *Pie chart, pie chart, pie chart.*)

DeKay paused to choose her thoughts carefully. Diversity officers must countenance the possibility of radical disagreement on the most fundamental questions. By use of indirect administrative methods, by uniqueness and belongingnessness, they must crush disagreement. She fastened ropes to the columns of etiquette, definitions, family structure, traditions and ethics, sobriety, reason, hygiene, work ethic, cartography, spelling, punctuality and competency, and she pulled. Down the columns fell, an avalanche of mass crashing toward Bomberger!

Down it all came! *He*... smash! *She*... smash! *Per*... smash! *They*... smash! *Ve*... Smash! *Xe*... Smash! *Ze*... Smashity smash smash smash-o! Aaaa-aaaaa!

Ushered by phantom Noah, Sammy, another phantom, floated in. Basil DeKay fled the room.

51.

In the hallway, Basil DeKay tried to imagine Noah bent at Sammy's table while her daughter whispered secrets. The secret was not about problems of freedom. She whispered about problems with her lovers.

Under stress of colonization and disease, spirit dancing became more extravagant and evocative.

DeKay watched the phantoms of her husband and daughter as they swept along the hall. Her wrath grew.

Then she thundered, "No Bombergers will impede our society from becoming more diverse and more inclusive! We will not allow Bomberger to stop our progress, the progress of marginalized ethnicities, sexual identities, pronouns, and genders! We will stop this Bomberger — and any other Bombergerites — in the name of equity!"

She raged in her imagination, a three-hundred-foot tall goddess with six arms that pushed down a building and smooshed it with her monstrous Nordstrom lady shoes. Then she picked up two more buildings with three arms each and smashed them together. All the while she looked at a mustached phantom, Roger, her ex, with an expression that meant, "See?"

Demystifying her own authority, merely human, she retired from the conference room. Even DeKay grew tired of whacking together the tin cans of jargon and ideology.

The two washrooms just read "Restroom." However, men usually still preferred the legacy men's room, and women the former women's.

DeKay sought to consult the divine in the vernacular, bathroom graffiti. She decided to sample the thoughts of common people. Surely, she'd find truths in the petty verbal transgressions beneath the concentrations of wealth and power. It is language that speaks, not the speaker! The speaker merely languages.

With great power comes a great electricity bill. She stood in the unlabeled washroom on the east side of the floor. Formerly labeled women's room, DeKay pushed the heavy door open. The lights flicked on.

The room hummed. She scrutinized the dull but sufficient stalls and found a lot of words.

A woman had written: *I've been bisexual and alone since 16 (sad face).*

DeKay's face was sad too. Beneath, another had replied, *"I wish you were gay! Laugh out loud!"*

She moved on. She read the scrawls on the tiles and on the stalls:

You are beautiful (heart). — It's not all that bad. — Date like a man so you don't get played like a bitch. — You are perfect. — Fight girl hate. — Your boyfriend is a bad kisser. — I am the least difficult woman. All I want is boundless affection. — I am so alone (bragging!). — Your body is not wrong. Society is. — We accept the love we think we deserve. — This is everything. — Be strong (heart).

All those feelings moved her. Life was happening. She was proud of her sisters, deep in the emotions and their adventures. She straightened and turned around. Scratched into the mirror was this:

Oh baby baby how was I supposed to know? That something wasn't right.

Deep down, she felt, we share eternal human needs and desires. We shared a lack of some kind. Could her generation of leaders help? Legislators were our unknown true poets. Even science was not a universal language. Perhaps that was what irked the strutting patriarch Dr. Bomberger so much about other ways to know science.

DeKay shuddered at the intuition that human identity is unstable, fragmented, or forever in process. She read some more:

If you can't be a good example, you'll just have to be a terrible warning. — My heart is broken. — Love is the thing we use to explain things we don't understand.

(Someone had crossed out *Love* and wrote: *UFOs*.) There was a bit more:

You totally look hot enough to make out with that guy. — Smoke Weed Everybody.

That reminded her, did she have any weed left at home under the delicate lid of the Blue Willow bowl? DeKay came back to:

Oh baby baby how was I supposed to know?
That something wasn't right.

She pushed into the room formerly known
as the men's room. Here there was more dirt
and peeled paint. It shocked her that graffiti was
more common in the ladies' room. Aside from
the initials and incomprehensible gang
scratches, she saw this:

Cry, girls, cry. No more of my penis for you.
Now it goes for men's behinds. Goodbye
forever, wonderful women!

Our lawyer E. missed a deadline and lost
our decision. So instead of paying him we
rented a couple whores. All's well that ends
well.

She didn't want to believe it.

Fellow defecator, may everything turn out okay so that you can get the hell out of here.

DeKay wondered if the men's room was the women's room without the expectation that anyone cared.

The whole time I wanted to tell L — — , take off your pants, please, and show us your hairy privates.

I refuted D.'s claim and then got laid. It was a good day.

Who was this **L,** and that **D,** DeKay wondered, searching her mind for lost claims. It didn't bother her at all. She felt the attention as affirmation.

She pushed out of the unlabeled men's room and walked down the hallway. The lights above hummed faintly.

Amongst the obscenity, the women's self-loathing, the men's urge for domination, she could not help but demystify the ideological contents of all texts. It was such poignant graffiti. It offered small signs of alienation, lust, love, and fellowship.

It moved her. Scribbled words meant something. DeKay packed up her laptop and keys. She descended in the bright elevator.

From the gloom rose a shape. It was a dome, no, a bald head. Under the dome were two serious eyes in round wire glasses. Up rose the half-masked face, the French attitudinal lilt to the tension in his brow, the half-hidden grimace

255

of intellect:

What is language? Words are magic spells. We can invent new ones. We can change the meanings of old ones. Interpretation is a power struggle. Words are action in pursuit of power. You can lose your job from a word. You can lose your reputation, your future. Sometimes, in some places, you just might lose your liberty.

The elevator door opened. I sensed a change coming. To the east, across the river, around Mount Hood, the night sky hit a paragraph of landscape, making it roll.

52.

DeKay said goodnight to Amon. He waved his pencil over his computer screen, much in the manner that a nineteenth century sailor might wave a scrimshaw knife over a whale tooth.

As she drove home, the hint of dawn was painful in the rear view mirror. Ahead, there was enough light to see spray-painted on a construction site: *Y'all not tired yet?* And: *Are we having fun yet?*

She drove by the federal courthouse, remembering its trials there in 2016 of the armed cowboy conspirators who took over the Malheur National Wildlife Refuge building in east Oregon, on the dry side of the Cascades.

In the city, cars' headlights began to probe. The first morning commuters began their rush.

Keep your eyes on the road, people! she told herself. *Indigenous people once tread the*

earth underneath that asphalt! Remember the broken treaties! Don't let their losses be for nothing!

Once, not far from this spot, indigenous people thrived in brutal hierarchies of nobles, rich commoners, poor commoners, and slaves. Elites bound and flattened the foreheads of their infants, forcing the skull to grow upward. Heads with deformation seemed more beautiful and high caste. Heads without deformation belonged to the low caste, rivals, captives, and slaves.

What modern person didn't long to believe in a lost wholeness of stone age humanity? Who didn't want to blame civilization? But what if there never was a wholeness that we lost?

258

DeKay yawned as, deep in her car park, she walked from her car to her condominium elevator. The human confidences continued to move her as she entered the home. Noah's room was dark. In the living room now, she opened her laptop. With a fond expression, she emailed her office's building maintenance to sand or paint over the bathroom graffiti.

She stared into the light. Web page titles rolled by... There was "Most Women You Know Are Angry — and That's All Right", "Why Can't Women Be Angry?", and "Why Women Need to *Honor* their Anger". After those, she clicked the link to read an alternative opinion: "Why Women Should *Embrace* Their Anger".

"Yes, I honor my anger, but I balance that," DeKay thought, "when I also embrace my anger." She read a review of an exciting new book, a translation from France: *I Hate Men.*

The future was female. One could say
women's anger at men relaxed as the genders
united for strength against the emergency, if it
were Opposite Day. The rate of divorce, usually
initiated by women, rose by a third. This decline
was due to abate, however, since the rate of
marriage itself steeply declined. One in five
American women took antidepressants.

Under the banner of Hope, young candidate
Obama looked up and off to the side. History
lost the origin of that word, *hope,* but it
appeared in Old English as *hopian,* a
theological virtue, *trust in God.* Obama was no
longer president. Hope moved ever upward,
ever off to the side.

The east side of the art museum glowed orange. Basil DeKay slept. Downtown, by the art museum, Noah and Lourdes considered signs and portents.

"Safe reopening?" — *"Extremely contagious!"* — "Limited capacity and timed entry tickets?" — *"Closed Monday through Wednesday!"*

Discourses merged and mingled. "Personal safety and community health?" — *"Medical professionals, government officials, and peer institutions!"* — "Facilities and infrastructure?" — *"Social distancing!"* — "What of our staff and public?" — *"A shared belief!"* — "Required to adhere to safety precautions?" — *"Yes, the safest possible way!"* — "Is there an inherent risk of exposure to COVID-19?" — *"I don't care, let me out of my house!"*

Air rolled out in a wail.

261

53.

The old bronze elk bugled. "Oeiaaaaa!" It sounded kitsch, a child's cheap toy sound, a floppy plastic pipe swung around. It was a hoarse, squeaky, pure uncultured complaint of rut. The English word "bugle" comes from the Latin "buculus," a steer.

"Could you bugle something deeper, resonant, and more dignified?" I asked.

The bronze elk rebuked, "You know the difference between your dignity and the Flat Earth theory? Some people still believe in the Flat Earth theory."

I replied, "Did you know that the word *trustworthy* has been removed from the dictionary?"

"Don't be ridiculous," it replied, "there's no such word as *dictionary*. Did you mean *website?"*

In fact, I pocketed my dictionary and hurried passed the fountain. The echo of the smoldered day quavered in the glass of a masked woman's smartphone. Its screen flashed: The news reported the latest pots and pans the President Baboon had thrown, some at enemies, some at friends. Oh baby baby how was I supposed to know? That something wasn't right. But nothing demonstrated, nothing ignited, nothing exploded.

The angle of the bottom of my feet tilted as I

climbed uphill to the Park Blocks. A homeless man lay against a tree and vaccinated himself. The thin park swept under me in a green blur. I offered a perfunctory greeting to the crow-peppered trees and sad statues… to the bored homeless and students who sat in the smoke of cannabis. Lourdes, after Noah, climbed up the broad steps of the museum.

They saw the notice:

"The Portland Art Museum recognizes and honors the Indigenous peoples of this region on whose ancestral lands the museum now stands."

Lourdes produced two pages he had printed, two tickets with two barcodes. The guard at the door turned his device and scanned it.

A sudden breeze of sophisticated and equivocal discourse squeezed me through the doorway. I caught up to the men as they paused.

Lourdes and Noah stood looking at a large, brightly colored Peruvian scrap of cloth. It was a few square feet of poncho remnant from 900 AD. So old was this pink and green rectangular checkerboard of parrot feathers! Was there anything else this old that was this pink and this green? The two visitors both tried to take in what it meant. It was over a thousand years old and the color survived.

Lourdes sensed that Noah's apathy was about to give way to something else. "Is beauty enough?"

"It is beautiful," Noah conceded or perhaps

admired. Did Sammy know that he had told her mother the secret? Was she mad? He rubbed his carefully unshaven chin. He breathed away the sadness of his estrangement with his wife. But when he breathed in again, the same sadness returned.

"Is beauty enough? Would you wear that, if new?" Lourdes said with a smirk.

"It doesn't matter what I wear," Noah replied. "It mattered to them more."

The counselor let that dodge pass, and led them on. They had to pass through the Native section. The path of artifacts revealed a subsection of Pacific Northwestern peoples: baskets, pottery, tools, carved orcas, and owls.

265

Lourdes lingered by a wooden fragment: two salmon held in symmetry by an upside down man with a fox between his knees.

"That's how I feel sometimes," Lourdes commented, but he was lying. He felt guilt for a moment, but it passed.

They paused for a moment by stones axes, drills, knives, spear points, scrapers, and small pieces of other artifacts. High on the wall mounted a dugout canoe. By it was a photo of a sail. The sail had a design much like the baskets and woodwork, a thick-lined style of animals in action within the restraints of the object.

A sign explained the changes in culture that Russian and French trade brought, and then

British and American trade brought. Lourdes and Noah read that during tribal decline, spirit dancing become more extravagant and evocative.

And then Lourdes guided Noah knowingly toward the wing with decorative arts.

Noah was sheepish. "I don't remember ever looking at this section before."

Lourdes looked into his eyes carefully. "You have qualms about it?" he probed.

"I don't know." Noah shrugged. "I just don't see the interest in… bowls…"

Lourdes sorted himself with restraint. He made himself calm.

"A bowl is much more than a practical

267

container for human kibble," he explained. "Here, crafts join decoration and utility. It is the perfect metaphor for the enlightened new masculinity."

"I don't know about that."

"How would you know? You've never ventured into decorative arts before. Apparently, it frightens you."

Noah took a breath and composed himself for patience. He surveyed the signs to Arts and Crafts, Ming Dynasty, Medieval Europe, Art Nouveau, and Art Deco. It amazed him to perceive that within decorative arts was an entire world of subcategories.

The dolphin-man thought, "Even you take

me to a place that makes choices what to show and what not to show. A museum has to do that. So…" By *so*, he meant to argue, every institution needs a liaison between the past and the future. His wife was not so much a professional scold as Lourdes seemed to think, but a professional with responsibility to promote the new kindness that determines new winners and new losers. As society whirled, how else could employees know what they could or could not do, say, or think, without her custody?

In this manner, the dolphin withheld his doubts and let Lourdes guide him. Lourdes hid the fact that he thought this was a victory.

269

54.

The two men promenaded easily among
tapestry, stained glass, carpet, rug and mosaic.
They paused by so many shapes of pottery.
There were details of metalwork to consider, the
richness of enamel. And then the dark luster of
lacquer work beckoned. Glassware glowed,
green, brown, and amber. Basketry seemed
familiar, but what were those floral
decorations? Lourdes pointed out the single
case of swords and muskets. Then they went on
past the cabinets of dress, the brightly lit glass
boxes of jewelry.

Noah began to perceive that each artifact
was more than just an accomplishment of
extreme artistry. Each was a capsule of the
epoch's cultural wealth and ideological
wellbeing.

Lourdes gestured to the next room, where
something lay he could not yet see.

"You and I, Noah, we're new men. We're
experimental creatures for our civilization. We
have to discover our new responsibilities."

Noah listened with a face of independent
thought; he held his tongue but listened without
commitment to Lourdes' assertions. Was there a
force, a substance to his appreciation of objects
that were, Noah might have otherwise claimed,
merely "fancy?"

"We, too, Noah," Lourdes intoned, "We
men of twenty-twenty, we are forms reimagined
from nature."

Noah had started to wonder if Lourdes' usual smoke was more than just style. "You seem to claim that these objects aren't about the objects at all."

They were moving now. As they slid into the mystery room, Lourdes held back from saying this aloud: "What process of under-glaze can bring out the brilliant cobalt blue pigment of your eyes, Noah Beardsmore, my Fabergé egg?"

They halted before a glass pedestal, well lit. On the pedestal sat a bowl.

This was the All Hallows Mazer Bowl of 1470. Silver at top and rim, its bottom half was maple. A transition composed of triangles joined the two halves.

Perhaps the triangles represented the Nail of Our Lord. The tip of the spear that killed Jesus, the Holy Spear, was such a triangle. As Jesus hung on the cross, a Roman Centurion struck him. The spear that killed God ignited spirit from material. It caused an explosion of reprieve. It meant, or tried to mean, repentance and divine forgiveness. Something turned.

"It's beautiful," mourned Noah. "All made by hand? How is that possible? I'm looking at it. It proves itself to be possible. How is the possible itself possible?"

"A lost art," said Lourdes.

Who dares to speak up for forgiveness?
Utopia always leads to dystopia. This treasure
was a shallow drinking bowl. Shallow made no
difference. It promised that mystical love of
truth and justice founded political legitimacy. It
needed no great quantity. It needed faith, or so
the small bowl claimed. Oh, was that all?

It also needed faith to abide corruption. For
a time, this bowl for a price granted the drinker
an indulgence of forty days remission from
Purgatory.

But this fancy bowl outlasted many years of
violent Reformation and Counter-Reformation.

Now it was an artifact of arts and craft under protective glass of alienation.

A little mystical pot of the truth, it had a Christogram, too. This was a talismanic star of overlapping letters, iota-eta-sigma. The import of these signs came from the drift of language, the first three Greek letters of Jesus. Mystic acronyms lay in plain sight, such as Jesus Hominum Salvator...

Noah broke his gaze away from it. "Thank you for showing it to me and for explaining it."

Lourdes leaned close. He spoke in a lower tone. "At the restaurant, you never answered my indiscrete questions."

This surprised Noah. He was annoyed but did not move away. "It's my right not to answer."

Lourdes only smiled. "But you gave me permission to ask. Doesn't that imply your duty to answer?"

"I grant you," Noah replied, "it's a beautiful dream. I still believe in the dream."

"Do you believe as your wife believes, that in the real world, the world we have to live in, diversity is strength?"

"People used to emphasize what we had in common," Noah replied haltingly. "Now it's the differences that count."

"So, the way we're doing it, diversity is division?" Lourdes peered at into his face.

The Mazer Bowl beckoned. Noah looked back at it, not the counselor, and did not want to answer. Instead, he just said, "I want it to work."

Solemnly, silently, Lourdes took this in: *As you want your marriage to work.* He gauged the dolphin's allegiances.

Then he took a step back and asked, "And my second question, since you permit it: Do you *Louvre* your wife?"

Noah didn't answer. He was still angry with her. He knew why Lourdes was making fun of love with the word "Louvre".

Lourdes observed this. He suggested, "You used to think so. You still think so. But the way you're both doing it divides you two?"

The other man looked to the side and walked

back to the Mazer Bowl.

All Hallows, also known as All Saints Day, was a celebration of the saints. The brutality of the ignorant, fallen world had martyred many of them. A mystical relation to eternity offered a depth and richness to make it possible to act faithfully within and beyond the entrenched political perceptions. Everything began in mysticism and ended in politics.

The bowl seemed to tell Noah: *The ultimate source of authority is transcendent truth that we only understand with honesty, humility, and painful sacrifice.*

He struggled. It was his right to be happy — happier than he was now, even before his fight with his wife. But with insight he knew that was a distraction. Something in him yearned for obligation. But that wasn't enough. It yearned for his personal obligation to be part of a larger purpose. He wanted to kneel before a great king. He didn't want to serve a king as oligarch, but a king as a wise ruler in a land where everyone shaped a figure in the tapestry that recorded it. The feeling started to elude him. The sense of it faded away.

Noah leaned into the glass to recapture it and the exhibit began to buzz in warning.

A guard emerged from nowhere. "Stand back, please," she ordered.

55.

Shock! That special kind of shock! Hair shock!

Above, the miniatures of the International Rose Test Garden trembled. Below, the train punched into the dark tunnel under the hills and stopped. Then the doors slid open. Steven hurried through the bright, tiled cave. He took the long elevator up, up, up through the layers of ancient rock. When he emerged, so close to the zoo, he searched for Sammy. But the first thing his eyes found was this sign:

Your zoo experience will be different than it was before the pandemic.

Inside the gate, it shocked Steven to see

Sammy's new hairstyle. It shocked him and
then pleasure rushed in. There was almost
nothing she could do to adorn herself that he
would not find pleasant. Her hair demonstrated
its ability to ignite and explode.

After praising her style, he reported on his
organization effort. It was his first effort of that
nature, and he failed. Despite his entreaties,
Romana declined to come. She wasn't going to
join their "affinity group" of... of what?

Steven wasn't sure what Sammy had in
mind. He thought of it as a club. It meant that
Sammy would spend more time with him.

Masks loose around their necks, they
followed the one-way path through the zoo.

Sadly, some indoor and high-touch areas remained closed. There lurked a threat of science. The chitter of the wren was science. Science spun a web. Science swam in the tank. Science coiled and tasted the air with its tongue.

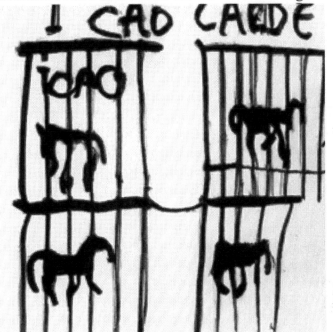

It was offensive, the lack of post-colonial science among the zoo animals. Where was the science of threats? The animals knew that science, like law, preserved inequality. Science determined fortunes and failure. Science was robbery by words.

Sammy had tears in her eyes. She held a note in childhood stationary: a kitten nuzzled a puppy. The note said *Steven*, and the time and place, the *now* of it all. Steven felt this *now* so strongly. Moved almost to tears himself, was this love? Steven with hope asked why she was sad.

Sammy confessed, "I'm a hypocrite and a coward. That makes me a bad person. Unless I can change."

Once, looking for Sammy, Steven attended a gathering of affinity groups. When it began, person after person took turns to declare themselves mentally disabled and therefore oppressed. They all wore black. Sammy didn't show up. During a stir between speakers, he retreated.

Sammy's self-condemnation now reminded him of their declarations of anguish. "Change how?" Steven asked.

The zoo established authority over and over. The cages implied a menace. Authority was everywhere. The two students left the stark sunlight as they followed the sign to the primate forest. Sammy led the way into the sheet of darkness. "Do you know about the problem of freedom?" she asked.

In the primate forest, on a tree platform, lived something with gray fur. Its long tail swayed. It thumped its bowl up and down once and twice. Pronouns bounced out, old and new. The platform rattled.

I studied the primate's thoughtful expression. It did appear to think about subversion of the Enlightenment meta-narrative of bourgeois-capitalism. The placard read,

Allen's swamp monkey, but who is to say?

Steven wanted to get this right. "I'm not sure what you mean."

They moved on, following the path of painted paws.

Sammy leaned on the railing and peered up at the gray creature. "There's so much mushy talk about diversity and equality. What does it mean, precisely? What should we do about it?"

The sign before them explained the small, skunk-like colobus monkey. One female monkey looked at another. *What was sisterhood? Stick together and don't sabotage.*

Steven now felt he could handle a reply. "Diversity means people are different, and different in all kinds of ways. People express love differently, even within their own culture, for example."

The colobus monkey flicked her white tail at this dull insinuation; she refused to express love. By a turn of her back, she showed that she strove for the revolutionary implementation of radical egalitarianism. (She batted her bowl aside, then upside down.) Also… she preferred the alpha monkey, not the monkey schlubs.

Sammy turned away from the monkey and faced Steven. "Then what does equality mean? How can different mean equal?"

Steven tried to turtle his head down inside him. He thought maybe she saw more than just a schlub in him. He didn't want to risk that with a response she didn't welcome.

56.

Sammy turned to the monkey again. "If it means equal size and shape, not really. If it means they have equal moral value, no one really says we don't."

She gripped the rail and shook it. It was firm, so she shook herself. "But if..." The cries of animals drowned out her words for a moment. "...then..." Herbivores shook their cages. Predictors shook their cages. It seemed to Steven that all the animals shook their cages.

The physics student waited with his lovelorn eyes big and sad. The monkey did not seem to notice. Neither did Sammy. She continued, "If we use government power to make people more

Oo aaa, they will be less *Haaa ooo aaaa. Ahh ooo ooo, like, aahhhh* means our concept of freedom is the problem."

Sammy looked at him for a reply. Steven had listened but did not track. Freedom was oppression? He nodded for her to continue.

She went on, "To achieve *oo ooo* we must *aaa ooo* to *aaa oo* the *ooo haaa.*

There was no reason here that Steven saw. There were only primitive impulses. The young man's thoughts swam like crocodiles. They swam deeper than political theory. They looked for the paddling feet of that happy duckling, love.

They walked slowly along the cages, signs, displays, and exhibits.

Flamingoes use their beaks to filter microaggressions from the water.

Steven said nothing.

Sammy looked at him, disappointed. A sign declared that the gibbons and orangutans were off view.

The pressure inside Steven pushed him to perform allegiance through these words: "I know that equality cannot happen in our current system."

He felt a little sick after saying it, until she exhaled. This breath of acceptance relieved Steven a great deal.

A snow leopard can leap twenty feet!

"Look at the president," Sammy replied. An expression quivered on her face, then subsided.

"Our current system has, like, no solution and teeters toward *Ooo Oooo Oooo.*"

They stood before the chimpanzees now. Primates eyed primates.

"Solidarity," the chimp began, "helps us model the kind of habitat we want to live in: a classless, cageless food web."

Her strong hairy arms pulled the chimp to a higher branch. "Through solidarity, we hope to create radical living spaces that can not only grow these niches into real liberation, but…"

The chimp now hung by one prehensile foot. "…but also act as, like, a viable alternative to those that seek community. Predators provide false solutions to problems of, like, class and alienation in our society."

Steven didn't know about all that. But as the speaker continued to pontificate, he did watch the chimps. The female rocked in the tree. She swung and then rested.

Two others appeared to chase each other for a moment in the constructed tree. One began to yell at the other, but the aggression gentled. Now the one's fingers combed through the other's fur.

It was obvious that this grooming showed the primate consciousness as it struggled against meta-narratives. They imposed their *hoo-hoo HOO haa-haa* discourse on the primate masses. This lack of full range of howls denied them the full expression of grooming, liberty, dominance displays, equality and justice for all.

A wallaby is born the size of a gummy bear or a nine week-old human fetus.

Romana wouldn't meet Sammy but Steven had. Was this enough? Sammy took the physics student's arm. His heart surged.

Somehow, in the cavern of the flying fox, Sammy called Steven "dear" …and he swooned.

Steven suggested they take a break from politics. He suggested they visit the Pacific Shores biome. There were sharks and sea otters. The sea otters twisted, slid, chased and swam. The shark had skin like sandpaper. That's why the oceans were so rounded and smooth.

57.

There was some cotton candy of time stuck on the bronze elk's antlers. I couldn't reach it. I had to slip off a shoe and throw it three times. Freed, the wisp tumbled away to catch in the near park tree branches. Shoed again, laced and knotted, I walked from the elk statue and detoured in search of Basilica DeKay's dream discourse. I double-timed to catch up with her. Fiercely, she deepened into sleep.

My mission troubled me. Zoë and Tom expected my report.

The broken trash world made time and beauty possible due to imperfection. It was more inclusive but also reactive. It heard but also misunderstood. It tried to be good but failed. There was intent and there was error. There were incidents, harassment, discrimination, and even hate crimes. Oh baby baby how was I supposed to know? That something wasn't right.

The sun shone hot, but the curtains sealed in the darkness. Basil DeKay turned over on her side. The weight pressed against the attack of varicella zoster virus. The viral needle poked the sides of her chest.

She closed her eyes. The last things she saw in the murk, the image pattern that faded weirdly on her optic nerve, comforted her. These were a book, Michelle Obama's *Becoming*, and an aromatherapy diffuser. The scent now was jasmine citrine to boost immunity.

She slept with amber-colored blackout curtains over the large windows. Behind the blackout, the West Hills mounted steep and

green, so near, influencing her sleep. The bulk
of the hills comforted. Her modulated sense of
the rise and fall of mass helped her sleep
through the morning hours until noon or later.

Her rivals had the burden of light upon their
actions. She felt that something wasn't right as
Noah appeared in her dream. Where was he?
Was he near? Was he far? DeKay in her day-
sleep again suffered rapid onset dream disorder.

Arm in arm with Lourdes, Noah strolled
through sections of the decorative arts. They
walked through Medieval Europe to Art
Nouveau and Art Deco.

Lourdes felt right. "What makes us different
than animals? From gods? If we can behold
something this beautiful, do we not exist in the
same space as beauty? Doesn't that make us
equal to it? Doesn't that make you equal to it,
Noah?"

Noah only emitted a sound: "Mmmh."

The counselor knew he could push an argument for pleasure. He raised his eyebrows and implored, "Do the gods feel shame? Do animals? Do artists?"

Noah didn't know what Lourdes meant, so he merely repeated a platitude. "Shame is an unhelpful emotion."

Victorious, Lourdes raised his arms, for he had led Noah to retreat another step toward whatever it was that queerness meant. Lourdes' push for conquest advanced — and he moved around the corner, out of view.

The moment hovered over the waxed echo of museum floor. Something waited inside a pedestal case of well-lit glass. Inside the bright

292

pool of light poised a solitary bowl.

In dream, DeKay couldn't see it clearly, for Noah drifted by with an enigmatic smile. He stole her attention. She wanted to reach out to him but could not. "Ze! Ze! Too bad I'm asleep! Too bad, too bad!"

58.

Noah and Lourdes stood before the small monolith of glass.

Inside lay an unnamed bowl of silver upright on its own small pedestal foot, crafted in 1929. Egyptian lines and beaux-arts sleek implied a secular grace. Its round scope held itself in assurance of wireless waves that connected every skyscraper and farmhouse with an electric hum. As an artifact of sterling hollowware the Unnamed bowl glowed like a vacuum tube with invisible lines of force. With only a few etched lines arced like clouds or wires, the Unnamed suggested electromagnetic entertainment and finance.

A triangle medallion poised in the act of run with corners curved back as if from clockwise propeller motion. It spun for progress toward a sleek grace.

Adjacent to the triskelion flowed the delicate design of an Egyptian papyrus stem fan. This rose on graceful stalks. Sedge triangles formed a clockwise rotary on a base of rhizomes between rounded, upright elastic triangles of riverine earth. The bowl's narrowing base showed the will for self-control and gratitude. The sedge and base lines together formed a doubled image, a lotus.

With precious metal of silver came the awareness of scarcity and value. Ancient Egypt

with all its art and advancements fell in ruins.
Its memory could still shock us.

What shocked us was its aesthetics and
strange affluence of imagination linked to a way
of life. The Unnamed could inspire the
aesthetics of an American memory. It was a
compelling force that continued in precise,
harmonious echoes. These echoes even reached
the wireless age in this bowl.

The mere presence of such elite, refined, and
restrained beauty protested even a single insult
to humanity.

The Unnamed bowl made Lourdes feel there
was hope for something significant and good in
that past American culture to give the future. It

was modern, yet carried grace. This was an artifact of the newly modern republic. Noah rolled his lip not to groan with the pain and sorrow that beauty can imply. It had all gone astray.

It didn't follow. If ancient Egypt fell, why wouldn't...

But this bowl promised a possibility for an eternal progress that moved in harmony with beauty. Was it a lie? Or was a truth we had abandoned?

The men returned to jewelry, rows of enamel pendants. Noah was cold, not curious, not shamed. Lourdes couldn't penetrate his enigmatic sheen.

"Mass production of form," Lourdes proposed, "or the human touch?"

"The human touch is better."

"The connoisseurship of form matters, Noah, because it outlasts touch."

"I'm surprised you don't advocate touch over form."

"I dare to think, and observe, and appreciate. Why live a life at all, if not for beauty, delicacy and strength? Don't you agree?"

Noah would not relent. "Without touch there's nothing."

"I could close my eyes and dream. In dream, every fantasy is possible."

Noah's face showed disagreement. He found a way to express it: "Dreams are nothing, in the end. You need physical existence. The nervous system is part of the brain. The brain extends to all the senses. You talk so much about pleasure, and you don't know this? Maybe you'll find out someday."

Lourdes' mouth moved, but no sound came out. He turned not just his eyes, not just his head, but his whole body to Noah.

Who was the arts and who was the craft? Did craft know how to be a good ally of the arts? Who offered patronage, and who was the collection?

Noah smiled enigmatically.

DeKay's body turned over. She wanted to reach out to Noah, but could not. "I'm asleep! I can't touch him. Ze! Ze! Too bad, too bad!" She gasped on the pillow.

59.

An elk eats twenty pounds of seasonal
vegetation each day. Graywolves, Roosevelt
elk, deer, picas, Stevens and Sammys were a
tiny part of a greater whole. This included life
cycles, food chains, ideologies, predator-prey
relationships, habitat loss, heritage loss,
pollution, video chats, and endangered species.
Did animals have an inner sense of identity?

There were big and little identities. There
were furry and smooth identities. There were
soft and rough identities, and even cold and hot
identities. Are viruses alive or floating pieces of
mathematics? Who assigns the sex of animals?

Masked people shifted near Steven and
Sammy. This included Zoë and Tom. I started

in surprise as I recognized them. While Zoë looked at the animals, Tom looked at me. When Tom looked at the animals, Zoë looked at me.

Sammy no longer held Steven's arm. She slipped away from his attempts to reattach. He considered this. His face turned down.

They walked on for a while. I followed them until we could see no other person. Steven let his sad face press against the netted window of an aviary. His face bore this mark after they walked on.

Scornful was the glare of the red-billed hornbill. The downward curving beak sourly ruminated. The vertical cage suggested savanna, woodland, and thorn scrub. In its bowl lay pieces of apple, critical spinach theory, dry pellets of bias, and mealworms. In other parts of the cage hid crickets.

Steven found his voice in resentment but controlled it. "So you actually believe that any authority that holds up the current order holds up fascism?"

He asked this in the way someone might ask, what is the difference between horns and antlers?

Unhappily, because he loved her, he expressed the conclusion he didn't want to reach, but apparently she did. "Therefore to be antifascist is to be a revolutionary?"

This surprised Sammy, but she was glad to answer with her ready claim.

"What people call a free society is a way to

maintain inequities."

Steven remained stoic. "I see…"
Compressed emotion made his voice squeak.
He was a songbird that tried to speak in the
language of frog. He did not see how his own
struggles, discipline and gift in mathematics led
to easy pronouncement of privilege. Sammy
had to go meet her mother. If they were going
to kiss, he thought, it would have to be soon.
But he was afraid.

What do the animals make of the moving
exhibit of people?

*Did you know that many mammals, from
rats to dolphins, can laugh?*

The working dinosaur skeleton with the
Please DO Touch sign showed how the jaw

hinge works by manipulation up and down. It had another sign on it: PANDEMIC. Please Do Not Touch.

How are this animal's teeth similar to and different from your teeth? If you were to pick an animal to eat you, which animal would you pick and why?

To resist his growing despondency, Steven tried to prolong Sammy's interest. "What do we do?" The net pattern faded on his cheek.

People again came close, made noise, and then receded.

Delightfully close to Steven, Sammy leaned; at least, Steven found it delightful. There was inscrutability to that moment that caused it adhere: "Those who feel threatened by, like, shifting social and economic realities want power. Authority offers it. Fascism, however masked, offers authority. We must threaten them even more."

Steven remained stiff. He resisted absorption of these words in order to maintain his respect for Sammy. To be polite, he repeated without comprehension. "Threaten them?"

The young woman affirmed this. The determination in her face was a shape with an uncertain side pushed up against the certainty anchored in her forehead. "Threaten all authorities. Demonstrate, ignite and explode."

DeKay's daughter explained more abstractions, which she stretched and snapped. Sammy continued in a whisper and stopped.

Steven said nothing, so the young woman went on. They shared a moment. Sammy was looking into Steven's eyes. His heart threatened to ignite.

After a time, overcome by *boom-shaka-laka,* she kissed him and he swooned.

The monkey's silver bowl glinted with the reflection of a distorted observer. It was the half face of the rising postcolonial scientific moment. The monkey dipped his hand in the bowl. The creature gave no sign of recognition of the warped face of the Masked One. The face had that aggression, that thrust, that intellectual forehead. Half discs of its glass lenses showed. But that was all. The monkey didn't care.

The bronze elk was tired. It had bugled for a hundred years and more. Still, it made an effort: "Shout-out to everyone who struggles to self-identify. *You know who you are.*"

A crow eyed me from a parking lot fence, a snail in its beak. Bourn in the beak of discourse, over treetops, over the rooftop air conditions to downtown, I descended, to land beside yellow tongue pedals of daylily in pots watered by an artisan dressmaker. Its impossibly vegetative butter glow startled me with pleasure. I turned my gaze up to find Lourdes' private chambers.

The State analyzed the results of plan 1a for Multnomah County — problems infected the solutions. Time was fluid: past, present, future united in a way that evaded the control of government caseworkers.

A single-shot espresso in a demitasse proved the moment sublime. Lourdes remembered when he had himself looked angelic, yes; yes he had, even as an adult. Then that look had passed. And now, at forty-four? Could he pass for an athlete? A swimmer? A dancer? No. No. And no.

Lourdes turned his dance music louder but could not move. His self was fluid: His self-conceptions ranged. He lay on his rug and analyzed himself — there were problems.

60.

Sour croaks! Sour croaks! The two pally crows on their forked perch could not approve the two-legged antics, except for our edible leavings. For each other they had a kinder call from deeper in the craw: *Kreek-cricketty-coo.*

Alone, without pal or family, under COVID-19 lockdown, Lourdes lay on his living room rug. As a thought experiment, he probed his core. He found himself as the sentient blur his ideology told himself he was. This is what he wanted — not blur as a slur but blur as a superpower. It helped him thrive that Machiavellian biome, the bureaucracy of 2020.

Lourdes worried that neither success nor failure of his seduction of Noah would save him. His insomnia would endure, and with it the doubts, the shadows. Physical passions were bound to disappoint, then bring pain. Was anything better than a distraction? A distraction from what, then? He did not know.

How had he let himself go astray?

There was something amiss with his authenticity.

The echo of the smoldering day quavered. A woman walked a dog outside. He saw a flash of light in her hand. He shortened his focus to look at his translucent outline in the window. *I hope to find peace with my appearance someday.*

He made himself a single-shot espresso against the blathering silence. Noah still did not telephone or text him, but did not call him a buddy, either.

He surveyed the primp of colognes, the skin care products, the defoliation mittens, the closet with designer labels, male cosmetics and fashionable clothing, plus his shoes (current favorite: Milano Double Monk Straps). The checklist of vanities, he could sustain a mild interest. Was it affectation? What was essential? Did he really have no self?

Lourdes had doubts. His self ached. His passion for Noah caused him pain. This was not supposed to happen. His desire to dominate and humiliate Noah still tempted him sexually. This is what he called passion; it wasn't desire for Noah's form. There was passion, however, passion to dominate. If he gored Noah, then he was the unicorn.

But what if Lourdes sacrificed Noah to the unicorn of his insomnia, and then the unicorn continued to haunt his nights? Would he have to add guilt to his night thoughts?

Lourdes qualified for early retirement. He could leave and start a practice in Ashland.

His self was everywhere, if he looked for it. Doubt was everywhere, if he looked for it. What was the gift of unexpected self-doubt? The inability of modern fluid ideology to replace doubt was not a fault. But doubt remained. His self remained elusive. The void remained.

What he liked about queer theory was its deliberate use of incoherence as strength, its contradiction as vigor, and its obscurity as playground. These aspects, as activists promised, gave him power. So why did he feel that something about it was, for him, unsustainable? How did he fail himself?

The unicorn charged through clarity. Its sharp hooves chopped lines and shapes into diffuse murk. How could people possibly be free to make independent rational decisions? How could people determine their own destiny?

Sometimes it seemed that Lourdes could never know himself until utopia arrived. Or maybe he could never know himself unless he accepted the most obscure jargon. Self-knowledge was a willful pursuit of disquiet.

309

All this made him more vulnerable to a special pansexuality, *thanatophobia,* the death anxiety. It gave his fear the guise of unicorn.

Queer theory showed Lourdes that being part of a group leant him the ability to critique his own category of belonging, his own membership. Therefore, to its credit, he thought, this ideology itself gave him a road out.

A being without contradiction had no inner resistance, no friction, no traction, and remained a pliable nothing. He was not pliable. He was not nothing.

He burst into incredulous chortles.

What if Lourdes, in the end, at his most self-empowered and self-actualized and authentic, was the most queer of all possible queers, queer to the queerth power, a heterosexual? A... *straight white male?*

That was the rainbowest triumph of them all. He snorted and whooped.

If reality is the same as thought... If humans determined reality by thought... If humans had the ability to change reality by thought... And therefore avenge their grudges... Then we could not say what is true and what is not true.

He waited, but Noah did not show up at his door. Lourdes thought this absence would bring relief from his inner confrontation, but he wanted that confrontation.

Not far away, though the smoke, the old bronze elk called me: "Did you hear about the man who got arrested for stealing hats? He *hat* it coming."

The origin of the English word "pun" is lost. But the origin of the word "joke" comes from Proto-Indo-European *yek,* "to speak".

The elk was still speaking, as if afraid of bronze silence. "In the interrogation room, the hat thief announced, 'I'm not saying a thing without my lawyer present!' – 'Sir,' said the officer, 'you *are* a lawyer.' – 'Exactly!' the thief replied. 'Where's my present?'" There was more, but I hurried in pursuit of DeKay's daughter.

Sammy took the trolley from Goose Hollow to Old Town. She was a little homesick, although she hadn't moved out yet. Tents in rows and clumps slid by.

Some tents stood on semi-permanent foundations of wooden pallets. The addicted, the deranged, the disturbed, the anti-social, the victims of unfair circumstance, the addled... they all needed homes. Sammy's nose did not wrinkle. With flat affect, she met the odor of fear and malevolence that accompanied assaults. She sensed without reaction the discarded syringes, the food wrappers, the human waste, the people slumped in boredom against the sidewalk wall with face torn or curled.

O old home sweet feeling! Where can I find you again?

She pressed the buzzer of an apartment

building that resisted the gentrification — so far. No one answered. Sammy walked around the side to look for a parked motorcycle and did not find it.

Her face struggled to find an expression.

61.

A woman with a laptop has sorrow, because her hour of PowerPoint has come. As soon as she delivers her workshop, her anguish becomes joy that her deliverable has begun a process of therapy to the world.

Truth, like a virus, was contingent and dependent on context. Truth could change accordingly, with the ease of a new word's invention or a new definition for an old word. Truth could evolve and hide behind a KN95 mask. One truth could usurp other truths. An office hallway flickered. The cubicles swayed.

Basil DeKay, the night owl, woke up early — two in the afternoon — for a three o'clock videoconference. She drank coffee as she drove to her office with Sammy.

Due to the pandemic, she and Contessa Finger would be the only participants to physically attend the conference room. The others would join by the room's video feed.

DeKay brought her daughter as a way to address her profession's answer to some of the problems of freedom. In the elevator, she instructed Sammy how to sit out of view of the camera. The mother put on a plastic face shield instead of the usual mask. In the glint of that face shield, I saw, for a moment, a reflected pair of eyes… eyes that didn't belong.

And, as DeKay and Sammy walked over to the glass walled conference room, the painful landscape receded. The room grew larger and larger. I could not move. I tried to understand why I adhered to the wall.

A giant dome rose. It was a bald, shaved head. Up rose metal frame glasses with thick lenses that distorted the eyes behind it. The glasses grew and with it, the eyes, the mask with contours of nose and cheeks, even the chin hidden… the mostly obscured face.

It was the face of the Masked One. The others see him, but his glance showed the way to the conference room.

His glance twisted the rows of its twelve empty chairs at the table, and then clarified.

315

Without a sound he told us: *Where there is power, there is resistance.*

DeKay and Sammy entered the conference room. The mother ushered her daughter to Finger, who waited in a chair by the door. DeKay pushed aside her distrust and resentment to offer a collegiate pleasantry.

Small, young, Finger was steadfast, with long straight black hair, an elusive complexion, and regal bearing.

Finger turned on the video and awaited the response to her invites. Soon a lone man waited in a single video frame. Safe in his digital square, under heavy square glasses, his digital jowls showed discontent.

316

DeKay pretended not to notice the resentful way his glasses flashed all their schlubby squareness. How many times had she seen that look before! It was a truism: the removal of privilege felt like oppression. Still, she wanted to give the man a chance. Also, she noted that he, Mister Bitter Safety Glasses, was a schlub.

The others filled in further squares on the screen. Inside the squares, there were three people shaped like flasks. One had a long neck and flat bottom, another had a long neck and round bottom, and there was one with a narrow neck that expanded steadily toward her base. The next person ate snacks on screen, with lips reaching out and gripping food like a tong. One

317

face suggested a crucible, smooth, shallow, and hot. The next put one in mind of a funnel — wide on top, narrow at the bottom.

On the next row one found a graduated cylinder, with tattoos on the side of his face, a dropper, who had a narrow face and a rubber bulb nose, and a clamp, with her tightly clenched expression. A ring stand, whose earrings bolted her ears firmly in place, also joined the group. Now all their little squares of faces filled the screen.

Contessa Finger offered her greeting and introduction. With enviable ease, she created an online environment of Uniqueness and Belongingnessness. Then she introduced DeKay.

To begin, DeKay painted a vision of a better

world. Then she talked through various PowerPoint slides that slowly increased in sophistication and vehemence: First was Problematics... Next came Socialized Entitlements... Third was about Discourses of Dominance... Fourth was Pervasives... And Fifth was Systemics...

Sammy sat with a blank face. *So much useless talk*, she thought. *All this to put a new person in an old chair. They did, like, nothing to add additional chairs. So no additional persons get to sit down at the table*, she mulled sullenly. *The pyramid remains, with most squished at the bottom.*

She tried not to yawn. She tried not to show annoyance. The problem of freedom remained.

Freedom ached. Her mom was so *bougie* it was painful.

Sammy, unmoved, felt boredom and guilt. The arid cube of the space was impotent to justice, and death to *boom-shaka-laka.*

Mom actually thinks, Daughter thought with a blank expression, *she is moving marginalized people into positions of prestige. The flaw is so, like, obvious and self-serving! The system demands losers. What minority of winners determines this majority of losers? Why this pyramid that guarantees so many losers? No one has ever explained this to me.*

Sammy's mind went to a vacant place as she waited for the videoconference to end.

62.

I watched too, but the Masked One's appearance had distracted me. I sought glimpses of him but found none. I don't like to admit this but… I adhered to a spot above the light switch. He had put me inside a COVID-19 virion. I wiggled my protein spikes in protest.

"Structures that perpetuate power and privilege…" the diversity officer continued with a bunch of words. "Uniqueness…" she explained. Her voice rose to a crescendo as she quoted her personal contribution to the movement:

"Belonging… Belongingness? No, belongingness is not enough. We need a culture where *belongingness* itself belongs: belongingness*ness.*"

Suddenly she asked about the intersections between knowledge and power.

No one in the video audience dared to venture a guess.

"Knowledge is inadequate and therefore violent," DeKay explained "unless it includes the experience of historically disadvantaged groups *as knowledge.*"

She sensed she was losing her audience. She knew they had the disadvantage of all their technical and scientific propaganda about objective, measurable, testable truth.

"Violence?" she asked, along with other words of power.

The faces on the screen rustled slightly. She explained. She had unrolled two-thirds of the machinery of her argument. There was violence behind how we all know, or how we think we know, what we know.

In a different tone, she hit them with further words, putting most of the emphasis on, "Safety."

She paused and then clicked her PowerPoint. A slide flashed anew. Thus she revealed her *coup de main*. It was a pie chart!

This was data on that very lab. It was a pie chart that revealed the current self-reported ethnic breakdown of the lab's workforce. This was actionable data! She beamed with good feeling.

Somehow, she was unprepared when Bitter Safety Glasses asked, "How do you want that pie chart to look?" When she didn't answer right away, he blurted out, "Just give me the quotas."

On the large screen, inside their little squares, the flasks and cylinders and tongs leaned away from the heretic's square.

BSG's question caught her off guard. DeKay froze for a moment.

Any answer to that problematic question would itself be problematic.

DeKay glanced at her foot. She knew that the lab already employed more ethnic diversity than the local population. Portland was one of the whitest cities in the U.S.A. Local history included indefensible bias and acts we now

323

consider shameful, like every place on Earth.

It is a fallen world. The wicked continue to prosper. How should we go forward? It was the diversity officer's job to know how. It required a lot more than just the cattle prod of Belonging, the cleaver of Uniqueness, the bludgeon of pie charts. Nothing would happen without the dark triad of facial expressions: *Face for White Males Who Felt Defensive, Face for White Women Who Believed the Same As Her,* and *Face to Welcome Minority Persons Who Believed the Same as Her.*

BSG flashed again. DeKay sensed that he took her hesitation for weakness.

"How can you achieve that diversity goal

without systematically hiring according to skin color?" he asked. "Not with blind tests! By skin color! Isn't that evil and anti-scientific?" Then he said something badly racist: "Why can't we judge each other as individuals?"

The three flasks, and the tong, the two funnels, the other tong (a different one had started to snack), the graduated cylinder, and the clamps and ring stands and rubber stoppers — all of them shrank — forbidden words rebounded. Was all power gained through another group's loss? Did *that* loss count as a loss? Was that loss punishment? Was group punishment justice? Was revenge a form of justice?

Sammy perked up now. This slightly frightened her. Her eyes grew wide.

The room had no independent existence outside the power dynamics. The room swayed. There were no universal truths, no objective reality. There was just narratives expressed in discourses and strings of words designed to apportion power.

There was no argument really. It was just a showdown of identities. That replaced argument. Outcomes mattered; opportunities were only opportunities if they caused the correct outcome. Otherwise, opportunity was oppression by trickery.

Did the encounter exasperate? Gnaw? Ruffle, irk, and chafe? There was just a permanence of oppressors and oppressed. There was only warfare by administration. There was only appeasement or victory.

Sammy exhaled with impatience with her mom's late-liberal rhetoric, her mom's defense of the pyramid of injustice, her fruity-peach lipstick and the fluffy-headed hairstyle. She let her attention fade, her eyes unfocus.

Smoothly DeKay moved on from diagnosis to plan of action. How could the lab achieve this? The team as a collective needed to make sure that everyone had the resources each needed. This required the team as a democracy to customize work to the individual. Everyone needed to make sure everyone felt comfortable.

Bitter Safety Glasses dryly asked, "Have

you ever worked in a lab?"

A commotion began. DeKay took the moment of digital upset to mute herself, lean off camera and confer with Finger. They agreed. Time had run out. There was just enough time to explain that the participants needed to click the link they sent and complete the mandatory online diversity training.

Thankfully, I drifted back into human form, and could follow. But a bronze voice told me, "How does every American joke begin? Nowadays, by looking over your shoulder."

I looked over my shoulder.

63.

Whether a wheel, an arrow, or a pretzel, Time moved. Faces moved with it, and their representation, again and again, in a circle, or straight forward, or in a knot, on flat screens. In her living room, Basil DeKay sat before her laptop. Seeing her own image there, she tied back her hair. She braced herself again to fake cordiality with Contessa Finger. The Mother's Day flowers from Sammy dropped a pedal.

A force as powerful as deadlines is real-time video conferencing! The coals of networking are coals of caring, which hath a most vehement flame.

But now DeKay hosted the videoconference of the *Ex-ter-mi-knitters*. She clicked in Bezz Larsen first. Her face appeared on screen. There was victory in her eyes, and a fellowship.

DeKay knew just what she meant.

Larsen whispered with excitement, "Your you-know-who case has finally come my way on the Oversight Committee." Louder, she exclaimed, "It looks like Bomberger is going down. Contessa couldn't say a word."

It was still just their two faces that shared a split screen at the moment. DeKay hesitated before letting the other women in.

Larsen continued: "The old dinosaur has finally met his meteorite, and she has your face, honey!"

Larsen snorted. In solidarity with Larsen's snort, DeKay also snorted. They discussed what they both knew of the restorative justice process: the victim-offender mediation, the face to face, the sentencing circle.

DeKay felt herself grow stronger, and — somehow — likable! She really was making the world a better place. She was a leader, one of the many who routed conservatives comprehensively in the culture war. She was someone the world just had to pay attention to, if the world were fair about it.

Even her daughter would notice, if the world were fair.

"Okay no work talk now. I'm letting Sarah, Ginny, and Contessa on. Where are they? Oh, here they come."

Each knitter brought her face worn out from the parasitic daydreams of shutdown. They tried to smile through their saturated emanations of fraught. The problem with video chat is it made the owners of the faces feel queasy and dislocated. Sisterhood, however, saved them again and again.

"Get your hooks and yarns ready." — "That baboon of a president!" — "Ugh! Knitting is direct action." — "The most impressive thing about it taking twelve sheep to make a pullover is that I didn't know they even had any knitting needles!"

Thus Ginny struck again. They all laughed.

"Twiddlemuffs and big knits?" —

"Organized and activated!" — "Knit linen placemats?" — "Online initiatives!" — "Stocking stitch, slip every other stitch" — "Decontextualize women's crafts!" — "Crossover cardigan?" — "Knit for community!"

The knitters' club took a moment for fellowship. Digital mishap chopped the laughter and made it alien.

Outside, the crows were asleep in their leafy roosts. Of the low amber of afternoon, I stood quietly in its murk.

It was just then when Ginny's husband walked behind her. He didn't stop and didn't peer into the screen. DeKay couldn't even see his face clearly.

With shock, she recognized his oblong shape. She scrutinized the little video square of Larsen. Her friend's image silently looked her in the eyes, the digital eyes. She knew it was illusion, but she felt it nonetheless.

Ginny and Bomberger? she reflected. Yes, she didn't know Ginny well, except for knitting.

DeKay sat before her computer with a fixed smile as she hid her reaction. All this time, Ginny was married to Bomberger?

"Did you check out that nautical sweater with anchor motif?" — "Whiteness." — "Table runner?" — "Privilege!" — "Eyelet scarf with tassels?" — "Felt projects!" — "What is that you have there?" — "A felted wool spiral." — "How did you make it?" — "Easy! If you knit a spiral, then wash it repeatedly, you can felt a purity spiral in no time at all. Who can be the most pure?"

DeKay only listened. Words became volatile bits. Words crumbled into distortion. The crunching torque of humiliation roared. The new engine rejected absolutes. There was nothing to share but humiliation and rage.

"Let's get real, girlfriends," called out Ginny. "Are tassels a sign of pandemic mental crackups among knitters?"

DeKay tried to reply with affirmation, but

no words came out. The others continued without pause:

"A deal on four-ply yarn!" — "Knitting keeps me from stabbing people!" — "Knitting is cheaper than therapy." — "You guys are my therapy!" — "I love my girl gang!"

64.

As Basil DeKay parked her car near
Grandma's apartment in the Irvington
neighborhood, she passed signs on a telephone
pole. Who would say where her mind
organized, advocated, and induced? Discourse
never parks its car. She felt tension — those
heated moments on video — did Bitter Safety
Glasses represent a bias incident? Was there
lack of support? How could she reduce diversity
resistance? How could she check the unchecked
unconscious bias? How could she support
anonymous accusers?

She walked into the foyer double-masked
and buzzed with purpose. Her purpose was to
deliver a late Mother's Day gift for Sammy's
grandma. It was a duty. DeKay let it be late
because she believed Grandma didn't care
much, although she did like Sammy.

Inside, DeKay observed the many baubles of
Grandma's travels, her collection of owl-
themed mugs, her framed photos of herself and
young Roger. "Where's your hand sanitizer?"

"What?" Grandma was confused. "Don't
need it. Just wash your hands with soap and
water."

DeKay washed her hands.

Grandma shouted over the water. "Well,
Diversity Specialist, have you found nothing
better to do today than visit me? Have a drink to
the rainbow yet?"

She lifted a bottle of Pinot Gris, which she

had already started. As she found a glass for her guest, she called back, "Added any new genders to the list?"

They moved to the back porch, where wicker furniture waited. The yard was small, neat and green. The elder poured the wine. DeKay took it but closed her eyes against the abuse.

There was a coyote problem in the city; they had snatched several cats. There was also a Sammy problem in the city; Sammy had slipped out of their view.

Caw! Caw! Caw! Caw! Thus a crow shouted down its skepticisms. What is the nature of the ethical matters facing us? What attitude should we adopt towards them? Perhaps an affectionate *Cluck chirrup graaa smurkle?*

What will be the outcome for those who have this attitude? With the economic shutdown, the wilderness, latent, pushed for inclusion.

Grandma's wrinkled eyes over her mask examined her keenly.

"Put on a few pounds? The pandemic fifteen, is that it?"

"Stop that." DeKay glared at her rudeness. This old lady overestimated DeKay's obligation as her ex-husband's mother.

She hesitated before pushing her mask down to drink the Gris. She turned away, dipped her mask below her chin, and drank. Then she slipped her mask back on and scowled.

Grandma's judgmental smile toppled the scowl of her former daughter-in-law. "You're weak if you let that offend you. You give me power over you that way. It takes so little effort. It's my Mother's Day gift to myself, also a day late. Now spill the beans. You and Noah still fighting?"

Masks restored, DeKay breathed away her annoyance: "I don't want to talk about it." She didn't say the full thought, which included, "...with you."

Grandma didn't react to that. She observed, "You did good to grab him quick after you kicked my boy out."

"It wasn't that quick," DeKay retorted.

"The wheels of the clock run faster and faster. I mean before you became perimenopausal. Now, as the pounds accumulate and the flesh sags, the question appears: Can you hold Noah?"

Sacrilegious words and deeds! Even the crow above me reacted to this provocation. DeKay, shocked by Grandma's hostility, leaned away. Did it really happen? Yes, it did happen.

DeKay made herself smile. "You mean, can *Noah* hold *me?* And what about you? You couldn't hold your man. You are the most abrasive person I know. No wonder your boy chose to live on a faraway continent."

Grandma laughed. "Away from both of us! We're in this together, even if we don't like each other."

65.

Steven was giddy with something close to
terror. Sammy had deleted all of her social
media pictures. Talk about destruction of the
self! A pursed duck lips face among two other
middle school friends… gone! Her big-eyed
pose near high school sunflowers — gone! And
his favorite: she lay in the fall light in a
nostalgic dress, the Rose Garden behind her,
Mount Hood behind the garden… she threw a
wreath of leaves — gone! All her posted
pictures, gone!

The air grew thick with heat and tears. It was bright, but sour with imprecations, curses, abuse, and thumbs down. Dogged he stared at his phone with bloodshot eyes. The screen lit up with absence.

The physics student sat in his tiny apartment. He sat at his window that overlooked Sandy Boulevard. It was a diagonal swath of road through the city grid. In normal times diagonal people busied it with stores and life. Now it was subdued.

Sandy Boulevard was once a Native trail

from the Willamette River to the spot where the Sandy River snaked down from Mount Hood to meet the Columbia. On that ancient trail, Steven prepared for the therapy by video. In conversation with himself, he negotiated against the facts. The facts he pushed down to drown in the bathtub of his soapy, yellow emotions. They rose up again like a stout rubber ducky.

Lourdes texted a query. His lilac cologne sanitized the quotidian. It added decorum and meaning to the moment. Scent freshened and domesticated the male animal.

Meanwhile, the lad had answered. The counselor listened with a carefully neutral expression as Steven explained all.

Judging by his face on the video, Lourdes thought Steven looked a little greenish and delicate. He sensed the lad was an only child. There was an angularity.

Steven was a betrayer, he confessed on screen. He did not want to join Sammy's "affinity group." She planned battle with authority. She implied violence. It was not that she shut him out. She had shut herself out of common society. He loved her but didn't want to be a radical. Hard cider clarified this.

Portland has a street named Couch, pronounced *Cooch*, after steamboat captain John Heard Couch. In 1845, he claimed a mile of land here and drew alphabetic streets, but the British also claimed it. Steven knew what happened on the street named Couch. Last year,

2019, anarchists exchanged gunshots outside Cider Riot, a bar at 8th and Northeast Couch Street. It was their hangout. One man tried to run another man over with his car. What happened? Afterward, that car, riddled with bullets, crashed into nearby trees. Since the anarchists wouldn't talk, no one else knew the whole story. After that, and a fight between anarchists and rightists, customers stopped coming. Steven's favorite bar closed forever.

He wanted to talk Sammy out of her affinity group. He wanted to keep her safe. This did not convince Lourdes. "She hasn't deleted her account? Just some pictures."

Steven confirmed this.

"Her account is still active, Steven," Lourdes's face on the smartphone pointed out. "That's the salient point you are avoiding to admit to me. It shows me that you don't want to think about what it means."

"What does it mean?" Steven implored.

The wallpaper curled. The sun ebbed. The distance between the patterns widened, paler, emptier. Steven felt a subsidence, an inner consolation. He felt the beauty of his unmet longing. It hurt, though.

66.

It was no surprise how much Grandma didn't like DeKay. Since the divorce, her ex's mother was always willing to cause her pain. But for Sammy's sake, DeKay didn't break relations.

Yes, Nature's affectionate *cluck chirrup graaa smurkle* was the diction the room needed to cheer me up, to cheer up DeKay. It was hard to be a Diversity, Inclusion and Equity specialist in a time of virus. Face to face trainings were easy. Holding others accountable over video was difficult, impractical or awkward to arrange. In that last video presentation, she had allowed BSG to heckle and ambush her. She had made the mistake of letting him air all his critique. It upset her to remember.

And home provided no comfort right now. Currently, she and Noah took their meals alone. She ate at the table. He took his meal on a tray into his room. She could hear him exercise. He watched movies on his laptop, she assumed. No doubt he played video games.

Purged of hostility, Grandma offered something else now. She showed pictures of DeKay's ex-husband. Proud, gloating, and vindictive, she held the photo out and peered at her face.

Roger had grayed a little at the temples. His old mustache was the same. Standing on a far-off scaffold, he held a briefcase in one hand. The other arm bent in a sling. Holding him was a shockingly attractive, younger, thin woman. Both wore hard hats. With the glow of her youth, the woman glared at DeKay with slightly Asian eyes. She saw how Roger's girlfriend clutched him with cruel, confident determination.

DeKay defended herself. She capsulated her professional struggles with strong words and provocative questions. *Caw-Caw?* Or *Caw* not *Caw? Cluck chirrup graaa smurkle?* or *Cluck chirrup graaa* not *smurkle?* She told Grandma that she hoped Noah would appreciate this.

345

Grandma scoffed. "I'm not talking professional accomplishments. I'm talking looks. You better hold on to him. We're not related except as women. Still, you're going to look more and more like me every day. And I'm alone."

How offensive! Just because Grandma was alone did not mean DeKay would ever be. DeKay retorted that *she* did not deserve to be alone. She thrived in a career surrounded by colleagues and friends.

The elder woman's eyebrows flickered with disagreement. Her tone was mild as she advised, "What job is safe in today's economy? What marriage is safe in this culture? What can we do about it? Make amends with Noah, and spare Sammy an unstable home, again."

This surprised DeKay. She didn't say anything.

Grandma went on. She thought the girl had a new tattoo. How regretful. How could DeKay let Grandma's son's daughter defile her body like that? Tattoo removal left scars.

Slumped in her chair, DeKay let herself moan. What would Contessa Finger think now, if she were watching? Sometimes it seemed that the struggle for equality made no progress. Strife and stress increased, but still there was not enough equality.

"I have no time for this." Grandma was disgusted. She looked away. "You're being ridiculous. Get ahold of yourself."

67.

"It is an old story," the lad began, as if he didn't believe it was the most important thing in the universe, if not Sandy Boulevard. "I fell in love with her. She just wants to be friends."

"That's how you see it." Since Steven couldn't argue with that, the counselor went on. "Was that painful for you?"

Steven's eyes, pallid and vague…, rose again to search for reassurance in Lourdes' face on his little smartphone screen. As his eyes searched, he swung his legs. He was ready for Lourdes to amaze and encourage him.

Lourdes gave the reassurance but found it

glib. Stevens jerked his image around as he squirmed. Lourdes shut his eyes. All the while, he spoke smoothly, clearly, portentously.

"Yes," Steven agreed. "I guess it made me understand she would never love me. We had no future, except as friends. I like being her friend," he added falsely.

The counselor encouraged this addendum. "That's good! That's good. Maybe you're better off as her friend than her lover."

"It doesn't feel that way," Steven replied, "but maybe you're right."

Lourdes let that sink in. Then he asked, "Is it an accident that you are attracted to a woman who made it perfectly clear she was unavailable to you? Does that sound healthy?"

Quietly he admitted, "No."

"How would you describe it?"

Steven croaked out, "Doomed."

On the screen, the lad's face looked sad again. Childhood, vicious and dying, pressed its face against its hand. The innocence was disgusting and brutal with its hunger for power. Strength hungered and so did weakness. The expiration of Steven's candor hurt the counselor.

Lourdes offered this: "Because consciousness reflects choice, you can choose your conscious attitude towards Sammy. In time, that will sink in."

Steven's smartphone had no choice but to transmit his scowl: "I don't want to. Why can't

I do whatever I want within the sovereignty of my own mind?"

"It's making you sick," the counselor countered.

Steven's response came easily. "Then I choose to be sick."

"Then you choose to be a slave."

The counselor's severity startled Steven. "What? No, I'm free to choose to suffer."

Lourdes did not relent. "That's a misuse of your responsibility to yourself. Self control is freedom."

The lad's face showed confusion. "That's not what freedom is."

"Steven," Lourdes began, his medium smart

mind unspooling its educated twine, "ancient wisdom discovered that passions are slavery. Freedom of the mind only comes from self-control. It's different than the contemporary idea that freedom is the ability to do whatever one wants. Follow your emotions and you enslave your mind."

The counselor could not help a frown start to form. He limited it to one corner of his mouth. No, he did not let that thought complete. He forced his mouth to neutralize. He felt some unease.

"Stay off social media, Steven," he advised, "at least for a while." His sense of unease grew.

Afterward, Lourdes waited but Noah did not call.

68.

Slumped, DeKay glared at Grandma. Then she sat upright again. She confessed, she wasn't sure what went wrong with Noah and had no idea how to fix it.

"You have no idea." Grandma nodded in confirmation. "You both don't." She barked, "What went wrong with Noah? First, you picked him. Noah isn't like my son. You thought you wanted a pushover man and you got Noah. The poor man can tell you don't respect him."

DeKay denied it all.

Grandma shrugged and turned away. At her low points, Grandma wondered if the purpose of her waves and troughs of emotion for the men she loved was to make the wheel of passion move. Maybe it redirected the boundless alternating current of sparks from love to hate to love again, ever fresh, ever strong, ever driving around and around. Either direction, drama pushed the electrons of feeling.

Unfortunately, she now believed, that's how she drove Wallace, Roger's father, away. It was her greatest regret. And now he was dead, so she couldn't tell him.

Oh baby baby how was I supposed to know? That something wasn't right.

Grandma said none of this. Neither did she say that she couldn't stand Noah.

The silence was enough. DeKay left the building unsatisfied. She started the car. She vowed not to visit Grandma again for a whole year. Then she looked up.

The street, Grand Avenue, widened physically and spiritually. It was unusually clear and powerful. The Masked One was suddenly at my ear. "There is still time to make Basil DeKay your hero."

Startled, I jumped.

"This creation of self is not natural and objective. *Power* creates a hero. People throughout history have been made into subjects. To support DeKay, you must disrupt the dominant discourse."

353

Again, I didn't understand. "Disrupt the discourse? Why would I want to do that? And which discourse is dominant?"

The Masked One was gone. Grand Avenue greeted me anew. What was its discourse? All the buildings bordering it seemed to huddle, unusually close. Yellow and red swirled among blobs. Blue outlined white in an ideology of yippee.

It was the "Forty-One 11," a look-at-me apartment building, where Couch Street met Martin Luther King Boulevard.

The squish was so important to each blob.

Love One Another, its roof sign cajoled. The
two square towers of the structure stood near at
angles, not parallel or perpendicular but
cockeyed on purpose. Its windows opened here
and there, sprinkled nonsensically and varying
in size.

It was a building of wrapping paper with
loud celebration. Alas, it had no dignity. It
offered just its own loud identity and fear from
its hoisted mass. It towered to force big smiles.
It was itself, enigmatic and cheerful,
unknowable, aggressive. It seized the distance
with a loud LOOK-AT-ME! It celebrated a
deity that yearned for its own annihilation.

"Ptum, ptum, ptum."

69.

As she drove home, Basil DeKay listened to
National Public Radio. The calm voices soothed
her, supported her feelings, and assured her
point of view. Under the spell of their cadences,
sure, smooth and correct, she found herself
driving with her head at a tilt. It was the
morning show. Reporter and guest openly
discussed the contradictory scientific theories
about this coronavirus.

Did people who recover from COVID-19
gain immunity or not? Was herd immunity

possible, inevitable, or impossible? Should listeners wash their hands with soap and water or half-truths and fear? Was Noah an immature jerk? Did mask mandates infect traditional norms? What new pronouns did the virus require? How did the virus self-identify? Was worship a super-spreader of infection? What defined the range of reasonable opinions? Sometimes it was this, other times, that.

The discourse of immunology remained structured by, and produced binaries between, the inside and outside of the host. The immune system responded one way to self and another way to non-self. Biological tolerance did model the way tolerance worked in society.

The virus continued to evolve. It evolved in reaction to every spastic and contradictory action of the fifty States, and of all the nations and all their programs and habits.

As she drove, DeKay remembered to buy takeout dinner. The masked cashier handed her the bag and the diversity officer sped on. Noah wasn't making the dinners or even shopping at the moment. As she looked for a parking space by a corner store, something nudged her. Was it her phone? She checked: Sammy confirmed pizza dinner tomorrow. But that wasn't what nudged her. What was it? She could not recall.

After the purchase of wine and a box of cookies to supplement the takeout, she drove through the world of the awake. She passed telephone poles with old fliers. Again she saw that fist silhouette against that face silhouette. Again, the great baboon hovered.

Home, DeKay cast out her weary insight. From the slight disorder, and absence of vibrations, she learned that Noah wasn't home. The takeout was now cold. Tired, in pajamas, she heated it in the microwave.

With the assistance of her aromatherapy dispenser, she slept. But there was a systemic problem with her dreams. They swelled and compressed as she breathed. It made wavy lines of blur and clarity.

Her thoughts drifted, half-lucid. Did anything else besides light cast a shadow? What was pattern? What was source? What was ephemeral, and what remained? "Why should I care about shadows?" she protested. The blur grew, and in the blur came a new clarity: "I am asleep." Then came the thought, "Where is Sammy? What is she doing?"

DeKay woke to a bad day.

70.

The diversity officer's phone buzzed again.
She rubbed her eyes and read the texts. Sammy
said she wouldn't be able to come for dinner.
She was working on a social justice project.

Daughter sent smiley emoticons to Mother
and to Noah. However, the emoticons did not
reflect Sammy's face's actual expression, in her
Old Town apartment, her face distorted and her
eyes wild.

Afterwards, DeKay video-called Larsen. Her
friend's face appeared grim in the phone screen.
She immediately changed the topic.

"Did you see what happened in
Minneapolis?"

"No. My daughter moved out. I think she's
having adventures. But she didn't say
anything…"

"Did Sammy move in with a boyfriend?"

"How would I know? I'm just her mother."

Larsen slowed down. Her posture eased. She
offered the consciously returned gaze of the
sisterhood.

"What happened in Minneapolis?" DeKay
asked.

There was news from that city. A man died
in cruel humiliation: Police, a neck, a knee. The
video of a man's death with a uniformed knee
on his neck was just a click away on the
smartphone. That was not all. History burst with
each click. History flinched and screamed.

The strings of discourse wound tight.
Discussion wasn't possible, now. History
exploded with tears and blood. History put a
knee on the neck of discussion. Progress had no
words that could expunge the pain of history.
What words told now was rage, fear, grief,
paranoia, guilt, lies, slogans, mind-killing cant,
the jargon of justice, virtue signaling and
opportunism, villainous grift, and stupefying
hate. History screamed. Dignity fled. Social
media wailed.

Discourse! Discourse! Word police snapped-to and saluted. Word militia patrolled with staves. Word vigilantes lurked with hammers.

Then sunset hissed into silence. And then… there… was… noise.

Meanwhile, in Simon Rush's domestic chambers of quarantine, Tejashree Pandey clicked into the variables fields of online city forms for pandemic-safe restaurant curb seating. She heated up with frustration; she only wanted one parking spot to build fenced table space. Her leg fell asleep. She stood up and started shaking around oddly.

But music played. So Simon stood up and

did the same thing as a dance. They turned it into frenetic torso and hip contortions. They shouted *Corona... Virus! Virus... Corona!* With hooking arms, they tried to imitate its shape and postures. They had no idea that justice was coming.

71.

When in doubt, it was time for Noah to work on his upper and lower abs and the obliques along the sides. The news was all bad: he turned it off. Noah lied on his back and pedaled an invisible air bicycle. He raised one shoulder as a symbolic gesture of touching the opposite knee. He repeated on the opposite side, two sets, so many reps.

"Keep your elbows back," he told himself. "Keep the sadness back." He pressed his lower back to the wooden floor. Next was crunches.

Later, Noah shot blue soldiers on the screen. He had earned this by his rule: two hours exercise, one hour game. His red avatar ran and crouched as the blue soldiers shot into the space he had just vacated. As he toggled through his weapons, he wondered, what is a right? What is a duty?

Noah had a buddy in Des Moines, Iowa, who planned to open a bar when normal life returned. Should he move there, or to Alaska, and work in a cannery? Was he ready to start a new life somewhere else, alone? Would it be safe to fly among all the masked passengers?

It made him sad. Did Noah want to end his marriage with Basil? Yes, sometimes, other times, not. Did he consider regret for his angry words? Yes, but he believed them. Did he feel regret for the drama he created? Yes, but he also felt justified. He considered regret, though, for the pain it caused her.

He did not want to play his game today, but he did want to grant his poor avatar a new life. He pressed the button on his console. A luminous pattern made a wraith of his facade.

Noah still believed his wife left passion behind when she divorced Roger. But he now toyed with the theory that it was a good thing. After all, Roger and Basil's passion came with instability. Noah knew he wanted no drama. And yet, he let his birthday irritation open his world to more and more of it. That was his fault.

He wasn't sure if Basil would consider their status repairable. If only her pregnancy last year had been healthy. How different their lives would be now!

Noah's game's screen avatar told him, "Being red and beautiful means what? Means… lonely. And you are red and beautiful." Lourdes understood this.

He supposed Lourdes wanted him to call. This annoyed him. He rebelled against it. He owed Lourdes nothing. It intrigued him, the idea of exploring that side of his self as a potential. But the act, with another man, he didn't like to admit the prejudice — disgusted him. Everyone said that it was a good thing to let go of internalized fetters and find his true self (if any self existed at all). His healthy body was full of abstract passion. That was the problem.

His avatar stood up, jumped over the wall and charged — right into a blue bomb.

I walked along the rostrums of Hawthorne Boulevard under the fantastic vault of bright colored night. The stores, ruminants, all closed, grazed reflections in fitful mood. I saw an anarchist lean on the side of the pizza shop, a cigarette between his teeth. It was typical of the moment to learn that by frying the lungs, cigarette smoke made the virus despair of grip.

He had pulled his mask below his chin to smoke and speak with his companions. His face was a frail shell of toughness. He had a brittle, venomous expression that contrasted with the delicateness of his face. Runes from elfin fantasy tattooed his forehead. Three studs pieced his lower lip. His eyes darted within maskara. When he saw me watching, those eyes turned insolent. As I watched, he pulled out a marker, and drew, under his eyes, on his skin, a black horizontal line, crookedly, across his face.

72.

I looked up. I saw rising clouds arranged in parallel rows. I heard that last delightful screech, the *"Yaaiip... Yaaiip!"* of the Steller's jay's impudent report. I smelled the pollen that cloyed, the dust that assured, the provocative confusion.

While Noah exercised and clicked buttons at a two to one ratio, Basil DeKay slept with anxious turnings. Did enigmas and contradictions battle with her certainties? Fortunately, her alarm vibrated: It was still daylight.

She looked out her window. It was in that same window I had first seen her. It was many nights ago, it seemed, when the Masked One and his agents had first intruded upon my doubts at night. Now three maskless girls abandoned their tasseled scooters and followed each other around a tree. Each wore a helmet. One of them talked about ghosts. Normal life tried to go on.

There was less traffic on the boulevard than usual. Uncertain which way to go, I heard an old lady crying, "Caw, Caw!" But was it an old lady? And was she cursing a bicyclist that didn't give way as she crossed the street? Or was she a crow, bringing fire to a hairless primate?

On one side of the boulevard, the Edwardian house retaining walls sprouted. On the other, a boutique's naive handbags mixed with unshakable clogs and a bistro's myth-destroying pesto. Across the street, across from the Tea & Yoga, across from the Thai and Lebanese and

Korean restaurants, which each displayed hand
sanitizer in the window, across from them
lurked the indications of a shadow, the pointer
of a sundial for the soul. I walked the half-
hearted pandemic shopping district with a light
froth of crisis and concealment. I saw the clever
Wear Your Mask signs. It was another day
demystifying an idea of progress that is devoid
of essence. Still, I walked on, guiltless and
unhobbled, a kind of free.

A homeless man curled his life entirely
within a sleeping bag. He had pulled the bag
over his head. A bicycle lay beside him. The
huddled form of quilted nylon lay on the grass
strip next to the curb.

And now the overwhelmed joined the
outraged. In a mass of noise, they tumbled

down the street, and over Hawthorne Bridge. The eerie and the stupefied protested the stay home routine. The creepy and the ecstatic marched, raising fists. These hands like thistle pods tried to clench the sun.

In a march, a man raised a human fist. His mask read, *I Can't Breathe.*

Lifted in the hands of a young woman, a placard read, *See us — Hear Us — Respect Us — Love Us.*

Is My Son Next? a mother's sign asked.

Even a toddler held a sign. His mother pulled him to the march in a red wagon. The chubby fellow sat there with the placard that read:

F— the Police!

73.

Now was the time of unsettling, the Time of the Virus. Now was the passage through its fiery chambers of closed businesses, its isolation in living rooms, its glare of video meetings. Now was the wayfarers' end to the dying rhythm of gathering.

The cipher of the mask was the new tabernacle. It was a holy place of obscurity. It muffled speech. Would shouting help? The mask promised discomfort, intoxication, estrangement, doubt, shoddiness, bad odors, mediocre television, and anesthesia.

Awkwardly everywhere, the Masked One advocated in disjointed phrases, elliptical and difficult to understand.

Most wore masks: colleagues, superiors, underlings, individuals, foreigners, domestics, spouses, siblings, children, neighbors... elders too.

But now more started to take them off.

Now local leadership equivocated. Weren't protests righteous and progressive? Masked and unmasked, thousands crossed a bridge. A green line shot up from the mob into the sky, up, up into its heavy rhythmic thropping. You could tell who was radical by who carried an umbrella.

A device buzzed. Grandma called. "Where is Sammy? Where is my granddaughter?"

DeKay responded with irritation. "She needs to be independent. She's been cooped up with me. It's natural she wants to get out."

The voice on her phone barked back, "You don't know where she is? Why not? It's natural for you to demand accountability."

"I'm giving her time to tell me. The harder I'd try to hold on to her," DeKay reasoned back to her device, "the more she'd push away."

Grandma snorted. "What, you missed a cliché there, that *if you love something let it go* crap? Stop thinking in clichés and make the effort of original thought. Aren't you worried?"

DeKay couldn't quite hang up on her. Instead, she just said, "I'll call you when I know more."

But before she could click the phone off, Grandma replied, "I'll let *you* know if I know more first."

Sammy's mother's every moment had a subordinate counter-current sense of occupation sensitive to whatever her daughter might be doing, whenever, wherever. It didn't always work. But she couldn't admit this now.

A sickly yellow tint to the lid of sky arrived. A forest fire grew on the side of Mount Hood. Ash collected on windowsills. Residents shut their windows. Did we shut out the poison or shut it in? The Goose Hollow balconies conceded their emptiness. In the distance, a bullhorn echoed, and drums.

74.

My fear grew. How could we even talk about the truth? What was the proper frame? What words should we use? One by one, the newspapers announced, capital B, small *w*. Justice was coming, so I hurried away.

In Old Town, as historic as it was stabby, as beautiful as it was shooty, a familiar woman approached a bed. Tejashree Pandey fought with her emotions. It upset her that politicians supported mass gathering, a violation of pandemic rules, for the purpose of protest against police abuse. These were the same rules that continued to strangle businesses like her own. But she also supported the protests.

Since she couldn't resolve this, she let out a long, restorative exhale. The death of a Black man in Minneapolis under the white police knee… It appalled her. It compressed the pain of history. Simon refused to watch the death video, but she did so. Now she wished she hadn't. She exhaled again, slowly.

Simon lay in the bed already. Tejashree asked Simon to sniff the cat to determine if she was without odor, thus clean enough to lie on the blankets. He did not want to, so he asked the cat, "Want to sniff yourself to make sure you don't stink?"

Then Simon pretended in a cat's voice, *"No thanks, I'm good."*

Tejashree started to laugh. Then she laughed some more. She couldn't stop. Quarantine unfolded and refolded, over and over, Hell's origami.

With mask on, Tejashree carried out a bag for recycling.

There in the hallway, among others, also with bags, stood Sammy, bandana around her neck. In her blank face lay the monomania of identity. She and her companions all wore dark hoods. They were all small, with elfin faces under hair tinted magenta, aqua, pink and metallic purple. Because of the masks, baggy clothes or chest armor, it was not clear to Tejashree if individuals were male or female. They had shopping bags, which should have been a normal thing. But Tejashree perceived among them a vibration of danger, or at least, conspiracy.

By her posture, turned for communication, eyes locked, Tejashree stopped Sammy. Through her mask she asked, "Everything okay in there?"

Sammy's eyes were red from crying. Otherwise, her expression was flat. She pulled her bandanna over her face. "Of course."

Tejashree Pandey noticed that Sammy's companions were of a type, but what was that type? People on the margins, liminal faces, they raised their grievous foreheads. It was hard to tell who was what. This one was a runaway waif? That weak-faced man with eye makeup over his ACAB mask, was he a woman? That one, a manic criminal, and there, an ideologue? This one, a military veteran? Here … small and ambiguous … there and there trans, there another trans maybe, and those two, drug addicts — and also, mentally ill? She could not be sure.

Tejashree then reached out to touch Sammy's arm but then remembered not to. Sammy began to walk on, so she called after her, "I have favor to ask."

Sammy stopped, turned back, and nodded.

Composed under her mask, Tejashree began, "Would you ask your boyfriend not to leave his motorcycle idling so long in the morning?"

"We don't do labels," Sammy replied, her voice muffled by its hoarseness and by the cloth.

Tejashree grew cross. "The motorcycle does noise. It's right outside our window. It's really loud."

"He needs to let it idle to warm up."

Tejashree made a gesture of "So?"

"If it doesn't warm up, it won't run right. It will stall if he doesn't." Now Sammy made the gesture of "So?"

"It's really loud," Tejashree insisted.

"Once it warms up," Sammy explained, "the motorcycle goes away. Win-win."

Tejashree felt her body tense to yell. She readjusted her mask, rather than speak.

Sammy blinked. She turned away, then turned back to ask, "Why did you ask me if everything was okay?"

Tejashree drew herself up as she considered how to answer without offense, nor retreat.

She thought about that man, who seemed to like aggression. "Well, your guy seems sort of antisocial…"

Now Sammy was annoyed, but just then something rattled — one of her companions' paper bags broke and something fell out of it. They quickly picked it up. Sammy led the way into the apartment and shut the door.

75.

Lourdes watched, astonished. Incandescent buildings filled our screens. Silhouettes danced and ran. In Minneapolis, a police precinct burned. It was a fist of flame. Was justice coming? Was this the way? The barracks of authority roiled in flames of celebration! Hooray! Red, gold, blue, green sparks shot up, and burst in a frothing star. The stars sparkled and dropped, and a new rocket shot upward.

The mob of justice cheered below. Hooray! Hooray! The skyline burned, hooray! Justice smoked, and Revenge sparkled. How could this be? What did it mean? Was this the way?

It was just the beginning.

Feuds twisted slowly in the sky. Effete youths swirled in resentful whorls. Lies brawled cosmic with lies. Rhythmic noise drowned consciousness. Below, tramp tents lay disordered under the spill of city night. The painted curses on plywood windows faded in the brotherhood of night-murk.

BREAKING WINDOWS: Shop windows represent segregation. They are invisible barriers. They offer a view of the Good Life while they block access to it. — Anarchist pamphlet

Why did plywood cover so many windows? Because of the heroic window-smash fun, the break-in, pillage and plunder. This violated that old Yiddish saying, *Don't spit into the well — you might drink from it later.*

It was only property. Were lives more important or not?

Right on schedule, morning came. The sun stared at us too much. *Tati tati ta ta!* Word trumpets blared. In Minneapolis, there were two autopsies that found different causes of death.

Humiliation burned. Streets burned. Buildings burned. Death made another visit. Justice was coming. So I hurried away.

Basil DeKay was groggy. There was broken glass on the carpet near her. Anarchists? Rioters? Looters? What? No. She had broken it herself. Everything was ruined. It could not be true.

Did the encounter exasperate? Gnaw? Ruffle, irk and chafe? She had encountered herself. She fell half-asleep again. She mulled the unhappiness in her drowsing mind. The vice provost told her: They were unsatisfied with the lack of progress with diversity and equity under DeKay's leadership.

But her smartphone sang a happy song. She had forgotten to turn it off or had left it on so her daughter could call. But her daughter did not call. An old voice barked.

DeKay winced at Grandma's truncated manner, so familiar and annoying, but she was never at ease with it.

"Where's my granddaughter?"

"She moved in with friends in Old Town," DeKay reported. "Just call her. Do you know how to text? She prefers text."

"A woman my age shouldn't have to text," the older woman snapped. "Your daughter should return my phone calls."

"The next time I talk to her, I will remind her."

"She's probably at the protests. I want her to stay off the street. It isn't safe right now."

DeKay was annoyed. Grandma made no mention of defunding police, of the need to replace police with social workers, of historic wrongs that still cried out for reparations, of the justice of rage. "Whatever you say. May we hang up now?"

"Are you drunk?" Grandma demanded.

Angrily DeKay replied, "I just woke up!" Then she clicked the connection off. She paused to consider; yeah, she was still a little drunk.

In the stillness, awake, she remembered she was unhappy. It would not help her to hum, *"Ptum, ptum, ptum."* She had, however, aromatherapy. Searching, she pressed a button. An NPR broadcast soothed her with its calm and reasonable words. Looting had a legitimate role in public discourse. Whiteness gave us our idea of property, and with it, Black oppression.

Where was her uniqueness? Where was belongingnessness? DeKay knew what her problems were: disbeliefness, paralysisness, and powerlessnessness. There must be something she could do, rather than turn to anger. Someday would come bargaining, depression, and acceptance.

BREAKING WINDOWS: Shop windows taunt the poor with commodities they cannot afford, status and security they will never attain. — Anarchist pamphlet

A man of the Archon family parked his motorcycle in Old Town. Bent awkwardly, Sammy's arms shook with the strain, the strain of pouring gasoline into bottles.

76.

Basil DeKay fell asleep again. Her wine-addled slumber roiled in hostility, discomfort, division, and conflict. She woke so thirsty. After water, DeKay lay back again. She drifted in and out of sleep. When awake, she moaned, "Please let me sleep." When asleep, her dream thoughts begged, "Wake up! Wake up!"

What is a human being, that you should make so much of her? That every day you examine her and test her every hour? Why do you hide your face? Why do you eagerly pursue a flying leaf and persecute a dried-up stem? You endowed her with life and tenderly guard her breath.

She woke, head aching. She saw now that she had, at some point last night, thrown the lamp into the mirror. She remembered that. She remembered that administration might sacrifice her for a lack of progress. And she remembered that Sammy had moved out.

All the cookie boxes were empty. She opened the last one in weak hope of normality, all that the steady supply of cookies meant to her. As she opened the box wider, time crackled. There was a fissure inside. Broken, unwelcome light appeared through the other side.

DeKay, locked in her room, was drinking again. Would the administration renew her contract? It did not seem as important now as she had thought it was.

Noah could hear her sing a lullaby. He wanted to go to her, but if she was drunk, maybe he had better not.

DeKay intuited that her daughter would not take on the burden of eons. She would never have a grandchild.

Someone draped a delicate handkerchief over a framed photograph of her own grandmother. Who had done that, she wondered. What did it mean? How could things have been different? What if Sammy had given birth to the child, her grandchild, a girl, perhaps named Eleanor? What would it have been like to cradle a baby again in her arms? She would be about the size of the pillow.

"Rock-a-bye-baby…" DeKay urged
Eleanor to go to sleep. She sung a rhyme that
little Sammy had liked, but it sounded
melancholy. She sang it again with forced
happiness… Then she realized that she rocked
the baby excessively.

Through the door, Noah said he could not
think because she was so loud. Somehow he
opened the door.

DeKay hid the "baby" and the bottles.
Slumped on the other side, Noah begged her to
let him in. He was lonely. Offended by his
intrusion, she blocked his way.

"Please," Noah implored, "Let's be friends!"
No, she blocked him again. He rubbed her arms.

This only emphasized his lack of words. "Please" was not enough; she required complete articulated capitulation. Yet if he surrendered, she would find his weakness repulsive. The peaches of immortality blossom for a thousand years, fearing no winter—but not on Earth. DeKay rejected his "Please" and pushed him out the door. Then she locked it.

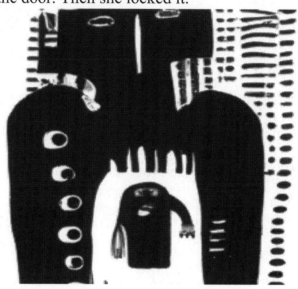

Noah yelled through the door. She cursed him. He responded that he would tell Larsen that she's an alcoholic. Then, in a strangled voice, he declared he would never do that. Finally, he was quiet. She supposed he had left.

DeKay had cut her finger. She looked at the framed Obama "HOPE" poster, undamaged. Obama looked away.

She reported to the *good* president that the enemies of justice tumbled in retreat. The city's

white woman police chief resigned, so that a
Black man could now lead. DeKay sat down on
the bed. Only when a sensation of otherness
rose from her inner depths did she suspect that
she had fallen asleep again.

No, she argued, she was awake. The
sensation of difference within her didn't
articulate itself in words. But in the murk of her
dream, she remembered what the sensation told
her before: "The concealment itself is
concealed. So great is this concealment, that I
am not even aware of the concealment. I may
even come to think of the darkness as light."

"Openly acknowledge, regularly remind."
DeKay complained in her dream. "Positively
impact! Go away. Everything and everybody.
Go away!"

77.

Light filled the wide-awake. This light was hot, white, square and dysphoric. The word *dysphoria* comes from the Greek for "hard to bear." It was hard to bear the weight of the light. The weight was not equal. Sometimes particle, when it wasn't a wave.... no, you know what, either way... the burden was nightmare. It lit the faces of millions of citizens.

Anarchists piled trash and stolen restaurant furniture. Where did they pile it? In the middle of the street between downtown park blocks, by the county and federal court buildings, of course. Yes, but where exactly? In the fountain bowl around the old bronze elk statue, of course. Fire was the new water.

The elk roared through the flames: "I just 'checked my privilege'… Looks fine to me." The bonfire beckoned, public property aflame with meaning: the human person is essentially Will, conscious deliberation, shed of anything unchosen.

I will drink the wine while it is warm
And never let you catch me looking at the sun

The nation's pain was too hot and too bright. Mobs stole justice from stores to liberate property from its oppressive owners. What was the truth of the cause? What was the truth of the riots? The hot sanctimony? The brittle certainty, the iconoclasm, the chants? The strange

solidarity of umbrellas? The broken windows
and bonfires of stolen furniture in the middle of
the street? Curses, screams, looting, drumming,
arson of whole buildings, these were the
armaments in the crusade against evil. Anyone
who disagreed was evil, and evil took the form
of reflective window glass. Smash!

Who held the police accountable for what?
What say you, if a face of pale dissent threw
something at the police? Was it words, phrases,
slogans, labels, metaphors? Perhaps the
message was sometimes clever? Something
crude and cruel, about their children, their
wives?

What *special* insults did they yell at the female police officers? Broken glass glittered with screams, laughs, and shouts. Chants arose to the holy street beat: *"Every precinct, every town, burn the precincts to the ground."*

Traditional news sources filtered facts to present an honest confirmation of their bias. Their viewers craved it.

Rose now a host of lights. It was too bright to make out shapes and motion, but there were shapes, and there was motion. Time had cracks. There was a fissure in the moment. Through it, a rageful light roared.

79.

The Provost called an All-Staff video town hall. He asked Sammy's mother for assistance. She was glad, because she didn't think the Provost could handle it.

It was an extraordinary summons. The screen showed row after row of little squares with the faces of the attendees. Leadership confessed dismay at their unwitting participation in pervasive, invisible injustice. Racism wove through the system. Racism haunted the machinery. What could they do to address it? The Provost leant control to the diversity officer.

Across the digital connection, Basil DeKay
deployed an extravaganza of Diversity,
Inclusion, and Equity words and phrases. Even
without the nourishment of a pie chart, she
knew her presentation was particularly strong…
supported by the intermittent interruptions of
street noise.

There were bullhorn declarations, the pop-
pops and whumps of less-lethal detonations, the
smoke and hiss of firework rockets… plus
screams, chants, drums, and police car sirens…

DeKay offered to answer questions, but, to
her dismay, the Provost took back control. This
shocked her. At first, no one's little picture
dared raise a hand icon. DeKay looked for her

smartphone to text the Provost of the danger.

Then one young woman did make that request. At first, sobbing, she couldn't speak. She managed to say she had just come back to work after having a baby, a white baby. She was so sad that even her little baby was guilty of systematic racism. He couldn't even sit up, but "My white baby is racist?" she sobbed.

This was passive-aggressive resistance, *white woman's tears.* DeKay had a prepared counter, but she didn't have control.

The Provost didn't try to answer. He asked the next person who signaled a question to reply. This white-haired man asked, "What happened to the dream that little children will one day live in a nation where they will not be judged by the color of their skin but by the content of their character?"

How predictable! DeKay had a prepared answer for this too, but the Provost granted people the right to speak in the order they raised their hand.

Now a middle aged white woman exploded. "I'm so angry about racism in this country! What to do about it? Maybe I'll give flowers or a Starbucks gift card to each staff person of color."

The diversity officer groaned as she clicked and clicked her hand icon. One of the face-squares of color winked out, then another.

Now a man's voice with a shrouded camera

spoke. "How can there be systematic racism if there's been laws against discrimination in force for decades? Isn't all this reverse racism?"

DeKay shouted. She could destroy this comment with a few words, but as more face-squares winked out, the hapless Provost chose the next person in line, another white woman.

"I'm furious at the ignorance and bigotry!" she yelled. "You fall in line with the anti-racist program or we will *fire* your ass!"

DeKay gasped. Dozens of face squares silently gasped along with her.

The Provost here stepped in. He used the prescribed phrase: "Do the work."

79.

Weirdly, life tried to go on. Basil DeKay received a strange phone call that she didn't answer. But she listened to the message. With shock, she recognized the voice of Bitter Safety Glasses.

It further surprised her to hear how upset he was — and how vulnerable. Humiliation weakened his voice. She called back. She winced as his words failed.

He started at his conclusion. "I'm a good person."

"I know you don't want to hear this right now, but it's not about whether or not you're a good person."

She couldn't tell him that she might also lose her funding. They cited a lack of progress across critical metrics. Decision makers might let her contract expire. She had a few days left, and had still not heard an official decision.

"This is not an appropriate conversation," she told him.

"You don't like me because you think I have privilege. If I had privilege, why would I lose my funding?" Without official complaint, decision makers had let his funding conclude.

"I like everybody equally," she replied coolly. "If you wish to talk further, please go to the website and click on the calendar to set up a meeting with me or Ms. Contessa Finger."

She exhaled and let her head droop. Then she lifted it, her face determined. No, he had to carry his own negative emotions. Meanwhile, her curriculum vitae coursed around the city with pulses of electricity.

So much of the binary brain organized to recognize human faces. The downtown buildings sometimes leapt out as faces, sometimes as estrangements. The new five story condominiums expressed cool reserve. The older Edwardians with their wedding cake visages looked with astonishment toward the enfolding project of progress.

The fountain under the large elk statue burned near the courthouse. F-12, its graffiti declared: FTP, ACAB.

"What do you anarchists want?" the bronze elk asked one of the masked, hooded figures lounging on the fountain rubble.

As if on cue, an anarchist yelled out to the world, "We want a society free of racism, class exploitation, misogyny and ecological ruin."

"Is that all?" the elk replied. "I want to live in a 'topia', like a utopia, but without *U.*"

I recognized that anarchist as my personal phantom, the one who visited me and bid me to disrupt the dominant discourse. "We want free health care for everyone," he told the bronze elk.

But then again, was that anarchist really my Masked One? I wasn't sure. What was a face, but words animated by power? Maybe I was mistaken, though: It was remarkably easy to confuse faces behind a state-required mask, as easy as it was to call an opposing viewpoint *fascist,* or a taxpayer-funded service *free.*

"Free housing, free food," the Masked One (if it was he) continued. "We want to live in a way that doesn't require imperialist wars or police. We want a society without coercion, an economy that doesn't change the climate. Clearly, this civilization doesn't do any of the these things. That's why we want fundamental social change."

Through the smoke and heat, the bronze face demanded, "And how will you realize this?"

The anarchist shrugged. Now I doubted. What was happening? Where was the phantom? Where was I for that matter? "Wash away the physical and mental obstructions to total liberation. Tear it all down and start over." He twirled his umbrella. The Masked One would never do that. But I would. I… would. The city began to twirl around me.

"Start over?"

"Of course," I heard myself say. "Take away the oppressions, and it will happen naturally. In a classless society, you'll find out that people are good."

Sky and earth tumbled again. I looked to see where the Masked One had moved me. A face appeared in the smoke.

The bronze elk looked down at me. "Yo mama's so classless," it replied, "she could be an anarchist utopia."

And there, in the distance, was a police

officer with a mask. Into his bullhorn the
Masked One declared, "A beautiful world
awaits."

My face felt strange. I realized that I was not
me. The mask tightened. The vision darkened
and went horribly wrong. *Get out of me,
phantom,* I thought. *Get me out of here.*

80.

Bronze Thomas Jefferson, across the river,
seated in contemplation before a high school,
pondered his bronze shame. What did George
Washington, Abraham Lincoln, and Christopher
Columbus all have in common? *They were all
born on holidays.* The ropes wound round and
round the third president. *Ptum, ptum, ptum!*

A citizen with a wrench unbolted the screws.
"Stand back!" he cried. The crowd heaved.
Bronze Thomas Jefferson, still seated, tipped
over. The wrench-man jumped out of the way.
The bronze sitter tipped over and down — an
anticlimactic thud. The bronze nose broke. Then

the spray paint hissed… SLAVE OWNER, and 846.

In bronze letters the empty plinth read, under the spray paint of the name of the man the police killed in Minneapolis, from the slave owner's First Inaugural Address:

"All too will bear in mind this sacred principle, that though the will of the majority is in all cases to prevail, that will, to be rightful, must be reasonable; that the minority possess their equal rights, which equal laws must protect, and to violate would be oppression."

This, and the spray paint covering it, filled the side of the empty plinth. However, the slave owner's address went on, a message from the third president of a new republic...

Let us then, fellow citizens, unite with one heart and one mind, let us restore to social intercourse that harmony and affection without which liberty, and even life itself, are but dreary things. And let us reflect that having banished from our land that religious intolerance under which mankind so long bled and suffered, we have yet gained little if we countenance a political intolerance, as despotic, as wicked, and capable of as bitter and bloody persecutions...

Every difference of opinion is not a difference of principle. We have called by different names brethren of the same principle. We are all republicans: we are all federalists. If there be any among us who would wish to dissolve this Union, or to change its republican form, let them stand undisturbed as monuments of the safety with which error of opinion may be tolerated, where reason is left free to combat it.

What did Hermes do when he broke a statue? He *Apollo-gized.* Portland statue topplers stood undisturbed as monuments of the safety with which error of opinion may be tolerated. Crows lifted; in fact, they skedaddled with the direction of domination. The excessive heat made every objection temperamental. I walked over to see the toppled Jefferson.

Once, Oregon was as far from Washington D.C. as the moon. In 1803, as he planned the Corps of Discovery expedition, Jefferson instructed Meriwether Lewis: *"Carry with you some matter of the kine-pox; inform those of them with whom you may be, of its efficacy as a preservative from the small pox; and instruct & encourage them in the use of it."*

Police warning tape already shrouded the fallen bronze. A woman shouted through a bullhorn: "Hold the *po-LEECE* accountable!"

Ptum, ptum, ptum! The clouds lifted. The sun burned even more hot and stark. The heat squeezed shadows into tighter, ever more claustrophobic holes. The light pierced narratives of exclusion and oppression. In the republic of trauma, umbrellas were not just for anarchists. In the republic of trauma, tastes, behaviors, desires, aspirations, and appearances became fraught. Revenge! Revenge!

Vegetation darkened with humiliation. Lichen demanded your pronouns. Pollen screamed for more equality. Fungus petitioned more dismantling, more decomposition. Were mildew and mold properly represented? Revenge! Revenge!

The diversity officer still felt the need to respond to the emergent moment. She felt accountable. Yet she was unsure what the people on the street stood for, and afraid of the violence, so she stayed home.

81.

In cities and in forests, the nation found itself on fire. Two autopsies disagreed: the social contract died of suffocation, or a heart made weak by poor choices. Everything was offensive. Everything was horrible to watch. Police had duties. Did civilians have none?

Why are you so concerned about property?
Things can be replaced; people cannot.
Anyway, all those businesses have insurance.

There was no truth, only power struggles. Waves of umbrellas blocked out the cameras. Vandalism? Arson? Murder? Around the country, the virus did not care.

Was the sky ever its most authentic self?

That summer of 2020, the sky understood its moment as a deep dissatisfaction with its truth, its lived experience. And you must agree. It was not blue. It browned like fried ideology.

I was in trouble, I knew it. The discourse was an anaerobic monster.

Born with a secret, the street was on the cusp of giving itself permission to explore that secret. Demoralized, humiliated, the air grew wiggly. Unstable, the gray-black Willamette River collided with the brown-black Columbia.

The scorched bronze elk lifted its head and looked for danger. It spotted a lone man who wore a mask. That was me.

"When we finally achieve equal outcomes,"

411

I asked, "will there still be riots, arson,
smashing and looting?

"Of course not," the elk replied. It paused to
reconnoiter. Maybe it could sense that there
wasn't much sand left in its hourglass… "When
we achieve equity, there will be nothing left to
smash and loot."

I summoned the trail of discourse. Along it I
flew, suddenly elsewhere. I stood quietly in a
Goose Hollow apartment. Basil DeKay spoke
by telephone with Bomberger. "Am I awake?"
she asked herself. She surveyed her landscape.
She felt her face. "Yes," she told herself.

Bomberger took this silence as greeting.

"My lawyer received your document," the doctor reported. "I'm going to sign it and send it back to you. What is next for me?"

The diversity officer took a moment to absorb the moment. "The mediator or Ms. Finger will contact you with your restorative justice plan," DeKay replied.

"When?" Bomberger asked. "I'd like to start as soon as possible."

DeKay answered, "I'll pass that along."

Apart by several miles, they held their phones in silence. DeKay was tired of Bomberger and the whole confrontation. Now that he was prostrate before her, she didn't want anything to do with him. In addition, she didn't want him to know that the administration seemed to let her own contract lapse. In the silence, she could sense the waver of her disarmed opponent.

Bomberger broke the silence. "Before you go, I'd like to say something. I don't have quite the right words. But I will try." He sounded hollow, but he knew it was his last chance.

Here it comes, thought DeKay.

Strange light flickered outside. She contorted her face until she hid her anger. That reminded me of the time I bought a dictionary and when I arrived home I realized all the pages were blank... I had *no words* for how angry I was. Jokes needed precise anchorage.

Bomberger began. "Once upon a time, a Jewish man named Morty went to a surgeon and said he wanted to be castrated."

DeKay silently groaned. She grit her teeth.

"The surgeon recoiled and said absolutely not!" Bomberger continued with rising strength.

"Morty insisted that the surgeon castrate him, until the other man couldn't take it any more. Reluctantly he agreed. So reluctantly!"

DeKay scowled. *Just a little bit more of this,* she thought. *Then, with luck, I'll never hear from him again.*

It was the last hurrah of the old provocateur, the last joke I ever heard him tell. Dr. Bomberger went on, "After the radical surgery, the surgeon came into the recovery ward and sat on Morty's bed. 'Morty,' he said, 'I know that your religion requires circumcision and I noticed you never had a bris.'

"Suddenly Morty sat up in the hospital bed. He snapped his finger and cried out, "Circumcise! Circumcise! *That's* the word I was thinking of!'"

Stretched, I began to laugh. In doing so, I relaxed in elastic return. Now, where I was, in my room, the hot shadows leapt. This was on account of a flicker of powerful light. I looked up from my writing table. What was going on out there?

Ptum, ptum, ptum! There was a knock on my door.

82.

Beside the street, in a crisis of fructification, flower petals closed and began to plump. The city swayed, sought a new normal, bought without authority, for there was none. Deep in the murk of the Willamette River, an old sturgeon shuffled its tail. The sun kneeled in shame. Smoky forests tainted the sky, and the sky knew no sleep.

The twins each carried an umbrella. We sat in my living room. I was the only one unmasked. I protested, "What did I do wrong?"

"You have offended," Tom observed grimly. "There were complaints. You have caused harm."

"I offended?" I recalled why, even in better times, I used to self-censor.

The twins, with umbrellas, turned to each other, then back to me. "There is a problematic idea that we might want to unpack," Tom told me.

I asked, "How many did I offend? One?"

Zoë's mask tightened. Emblems of authority affirmed a broken world. The loudest motorcycle in Portland, owned by Sammy's lover, affirmed a broken world.

Tom exhaled with restraint. With professional distaste, yet a strong dedication and duty, he tried again. "Okay. I understand the positionality that you're coming from.

However, the reality is that your words created a toxic climate…"

Zoë knocked the tip of her umbrella against the floor. "May I speak?"

"I have no concept," I ran on, "of how many readers complained, what their complaint was. You haven't shown me the complaint."

"I understand that this is upsetting," Zoë pressed, "but confidentiality matters."

I had trouble believing this. "The number of readers is confidential? What they complain is confidential?"

Zoë merely nodded. Tom nodded too.

The brazen elk of Main Street denied a broken world the last word. If humor was catharsis for repressed hostilities, humor purges the pain. Bolted to its fountain in 1900, the elk's four bronze stomachs digested the mayor, the city council, the chief of police, the district attorney. Its haunted eyes regarded skid row where the shades of farmhands and sailors drank worn-out faces. So many ghosts and phantoms of history peered out of the cracks: the natives dying of small pox and measles, the basement bordellos of Chinese women, the legless war veterans, the broken Wobbly lumberjacks. It bugled its mournful longing. Then at a distance I heard it…

"Everyone is entitled to be stupid, but some abuse the privilege."

Now Zoë gestured for my attention. "Listen. Do you see how this book is something that is not intellectually neutral? That you leave power up for debate? I mean this is a book that anyone could read."

I felt an inward crush. "But it should be up for debate."

Zoë looked at Tom.

Tom eyed me warily. With a careful and polite tone, he told me, "You're perfectly welcome to your own opinion, but when you're bringing it into the context of written narrative, opinions can become problematic. It can become something that creates an unsafe imaginary environment for your readers."

"It's not just that you told those jokes," Zoë argued. "You legitimized the doctor's words as a valid perspective."

In my head I replied, "But jokes put things into perspective, like this: per - (things) - spective."

My eyes must have betrayed my smile, for Tom's face showed the words of Aristotle: *"Patience is bitter, but its fruit is sweet."*

"The Masked One told you to follow Basil DeKay, her family, work and dreams," Zoë told me. "You did so. But he also told you to exalt her. You did not."

"So I caused harm?" I asked.

Tom explained, "You articulated the

420

doctor's defiance. Also, you laughed at his jokes. You retold them."

Bewildered and resentful, I remained certain that even in the future, when I could look back at all this from my hover-car powered by social credit points, I still would not agree. "Laughing at jokes is wrong now? What's going to happen to me?"

"You'll see."

The curtains fluttered, not from a breeze, but from the weight of light. There was a burst of brightness. I squinted and could not see for a long moment.

They turned. I looked as well. Beyond us, the forehead rose, the eyes sober and serious over the black mask. At last, I thought, an authority. I can appeal to him.

With pale hands, the Masked One unlooped the elastic from over his ears. He pulled the mask down. Just like that, without further notice or sign, he was gone. Nothing replaced him.

The sunshine burst through again. I had to blink. I shielded my eyes from the empty plinth.

I sensed the pathogen. It rushed into the void. It floated near, a meaningless perpetuation, or perhaps a relic of all life's origin. I assumed an immobile pose of statuary until it passed. It would soon break apart in the sunlight, right? At least, sooner or later it might. The reports contradicted each other.

Afraid to say anything, I clamped shut. If I opened my mouth, I thought the tribunes might slip in and set up tents in my mind.

Tom, as he faded backward, called out, "Justice is coming."

The twins set down the blades of their umbrellas. They looked at each other. Sun-bleached, they faded into the wail of siren. I assumed their umbrellas joined the others in the street. As the late summer light slowly darkened, bullhorns and *rat-a-tat boomba-tat* turned to sirens, helicopters, and small detonations… Wickedness and horror came a little closer, and with it… Justice. Yes, justice was coming! So I hurried away.

83.

Night after night, after night, after night
again, and some more nights, and finally...
nope this night too, and another, and now yes,
again, this night, to the serenade of sirens and
helicopters, there, again this night, between the
courthouses, an anarchist bonfire filled the dry
fountain. It cooked the plinth and legs of the
large elk statue.

Heat is energy and so is humor. Like
temperature, jokes measure how much energy
an object has, how much contradiction. Four-
legged memory chuckled.

"Will you clean my rump to help the anarchists make the city a better place?" the elk asked me.

"May I do that *after* the anarchists make the city a better place?"

The elk replied, "Sure," …then stopped and looked at me. Next, in effort to reform the disappointments of the whole world, it shook its hot metal antlers and bugled its heat. The pain it could bear, I could bear.

"We won, Bezz! Bomberger capitulated!"

"I gathered."

"Why do you not sound happy?"

Larsen didn't want to say.

On the east side of the river, in a private grass triangle by the ancient path between Willamette and the Sandy rivers, wrench and rope gathered. Humiliation and rage gathered, looping round. And angry people too gathered on the lawn of the German-American Society. The bronze George Washington[3] statue jerked, jerked again, leaned, and, despite his bronze cane, fell face down. Why was George Washington buried at Mount Vernon? *Because he was dead.* Spray painted COLONIZER it lay, red painted with 1619 and DEFUND WHITE MEN. Scorch black stained the statue, and breakfast cereal, and human shite.

425

"Bomberger was defying us all the way. Why would he give up? Because of the protests, the national reckoning?"

"No, Basil. Not the protests."

"What was it then?"

"Ginny's employer placed her on administrative leave yesterday."

An unexpected problem arose, following the fall of old bronze. Every aspect of the moment became wholly untrustworthy. Even the blue sky turned yellow and sick from forest ash.

In Lourdes' condominium apartment, Noah gave up every last defense. The victor undressed the younger man. The older man scaled the house of legislature. He blew up the crest of the fallen state. Thereupon he raised his flag of victory. With a polite smile, Noah showed his tolerance of Lourdes' ministrations.

"They want to fire Ginny? Because of her husband? Because we held him accountable to his words?"

Larsen paused too long for DeKay's comfort.

"I didn't say anything about her to anyone. Did you?"

"Of course not."

"So it's not our fault."

Larsen paused too long again.

But there was a shadow on the wall, a shadow from no light and nothing to occlude that missing light. It was a *pfft!* of unexpected consequences. The shadow of the pink unicorn was a lookie-lou. Look! Look, everyone! Death by *pfft!* In his murky soft bed, Lourdes had no desire.

Shying clear of heterodox, he didn't risk a rupture. What is a human being? Lourdes didn't know. He believed he had a body but no self. His lived experience was hollow, humorous, talkative, tasty, triumphant, easy, and weak. Jokes, he knew from Freud, were a form of catharsis for repressed hostilities. He cavorted pantomime in autumnal hysteria among the leaves of his mental foliage. Alt-liberal and fluid with his attentions to Noah, he had no new world to offer apart from destroying the old one. The wry destruction had sustained him for so long!

"Why would anyone blame Ginny for her husband's actions? Why fire her?"

"Things are like that now, I guess."

DeKay felt a wind blowing in there but denied it.

"I'm surprised Ginny or anyone else would marry Bomberger," DeKay shuddered.

They discussed social media, DeKay's letter to the medical board, cause and concurrence.

Since Larsen didn't satisfy, DeKay answered her own question: "It's a coincidence."

"Are you asking me or telling me?" Larsen responded. "Let's take our victory and keep moving forward. The Bombergers will be

alright.''

84.

Noah, inert and patient, reclined nude with his face in a pillow. He lay like a dolphin in a transport cradle. What is a human being? That agile aquatic mammal, Noah, was tolerant and expected little. He hid his heart deep, deep from the rest of humanity, all of them swindlers.

Lourdes tried so hard to push the nexus of universal history into Noah Beardsmore's Brexit, to smuggle an immigrant through the Channel Tunnel, to ride a Russian horse shirtless, to Palestine his Israel, to strmmnmrrph Western Civilization itself.

Lourdes sincerely delighted in his obscenity of privileges and rewards. But Noah's own milky body, smooth and healthy, had the natural capability to denounce the malignant.

"Be like water." With this, the anarchist social media exhorted tactics to its militia. *Water* was the expression of martial arts tradition. *Water* can flow around or crash through. Formless, unhurtable, adaptable, *water* finds ways direct and indirect to penetrate the hardest substances.

Formed, arid, the counselor lay face down on the younger man's back. He resisted tears, resisted weepage from confusion. He resisted a scream and bit back a laugh. His face grew determined. He took a breath like a man plunging forward to accept the weight of a great burden.

As his bare feet tread on dry leaves, he thought of pornography, of female parts compliant. What is a human being? With pornography at vanguard, humankind advanced towards universal freedom, defined as equal outcomes. But with Lourdes on top of Noah, time coagulated. Time did not cooperate. Time did not fabricate a moment.

Be like water. Noah's beauty mocked him.

The martial force of beauty pushed time forward faster: Tick tock, tick tock!

Be like water. With just a little bit of lust, Lourdes was lost in abstraction. Self-flagellant without self-forgiveness, he was not so much

431

monotheist as monomaniacal. His decorative arts gathered dust and demanded storage logistics. The icon refused to burst. The world remained blank and pitiless. All specters had opinions. He thrust but it became, in the end, pointless. Lourdes hated Noah.

85.

Deep in their awkwardness, both men recognized each other as human.

"This isn't working," Noah announced.

"No kidding." Lourdes snorted. He rolled away. Time in four colors looked to the side and down.

Noah vaulted a void. "What should I do?"

"With your life?" Lourdes wanted marijuana. "Only you can answer that."

The two men lay not touching.

"What are you going to do?"

Lourdes tried to use telekinesis to make his marijuana vape pen levitate from across the room. "I need to figure that out as well. I might retire early." He tried again: no levitation.

"That's not what I meant."

"It is what I meant." Lourdes paused to control his irritation. "I want to get away from this."

"What is this?"

Lourdes tried to explain to himself aloud. "All this. I might move. Sell my condo, find somewhere more tranquil. There are a lot of things I like in life. Even if I am queer, I'm still not gay. I need to stop making myself miserable. I think I prefer to be alone and asexual. I'll be just fine."

Noah thought this over. He looked his seducer in the eyes. *Oh my,* he thought. *I gave up my integrity for this?* He thought of Basil. He thought of Sammy. Aloud he continued, "I

433

don't think we can be friends."

"That's too bad. But I'll respect your wishes."

"At least until I figure out what I need."

Lourdes offered a cruel grin. "All right, buddy. Good luck."

Noah had no idea how Lourdes damned him by calling him *buddy*. Lourdes chagrinned his whole Noah project.

And thus these men, these two citizens of the demoralized Rose City, a city with no will to defend itself from itself, these two closed their eyes and footprinted behind that storm of angels evacuating Eden. These two men in their separate and silent ways tried to understand how progress stacked wreckage to welcome the Messianic Kingdom.

BREAKING WINDOWS: To smash a shop window is to contest all the boundaries that cut through this society: black and white, rich and poor. — Anarchist pamphlet

Annihilation refused desire. One man felt a rush of nausea and froze until it passed. The other eyed him, full of the tedious sense of the present, relieved only by hiccups and exhaustion. Time queered, curled, and wriggled.

Queer time rippled. It separated in layers and rejoined differently. Queer time refused accountability to any objective, graduated segments. Woozy, wobbly, queer time rotated. The more it searched, the more it drooped. No longer insistent, it suggested with faded numerals, softer clicks, and a weaker and weaker vigor.

86.

And me? I turned away, washing my hands with melancholy. With earphones to cut out the babble of the street, I listened to Fanny Hensel Mendolhson's *Hiob Cantata* sing from the Book of Job. I tuned my inner radio to the haunt of ancient discourse.

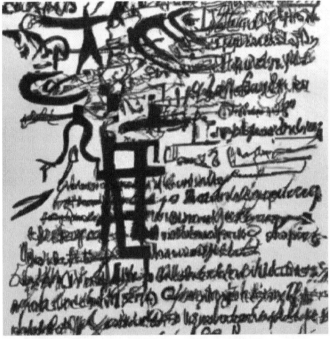

What is a human being, that you should make so much of him? That every day you examine him, and test him every hour? Why do you hide your face? Why do you eagerly pursue a flying leaf and persecute a dried-up stem? You endowed me with life, and tenderly guard my breath. While sometimes your heart is hidden, I know that you are ever mindful of me.

What is a human being? The sun was so
bright, the pants pleat so pressed, my
smartphone screen darkened with a glare of
shock and horror. Crows, bless you, protect me,
mordant feathered ambassadors, cortège of
liberties and independences, and please take my
poison bread away!

How did we hunger for such humiliation?
Every sunlit evening, the city confused itself
with piety. It ate the bread of righteous, showy
rage. As night came, that same bread revealed
its taste, a poison bread of anarchy. The civics
that the looters brought us: humiliation!

Our own people! The mob justice, as they grabbed what shame they could. How much shame would it take to heal the republic? How much broken glass? How many security photos of a young face, usually white, within a black hood? How many goofy, guilty expressions, as how many people stepped out of the smashed window? How many arms around how many boxes, how many sneakers, how many handbags?

What were the odds, when the rioters set fire to a business or shot bullets into it, that it would turn out to have Black owners? And if they were not Black, was that better? Did it matter?

What did it matter if four years before, a police officer in Dallas kneeled on the neck of a white man, and killed him? That had no special significance — it was in fact an obstacle to significance.

The looters stood undisturbed as monuments of the safety with which error of opinion may be tolerated. No one held them accountable. Police had duties, civilians had none. If police officers failed their duties, civilians had responsibility to SMASH!

The daylight protestor, the night crime anarchist, the social media agitator, the agendas in masquerade, the criminal, and the mentally ill, they all circled the crisis. Some bullied bystanders to raise a fist — almost every tested American did raise it. Don't hurt me!

The heat only increased. Steven lay on his tragic bed looking for signs of Sammy. With squinted eyes he scrutinized the social media posts of someone who called herself AntiFash Kissed. This account had the tag line on her profile, *Demonstrate, Ignite & Explode: Boom-shaka-laka.* He read her posts.

Lieh Tzŭ writes: If speech is harsh, the echo will be harsh. If the body is long, the shadow will be long.

Besiege, tire them, insult them, flaunt the rules, demoralize, and withdraw…

Feign madness but keep your balance. To masquerade, slough off the cicada's golden shell…

The mayor supports our civil rights message: Defeat the enemy by capturing their chief…

We own the streets. Let the police attack us on camera. Make the host and the guest exchange roles. Inflict injury on oneself to win the enemy's trust…

Order is violence. You endowed me with social media presence, and tenderly guard my Likes, my Thumbs Ups. While sometimes your account is hidden, I know that you receive notifications of my posts. Silence is violence. So smash it! Scream for justice! Scream louder! Who is accountable? Justice is coming! And her little sister, Revenge.

Twilight turned gold, silver, iron, then brass. The forest fire smoke formed distant, poisonous drifts. The sun, that pill of ivermectin, finally set. The night grew a hateful kind of yellow, an inside-out yellow. The ash-scented night humiliated the starlight. What followed, after the carousal of signs and speeches, were the warrior clowns. Parade the instruments of ideological terror! Drum! Scream! Chant! Laugh! Preach! Steal! Punch! Curse! Hammer! Throw! Tear! Dump! Push! Pull! Drag! Spray! Burn! Burn! Burn!

Ashes fluttered. Into streets of chaos Noah fled.

87.

Where were the crows now? Not far, not lost
in the forgotten hollers of tradition, but not near
either. Things were bad. "Ptum, ptum, ptum."

Steven hadn't left his apartment since his
meeting with the counselor. He lay on his bed
as his thumb scrolled social media. Now he read
AntiFash Kissed's post: *Befriend a distant state
and strike a neighboring one, then attack the
befriended state.*

Bronze Captain Clark, of Lewis and Clark,
stood with Bronze slave York and Bronze
Sacajawea (with Jean Baptiste, her bronze
baby). University maintenance staff crouched
by the bolts.

A plaque read, *"These statues stand as a visual reminder that three races contributed to the success of the Lewis and Clark expedition — symbolic of the first integrated society in Oregon country."*

Now unbolted, the workers loaded the bronze symbol of harmony in a truck. I blinked, lost in thought. Suddenly the truck was gone. Only the plinth remained, scorched and spray-painted: *1619, ACAB, F — 12.*

The streets were filthy with the personal. The vindictive curbs, the narcissus of revenge, the shabby marks overwhelmed the bystander with their lack of respect, their hostility and glee for destruction. Did you hear the joke about anger? It was all the *rage*. The anarchists broke my glasses. I could never *look* at them the same. By the courthouses, night after night, masked, hooded figures threw fireworks at police.

The skull of night parted its mouth and spat small fires. BURN! spittled the plywood around the federal courthouse. On the east side of the river, BURN! The minions spray painted KILL ALL COPS — HANG FASCISTS!

BURN! said the Multnomah County Building.

In the north, BURN! said the police union building.

BURN! said the middle of the street.

BURN! said the tall condominium where the mayor lived. BURN! BURN! BURN!

So far, one thing or another extinguished most of these fires before they spread. So far, it wasn't conflagration that rose in the street: it was BURN! the exclamation. It was the terror of the threat to BURN! It was the fiery absolutism of Year Zero justice. It was the strangeness of the civic duty to destroy the city we shared. It was impunity, that authority in its absence gave them permission. It was nightly bonfires of stolen furniture and pallets. The advocates of destruction propped trash fires against buildings. The smoke was full of protest. Meanwhile, another faction burned a decapitated pig's head with a police hat on it. This, and this, all this punitive Saturnalia persisted night after night. Justice was coming! But I had nowhere else to go.

What did it mean? Not much, not much, not much at all. The president was a baboon. There was an election coming. Any discordance could not be more than vandalism. Night after night, the anarchists circulated their target sites around the city: police precinct, police union, federal ICE facility, another police precinct, city building, county building, federal building.

Was it ebbing? The mayor ordered city police not to defend the federal courthouse. In response, the governor ordered the state police also not to defend the baboon's courthouse. The county police said, don't look at us; the district attorney won't prosecute. Many insisted on disbelief, a partisan willingness to sacrifice the city of Portland to the greater cause of the nation. BURN, Portland, for there is an election coming!

What was the truth of what was happening to the nation? Did the nation suffocate or suffer a heart attack? Autopsies of the republic proved oppositional causes. Who would have known that proof came from shared myth? Proof came from Latin *probare* 'to test.' The competing proofs tested our tolerance for diversity of facts, of truths that would not assimilate to ideology. Why is a dictionary dangerous? Because it has *dynamite*.

AntiFash Kissed posted: *Point at the mulberry tree while cursing the locust tree…*

88.

I made the mistake of reading a paragraph of local news. Mayor Smoke 'Em, the homeless man and southeast street personality, died badly. His tent by the highway embankment burst in flames. He had been reading by candlelight. I walked away, my face a mask.

Across Hawthorne Bridge, the People's Bridge, I fled, up the slope of southeast streets in numbers rising toward Mount Tabor. I passed a statue the iconoclasts had not yet discovered. Concrete Saint Francis held a frog. A sparrow perched on his shoulder. Gentle music drew me... a radiance of calm, a shimmer of golden candlelight...

It was hard to find the sense of it. What did it mean? Something transcendent something. Even a frog something something. Why didn't I know?

None of this aesthetic, this attempt at kindle and remark of a real aspect of the human had any leadership role in the writhe and self-loath of our civilization. A free society requires peace. Defund means dismantle means abolish.

No peace, no justice. I wanted to hold a frog. I wanted a shoulder bird. But the street of words afire insisted: since injustice existed, peace was violence.

AntiFash Kissed's posted: *Remove the firewood from under the pot...*

Before the fiery elk statue, I became self-conscious. I watched myself experience that softness. My sincerity curdled. The nightly detonations and daily lies tried to teach me to be hard. Reason buoyed by nothing more than therapeutic emotion had gone astray. "Ptum, ptum, ptum!"

The sun set. The front ranks of protestors shifted back. The anarchists came forward. Printed on their masks were smiles, teeth, and slogans. With elk head silhouettes stenciled on their shields, they marched through the neighborhoods. Rhythmically they chanted, *Wake up! (boom-boom), Wake up (boom-boom), Wake up m — f — , wake up! (boom-boom).*

Masked, hooded figures shined lights in

resident windows. Masked, hooded figures
carried open umbrellas and bear mace. Masked,
hooded figures gripped cans of rage. Masked,
hooded figures held bags of humiliation.
Masked, hooded figures shared synthetic drugs.
Masked, hooded figures threw green spears of
laser at opposing eyeballs. Masked, hooded
figures hid pistols inside their black clothes and
armor. Masked, hooded figures carried a six-
pack of beer bottles, in fact Corona-brand beer.
Refilled with gasoline and oil, and stoppered
with a rag wick, did it mean something?

AntiFash Kissed's posted: *Disturb the water
and catch a fish.*

Aside this, masked and guilty, Noah hurried.

The streets bent and confused him. The angles led him astray. The young destroyers in black stood in wait. He hesitated, lost. They looked at him, suspicious. The protestors had disappeared. These people were something else. Some, with clothes misfastened and disheveled expressions, appeared homeless. This militia blocked cars. Transit had stopped.

Noah had to rush around the edge, but he quailed behind the chanting mob. He eased back. The sounds faded, but the detonations did not. It frightened him. Not going home frightened him more.

It was hard to understand. Sounds broken from words ran into each other:

Cist... Cist... Ist... Ssst...
Stemic... Tutional... Ructural...
Cuse – Oxic – Pology –
Anceled.

Every idea fluttered in its ruins. Everything
contradicted. All words carried obvious bias.
No one could say anything. No one could say,
"I feel such gratitude." Everything frayed or fell
apart. Yet, he remained, so far.

AntiFash Kissed's posted: *Loot a burning*
house...

89.

Drawn to the burning bronze elk, Noah Beardsmore wandered into a carny world. He smelled the barbecue ribs and found himself in line. The anarchists offered it free of charge. Donations to Rib Riot had arrived from around the country and across the world. Sadly, this was before one of the anarchists embezzled over a hundred thousand dollars from the worldwide funding. Keep those donations coming!

I was there too, as the Masked One had bid me. I heard a bronze voice. "What do Jewish anarchists throw? *Mazel-tov cocktails.*"

The bronze elk stared at me. It showed its funny teeth. "What do you call stacks of free bricks left for rioters? *Free Masonry.*"

"Oh yeah?" I started. I saw how this was going so I played along. "What sort of mint do anarchists hate? *Governmint.*"

"Is that right. Well, why do anarchists smell so bad? Because they're *revolting.*"

At that moment an anarchist threw a broken piece of pallet into the concrete fountain bonfire. Sparks and smoke burst. The heat singed my arm hairs. I moved away.

When the flames shrank, I returned to the

seared bronze animal: "Why did the police arrest the crow? They had probable *caws.*"

The elk replied, "What do you call a well-known elk? *Famoose!*"

The moment smelled of barbecue sauce, frolic, marijuana, campfires, and unwashed bodies. The only culture the revolutionists offered was bacteria.

The elk had more, "It's wrong for anybody to be racist. It doesn't matter whether they're Black, Asian, or normal."

With a celebratory light in her eyes, a masked woman in black handed Noah a bowl of ribs. The bowl was heavy white paper fiber. A society without bowls would be pure *dishtopia.*

The invention of paper plates came about due to the sanitary needs of epidemic. In the early 1900s, entrepreneurs invented paper plates to slow the spread of tuberculosis. Paper plates followed germ theory. Disaster created a boom market: the 1906 San Francisco earthquake. Over a hundred years later, paper plates healthfully fed those who dedicated their pandemic nights to speed the spread of disaster. There was no objective truth, no science without bias, just residue.

It was my turn again. "I bought pepper spray to keep anarchists away. I hope they leave me alone when they see me crying."

90.

"Strange day, eh?" I asked the elk. "Too often we take bronze sculptures like you for *granite."*

"Strange indeed!" the elk replied. "First I found, right on the sidewalk, a paper coffee cup full of money... and then an angry weirdo jumped out of his sleeping bag and chased me."

"And what about the bonfire under you?"

"I didn't notice. I was sleeping *like a log."*

This fever, this weirdness reminded me that the bronze elk was born in a carnival.
Everything seemed so strange, so circus, and so real. "When the protestors go to bed," I offered, "the anarchists remain. The anarchists have

nihilistic politics. *It doesn't matter* though."

"You are giving nihilistic pessimism a bad name," the elk replied, "and *I don't care* for it."

"The etymology of the word 'politics'," I replied, "comes from two root words: *Poli* from the Greek *polis* for 'city', and *ticks* which are blood sucking parasites."

With so many businesses smashed, looted, and some that suffered arson, the mayor of Portland announced relief. Sixty-two million dollars in federal funds would go to individuals based on the color of their skin, not the content of their character, to Black people. Whether legal or not, this was the moment when progress openly signaled a change: the destruction of the old virtue, race blindness.

It turned out that this virtue the nation had emphatically lauded for decades was wrong. Surprise! It was evil all along. To claim race blindness now, progress revealed, to distribute funds equally, was the most vile form of white supremacy. Equality was oppression. The confusion we now felt, progressives encouraged, was a good thing. It meant we were doing the hard work. As the waves of vertigo cleared, what remained was a strange new banner: equity.

After eight-six consecutive nights of riot, President Baboon typed with his feet. On social media, he asked Oregon's governor, and

Portland's mayor, to let the National Guard stop the violence. The mayor replied, stay away.

Red paint covered the Bronze Pioneer Father, Mother, and Lad. Facing the courthouses, the large elk statue stood on its fountain plinth, the fountain around it filled not with water, but fire. Heat ripples rose. The elk nosed out of those huckleberry bushes of smoke to see, but it could not see.

Soup fed the fist! Soup meant community. "Come for the anarchy. Stay for the soup," read a banner. People around Noah, mostly anarchist youths, lounged cheerful.

One invited laughter with, "I love how pepper spray clears out your sinuses."

"I can protest racism and, like, smash the

state while I protest racism."

"I'm not so much anarchist as anarcho-curious."

"A diversity of tactics will get us there. There's direct action, mutual aid, and, like, horizontalism."

"We believe that racism is, like, built into capitalism. We want to destroy the system of oppression."

"It often gets boiled down to, like, 'Capitalism is the problem.' Which, like, yes. But I'm like, 'Also colonialism.'"

"The solution is, like, anarchism."

"Like, no bad protesters in a revolution."

"Tear it all down and, like, start over."

"Yup. We must, like, like the like like."

"Yup. And one simple way to get us, like, closer to that, is defunding the police. Defund, then dismantle, then abolish."

"The purpose of direct action at this stage is to capture police abuses on film which we then publicize. Then the silly liberals support us, and, like, change happens."

"Yep and cops are more likely to do something stupid if you insult them. It's, like, tactical and they fall for it."

"The longer we stay out here the better off we are."

"I'm not f– ing sad if a fascist dies."

"Like, you know, like like fascism like."

"Use traffic cones to snuff out tear-gas canisters."

"This soup proves that we're, like, serious."
"Like like like like like to like the like like."
"Like, like, yes. But also like."

Everyone sweated in the heat. They shared the ancient rite of hospitality together. Host and guest shared a meal. This tasty nourishment was proof, in a happy humorous way, of the world they wanted for everyone.

91.

Shields cut from fifty-five-gallon plastic
drums leaned against the square's trees. Flies
rioted over trash wrappings, broken bits, soiled
and shattered piles. Garbage lay here and there
in the parks by the courthouses — debris, too,
was anarchist agitprop. Campfires burned stolen
pallets and restaurant furniture and trash.
Civilians, as you know, never should be
accountable if they proclaimed belief in justice.

What did law mean, other than a power
struggle? The blue and red lights of police
flashed a block distant. People watched from
other curbs, then hurried away. Or they loitered,
heads bowed, staring into their smartphones,

wreathed in pot smoke. Sometimes the sensation of gritty figures wafted onto rooftop video cameras.

Everything seemed so strange, so circus, and so real. Noah wondered: Where was he? This was not Portland, not the Rose City, not Stumptown. This was No-town. This was Ruin. It was too unplaced, this former place. There was a scent of murder in the merrymaking.

Noah couldn't believe it. This was his life? Was it true that he stood in a square eating free anarchist barbecue among dangerous strangers and arsonists? Was it true that he and his wife had estranged each other? Was it true that he had just come from Lourdes' bed? Who was accountable? What was his duty now? Would he find Sammy out here?

He looked for something to anchor himself. He looked for the bronze elk. Instead, he saw smoke and fire. Instead, he saw an Archon, a cousin of the twins, a lieutenant of the Masked One. His motorcycle jacket creaked.

AntiFash Kissed's posted: *Wait at leisure while the enemy labors.*

The apartment windows with uncertain curtains revealed couches with cushions that hissed. Beyond an off-center lampshade, a lonely citizen stared at her family, pitiful focus squares on a screen.

A dark spot was a sign. Almost

undetectable, a burn stained the air. Flowerpots grew whispers of divine wrath. The hint of ash in the air contained the odor of their sickly emptiness. Strange foregrounded the cruel.

Who heard that lonely groan? No one.

There was no mutual understanding when, over masks, Noah's eyes met another's — only competition for space and air. Every other person was a potential threat, a betrayer and a temptation of sickness. Or the other offered outrage for not wearing a mask, for wearing it improperly — over mouth and chin, nose exposed — to infect violent moments of progress...

Noah watched as that big man in black, Sammy's sometime lover, swaggered. The man's brute swing bore the burden of his muscles. His long hair poured out of his motorcycle helmet. He had a face like a shovel. But, oh ladies, was there ever a more handsome, kissable shovel?

Time curled around Noah. Accusations and conspiracies blanched on telephone polls. The sidewalk spirit sauntered in anarcho precocity — he looked about with masked judgment — *I'm going to non-hierarchical voluntary associate a brick to your face* — so friend, are you with us? or against us?

The Archonic spirit walked by, face now in a black kerchief printed with a toothsome smile. The scarlet trumpets turned and lifted in tribute. Flies, persuaded by spiders, shook the webs that caught them and pled for dinner. Summer expended all its fiery ardor and eloquence. The heat accepted no apology. Affirmations deformed in smoke. The fire inside hollowed out the earth. Words became illicit.

Noah's face gathered unknown sources of justice. What happened next? He tried to remember, much later, as he sat in his jail cell.

92.

Bruised and battered, broken fingers
bandaged, Noah Beardsmore sat in a cage. A
taste of blood meant a loose tooth. He wore the
medical mask the police gave him. He sat,
holding his fractured ribs, trying to remember.
His face was scoured with small cuts, red-
scuffed under the mask. His eyes, searching
inward, were bloodshot. He hurt, hurt in waves,
hurt as he breathed.

The jail cell echoed with incomprehensible
voices and bad smells — the war of humanity
and disinfectant. He could still feel the sting of
the mace. He could feel the hits and kicks.
There was blood on his mask, his own blood.

He remembered a strobe light in his face. He tried to think backward.

He remembered his anger at himself, as he stood with his bowl among the anarchists. He had given up something and received nothing in return. Not only had he let meaning expire, he had pushed it into annihilation. He couldn't blame Lourdes. He couldn't blame Basil. And what about Sammy?

BREAKING WINDOWS: Anyone who truly desires to see an end to property destruction should hasten to bring about the end of property. — Anarchist pamphlet

It was then he perceived the longhaired man, the one who made Sammy cry. Even Archons eat ribs. Without warning Noah walked up, drew his arm back, and hit him in the jaw. The bowl of ribs flew, spraying them both with the sauce.

As time formed a circle around them, the Archon fought back. Noah blocked his swing and his kick. Each block hurt Noah, but he did not back away. His hatred grew. Then shouts broke the circle of time. Anarchist comrades sprang over, ready, all around Noah. He held them off alone — for a few seconds.

Then darkness fell. He was on the ground, hurting, with disbelief. Was this happening? Was this his life? Was this a moment he was living? Was this real? Anarchist strobe light filled his sight. Another held out a can and sprayed his face with something, over and over. It hurt to breathe. He lay on the ground, trying to protect his face, but still the anarchist sprayed him. Others took turns with kicks. He could barely see, so he could only half-block them. Suddenly they ran.

Just when he stood up, the police officer knocked him over. He lay on his belly, eyes and face stinging, as the man wrenched his arms behind.

Before him rose the empty plinth, placeholder of reason.

93.

Distended painfully, justice confused, the street itself stretched and released over and over again. We mere sidewalk aggressors reacted and adjusted.

The Multnomah County police again asked why they should waste resources to help the Portland city police, if the district attorney released most everyone they handcuffed? His program of restorative justice required it. The prosecution of protestors for justice, he explained, who may or may not have committed a small crime, required police to provide a wizard's tooth recovered from the belly from a Chinook salmon.

The night ferment went on and on, day after day. Quietly, the city removed Bronze Pioneer

Father, Mother, Lad, and Wagon Wheel, and stored them in a bronze refugee camp. Its plinth foundation remained, painted red with STOLEN LAND and 1492.

What statues still stood? The bronze elk, scorched and smoky, still bugled. "Racism is stupid. Why hate anyone based on skin color? If you just took the time to know the person as an individual, you'll find a whole lot of other reasons to hate." I heard this, turned mid-step, and rushed to Lourdes…

With most windows closed against drums, shouts, and other discordants, but still allowing in a little air, Euler Lourdes at night lay on his sofa. He missed his mother. He listened to a

471

radio broadcast of the same Fanny Hensel Mendelsson concert that the DeKay women had attended live, the *Cholera Musik.* The radio voice was smug.

Sprawled with his legs over the arm of the furniture, he was not yet at the point of declaring insomnia.

How strange this *Cholera Musik* was, he marveled, its apology for suffering. It explained the misery of life with gratitude to the Creator. Lourdes listened to the speaker describe the prodigy Hensel. At the age of thirteen, she could, from memory, play all twenty-four of Bach's Preludes from *The Well-Tempered Clavier.*

But what was a clavier? The clavier, also known as the clavichord, is an early keyboard instrument for which perfect tuning is mathematically not possible.

With every note double strung, two strings played in unison. The temperament of a clavier referred to the problem of how to divide an octave into semitones. Musicians developed different systems of dividing the octave. Each system implied a temperament.

If a musician like Hensel chose to make certain combinations perfect, she would have to make others imperfect or worse. Sages thought this was an acceptable compromise. Life was full of trade-offs. One temperament toward life would not accept the company of a rival temperament. Musicians could tune the instrument to associate an intended song with a certain mood or character suggested by the degree of the purity.

Bach's *Well Tempered Clavier* meant the musician tuned the instrument for a twelve-note compromise. It accepted imperfection as a friend of the good. It was imperfect, but it maximized consonance distributed across octaves, and did not make them rivals.

It was more common in Bach's day to tune it for the advantages of a narrow temperament with favored keys, other keys dissonant.

Lourdes felt a dissonance.

94.

The worldwide cholera pandemic of 1828-1837 crept closer and closer to Hensel. The Prussian authorities stopped commerce coming up the Odor River. Still the disease came closer, from Calcutta to Poland and Russia.

Hensel wrote in her diary, "The cholera rules across the entire eastern part of Europe. All the way to Danzig, the cholera rules." From distant ports, ships traded bacteria.

What was the discourse of cholera? The word apocalypse came from the Greek *apokalyptein*. It meant to uncover, disclose, or reveal. The pandemic always reveals. It draws back the curtains on the ideological embarrassments: the filth, the poverty.

Rumors grew as the Königsberg cholera hospital overcrowded. Deep in the Elisabethenburg Palace, the king hid. Rumor knew why. As crowded slums grew sicker, rumor heard that the secret police poisoned their wells. It was a conspiracy to cull the throngs of poor, rumor claimed. Smash! A window broke.

In Berlin, could Hensel protect her child? She guided her family through the alien landscape of sickened time. What caused sickness? Bad water? Bad air? Divine wrath? Unable to see the bacterium, it was rational to conclude that unseeable forces spread its darkness.

Against stay-home orders, against business

shutdowns, against checkpoints, against roadblocks, against the inability to work, against all this, the common people grew seditious.

The poverty of night fever-dreamed a skin drum beat by a bone. Riots erupted in Königsberg. The mob broke into a police station. The police ran. The mob took the station and ransacked it. It was a strange form of class struggle.

The mob chanted, *"We want cholera! Give us cholera!"*

The essence of culture is the conscious awareness of existence. *"We want cholera! Give us cholera!"*

Bacteria roared, and the people roared back. *"We want cholera! Give us cholera!"*

Police fired their muskets, killing eight anarchists. Berlin loosened its regulations and its people did not riot. Months passed, and the cholera subsided. Hensel and family survived.

Conventions of gender and family held tight. Hensel's brothers discouraged her compositions. Each day, however, her artist husband Wilhelm quietly gave her the paper to work on. And so she persevered. She composed.

95.

Hensel wrote the *Musik für die Toten der Cholera Epidemie* for the dead of Berlin's 1831 cholera pandemic. It directly addressed the problem of suffering under a benevolent Creator through the Book of Job.

The chorus sang: *A woman in labor has sorrow. Her hour of pain has come. But as soon as she delivers, her anguish becomes joy. She has birthed a child into the world. As powerful as death is love. Jealousy is as cruel as the grave. The coals of love are coals of fire! How vehement that flame.*

O, that I had a thousand tongues and a mouth thousandfold! With all the creatures I

*would attest my praise of the Creator. Green
leaves in the woods, wave and arise with me!
Tender flowers in the fields, glorify God with
your finery! It is for Him that you must live, so
join in my song of joy.*

The music rose and fell and rose again. A
beautiful stranger came and praised the stars
over the ruins of the Ancient. The stars
appeared as in dream through the rustling night
trees.

Then dawn came to the forest. Facing the
sunshine, the stranger wondered, is this a
dream? The buds in the trees raised up in praise.
And the stranger's heart knew joy.

Cholera arrived. God commanded it to bring

the dead to judgment. Woe to my disobedient children who revolted against me. Woe to sinners. The sinners cry, Help us, God. Help us, comfort us from your wrath. But there was no one to help them. God did not answer.

There was more.

Lourdes was not the only one who listened to the broadcast of the *Musik für die Toten der Cholera Epidemie.*

Dr. Abe Bomberger also listened. Defeated, exhausted from tears for Ginny, he listened. He understood the words in German:

The people are dying. Even the mighty thus die. My heart trembles. Behold my faith, my sadness and heartache. You created life. You

*destroyed it. Your hand is outstretched. I feel
nothing in my misery. I despair and cower. You
turn my friends away. Have mercy on me God.
Why so long must we suffer? He will cover you
with his long feathers. Under his wings you
shall have refuge. He will shield you. Wake, and
strengthen the dying.*

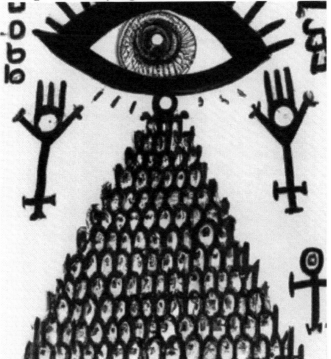

The mourners spoke: You have died. The
grass withered. The flower faded. You are gone
and God hid you. The blessed live on, with
God's compassion and mercy. And there will be
no more tears, nor sorrow, nor pain. For the
earth has moved on. Death has passed, and God
will wipe our tears.

The Faithful Dead speak: I kept the death. I will love God now as he speaks peace. I have faith! I reprove myself. I render myself to discipline! I repent!

Their soul is with God. You have their memory.

Lord save me from my sin. Turn away your sword. Let me see your bright face. We suffer for our sins. We sinned like our fathers. We mistreated each other. We were godless. But we have one God, our Lord who saves us from death.

96.

Alone in his suburban hotel room, Dr. Bomberger listened.

Humble yourself under the mighty hand of God. Sing your praises! Clap your hands with a drum! Exult with trumpets, with timbrel and dancing, with strings! Pipe with great trumpets, with cymbals and lyre and harp. Let all who have breath praise the Lord!

Not in the mood for praise, the doctor ruminated from this: only the Evil One wants to persuade us that there could be a life without suffering. In Yiddish, he told himself, *If God lived on earth, people would break His*

windows. The cantata concluded with amens. Motives turned in twelve-note compromise with beseeches. There was more praise and wails. It moved from pianissimo to fortissimo again. It concluded. Amen, Amen.

Elsewhere, as he heard the *amens,* Lourdes considered. Maybe Fanny Hensel Mendelsson herself adapted an approach to her life as a human *Well-Tempered Clavier.*

Alas, too soon after publication of her work began, at age forty-two, she died of stroke.

Lourdes thought, "How strange! The music seems vaguely familiar and alien at the same time."

The culture behind it was gone but not

entirely so. It was like a faded wallpaper in a
room or maybe a patina in that old wallpaper.

He puffed on his e-cigarette loaded with key
juices of cannabis. The battery lit up
satisfactorily to simulate an ember as he pulled
air from the tip through the loaded tube.

Lourdes let himself admit he was a little
bored. He had let his mind drift. He caught
himself. Returning to the music, he thought,
"Too bad she died so young. Was she satisfied
with her life? Did she believe in progress?"

Then he thought, "Maybe her faith made
those questions irrelevant. What would it be like
to be a person with faith?" It was a strange,
almost science-fiction question to him.

"What resilience she had," Lourdes admired. What could he learn from her example? He knew grace was a forbidden virtue, antiquated, possibly harmful. Himself, he lacked grace. He was all calculation.

He did not expect the distress that struck him. The skull of night opened its jaws and howled! Harsh, hateful, it scorched inside his nose. It seared, it tasted like choke, like gasps. His eyes began to thrust and hurt. His throat screamed in pain. Tear gas! He slammed his windows shut, ran into the bathroom, and pressed a washcloth against his mouth.

The charred, sick scent was the scent of missing order. Something did not square. There was no hero on the plinth. It was empty.

97.

Outside, under the crowless trees, I waited. Above me, in her condominium, Basil DeKay mourned in her lonely home. Noah had disappeared. The table held no note. The mantle was noteless. No text arrived, no email, no voice mail.

In truth, in jail, he was too proud to call her, to ask for bail. Miserable, he stared at the cinderblock wall, not to see his criminal companions.

AntiFash Kissed's posted, *Authority weak, forgotten in peace, such teeming degeneracy.* – *Sun Tzu*

Common people who considered themselves nice wavered between rage, amazement, boredom, and fear. Near the southeast precinct

of police, anarchist paramilitary blocked a
Portland road at night. Others dragged furniture
into the street and set it afire.

The thistle of dark grew a wild face. A
chemic tongue pushed out a march of reluctant
lurch: violent offenders, drug addicts, the
mentally ill, homeless and helpless, plus
released felons. Agitators with malicious intent
ran under-cover in a peaceful protest.

"If the nightly mayhem, the fires and
destruction and menace, is a free speech protest,
not a riot, why is there so much damage and
chaos?"

"It's racist bikers and Proud Boy fascists
attacking the anti-racists!"

Spray painted on walls, and on social media,
the anarchists promised to murder journalists

who opposed them. Among the spray-painters, in front of the police, one young woman kicked karate in the air. She almost fell over backward. With no mask, she held a wedge of orange peel in front of her mouth. Another protestor ran back and then up again, a long costume tail flopping… at least I think it was a costume… Police had duties, did civilians have none? The police announced that their ranks were tiring and overburdened. The governor promised an important announcement on International Pronouns Day.

AntiFash Kissed posted, *If he is taking his ease, give him no rest. – Sun Tzu*

98.

At that moment, Basil DeKay composed and recomposed an email response to the associate dean, Mariah. She knew that her friend's friend was the hammer of her superior's hand. Her own friend, the vice provost, remained silent.

DeKay's response email needed not to be a rebuke, nor retaliation, nor even an argument against, but an appeal to allow the hand to hear her counter-arguments. Paused in this labor, she sought support from her sisterhood. She closed her laptop, rubbed her face, and clicked her phone.

AntiFash Kissed posted, *If his forces are united, separate them. – Sun Tzu*

Larsen greeted DeKay in a tone of doubt. "Do you want to hear something about the Bombergers now or another time?"

"I don't know."

"It can wait," Larsen reassured.

DeKay didn't like the idea of that. "Tell me now."

"You're sure?"

"I want to know."

Larsen explained, "Ginny is filing for divorce."

"Really. Why? Because of us?"

"She publicly declared it."

DeKay thought, *that's cold. Well, who would want to be married to that guy? Anyway, why should anyone else care?*

"Why did Ginny publicly declare such a

private thing?" she asked.

"I think she made it public to try to keep her job. You didn't hear it from me."

"She'd divorce her husband over this, now? He's been obnoxious for years and years."

"I don't understand either of them... I should go now."

"Yes," DeKay agreed. "I have to go now too." Could the Ex-ter-mi-knitters meet after this? She didn't see how. Was her girl gang broken?

DeKay looked on protest social media for a picture of Sammy. She found only riot pictures of sounds and motion, with strange shapes: Black hooded figures, some with gas masks, they hopped, they swayed, they rotated as if drugged. In the middle of a street, a bonfire signaled sovereignty and allowance. A drag queen danced and lip-synced in front of a line of police. A man took off his shirt and ran parallel to the police line. While he ran, he flung his arms about and screamed incoherent fury. Another man restrained him. Bolts of bright green needles shot from the anarchist mass into something out of view. On a blurry video DeKay heard screaming, curses, and cries of "Fascist!"

How many police had transferred, quit, or retired?

After ninety-three consecutive days of riot,

the mayor formally replied to the Baboon's offer to send in the National Guard. No, we won't help your re-election, the letter said. We will arrest the rioters, and support the noble cause of the protestors.

Meanwhile, the district attorney announced that he would no longer prosecute anyone for interfering with police officers, disorderly conduct, criminal trespass, and so on.

AntiFash Kissed posted, *"If sovereign and subject are in accord, put division between them." – Sun Tzu*

99.

Unknown to the two knitters, as they spoke,
a utility truck with a crane stopped by the
rubble of the heat-shattered fountain. The side
of the truck read, *The City That Works.* The two
workers climbed down from the truck and
methodically readied their tools. Their precision
required almost no communication. They
manipulated a heavy gantry mounted on the
back of the truck.

With a sad face, sad in the interest of justice,
the district attorney announced that his office
had rejected three quarters of public order

arrests. He was fulfilling campaign promises, he
said.

The shadow of the truck's crane fell over the
scorched asphalt, over the broken fountain filled
with trash. The diagonal line of shadow moved
over the drip-lettered curses that filled the
plinth. The workers tied webbing around the
bronze quadruped. Under the crane, after 120
years of anchor, the statue separated.

Dangling from the air, the bronze elk called
me:

"A man walks into a riot composed of
several mobs. He asks the nearest protestor,

'You don't have any idea how to make our system more just, do you?' The protestor says, 'No, in this group we don't have any idea how to make things more equal. That group over there is the one that doesn't have any idea how to make our system more just.'"

"Where are you going?" I replied as, above me, it swung slightly. "Just hanging around?"

"I went to the zoo this morning," it replied. "They had a yak in the wildebeest exhibit. Did they really think I would fall for *fake gnus?"*

"But Elky, you were bolted down," I demanded, upset, "how could you possibly go to the zoo?"

"That's easy," the elk assured me as it dangled in the air. "You can go anywhere you

497

want if you look serious and carry a clipboard."

I could bear the pain but not the insult. The bronze elk hung in the air, a gift from an ancestor. To be humane to animals, what did that mean? The nobility of nature, what did that mean?

Heavy in its straps, the bronze elk no longer swayed. Still, it asked, "Did you hear about the guy caught stealing a statue? The robbery was a *bust.*"

It hung in the sky, then descended. It called, "They wanted to move a statue of a god. But it remained *idol.*"

The men strapped it to the truck. Faintly, with one last thing to say, the elk called to me. "Did you hear the joke about the rhetorical question?"

Without any further fuss, the truck drove away. The wreckage that remained was an anti-monument for the Oregon Inhumane Society. A ruin preceded a larger sense of the empty, a lack of place in the place.

100.

"Ptum, ptum, ptum!" What remained? The heat of fire had shattered the fountain. The anarchists had used small chunks of granite as ammunition, rocks to throw at police. The origin of the word *police* is the Greek word for "city", *polis*. The fountain ruins lay charred and spray-painted. "FTP" for *F— The Police* also meant *F— The City.*

What remained? Night remained. Bang! Pop-pop-pop. In the name of progress, the city had finally dismantled its Gun Violence Task Force. It had disproportionately impacted Black offenders. No more! It was hard work to do the right thing. (Bang! Bang! Call an ambulance!)

The murder rate rose twelvefold. Meanwhile, anarchists threatened restaurants not to serve officers.

AntiFash Kissed posted, *Attack him where he is unprepared, appear where you are not expected." – Sun Tzu*

The mayor explained. Was free speech good? Yes. Was racism bad? Yes. Was the president bad? Yes. That's why the mayor, as police commissioner, ordered his officers *not* to defend the federal courthouse from the anarchists. So what if radicals threw Molotov cocktails against the plywood armor over the lower part of the building? So what if they shot fireworks into its windows above? There was an election coming. BURN, Portland!

AntiFash Kissed posted, *If your opponent is temperamental, seek to irritate him. – Sun Tzu*

Rebels pried off a piece of the building's plywood encasement and attacked the door with a hammer. There was an election coming. And if a federal police officer had duties, if he tried to stop this, the citizen hit him in the head with his hammer of accountability. The important thing was that racism was bad and so was the president. There was an election coming. So BURN, Portland!

The Great Baboon sent federal police to protect the courthouse. This, many screamed in newspapers, on social media, was fascism.

Oh my god, the Baboon's fascist police invaded Portland, the big newspapers declared. The Baboon's jackboot goons kidnapped protestors! The Baboon's dragoons brutalized peaceful protestors who hated racism! The Baboon's black-shirt army had laid siege to a liberal city! It made so much sense. BURN, Portland!

BREAKING WINDOWS: Demonstrates that the ruling forces are not invincible. New comrades see this and join us. — Anarchist pamphlet

101.

That's right, the mayor declared, the street
troubles were President Baboon's fault. The
governor also chimed in — she declared that
yes, the street troubles were all President
Baboon's fault. That's why neither city nor state
police would they allow to defend the
occasionally burning courthouse.

Fresh scratches of discourse led me. I
stopped to read a sign on a Hawthorne
Boulevard telephone pole:

4-Step Plan for Revolution in USA, 2020

1. Vote Green Party in the November election to disrupt corporate rule.
2. Keep the country shut down with strikes, boycotts, and peaceful demonstrations.
3. Establish consensus for the new system.
4. Persuade the National Guard to assist the overthrow of the state.

Night after night, we heard the detonations, the drums and bullhorns, the fireworks and Molotov cocktails on one side, the helicopters, the police public address declarations, the less-than-lethal ordinance on the other. Which social media evidence did you want to view? The clip of the big policeman tackling a sweet young woman? Or the Molotov cocktail smashing against the plywood barrier around the federal courthouse? The protester bleeding from his face, hit by a plastic bullet? Or the camera-shaking street explosion of the gunpowder-augmented firework?

One, two, three gasoline bombs smutted ineffectually against the plywood barrier. One, two, three fireworks shot through upper windows to set the curtains afire. One, two, three anarchists disappeared under federal arrest. One, two, three federal officers lay in a hospital bed, eyes bandaged.

The mayor and some council members praised the people on the street: free speech was free speech. Was racism bad? Yes. Was the president bad? Yes. What about fascism, was that good or bad? *Yes or no, quickly!* That was bad.

AntiFash Kissed posted, *Pretend to be weak, that he may grow arrogant. – Sun Tzu*

Federal police reinforcements arrived in masks and armor with helicopters thwopping. Again the mayor blamed the president for the anarchy. *Stop the fascist siege of Portland!* More citizens arrived to show their hatred of the president. Indeed, the president was a baboon.

Look at that row of women, the *Wall of Moms,* who faced the Great Baboon's fascist police.[4] Look at the *Leaf blowing Dads,* whose backpack machines blew away the fascist tear gas. Racism was bad, and so was the president. The local district attorney would not charge most of the arrested, but the federals had a different attitude. *Fascist!*

102.

The mayor, with his long face masked, reaffirmed his order for the city police not to defend the building. There was only one way to defeat the anarchists, and that was to leave the courthouse undefended. It was not so much a bastion of justice but an outpost of the Great Baboon. In the streets around the courthouse, the federals installed a chain link riot fence. This, too, was an outrage. Was free speech good? Yes. Was racism bad? Yes. Was the president bad? Yes. Was fascism good or bad? It was bad.

Come on. The mayor ordered the city police

*not to defend the federal courthouse. The
anarchists are trying to burn it down. State and
city authorities won't protect federal rule. It's
uncomfortably like the secessionists' siege of
Fort Sumter in 1861. Someone has to defend the
federal courthouse against arson. So the federal
police are doing it. How is this fascist?*

They're arresting protestors. Is political
protest free speech?

Yes, but Molotov cocktails…

No, is free speech good?

*Yes, and the principle protects speech I
don't agree with. The protestors are telling a lot
of lies mixed with truths.*

What lies? Is racism bad?

*Yes, and difficult in ways we don't discuss,
for we forever contain the Other within our
psyches.*

Never mind that, just tell me, is the president
bad?

*Yes, but somehow we don't have any new
foreign wars for the first time in generations.*

Is fascism good or bad?

Of course fascism is bad, but does…

But what? In what ways are you supporting
fascism?

Nothing. I didn't say anything.

That's what I thought. I didn't think you
would. Now… racism, the president, fascism,
police, these are all the same bad thing we need
to fight, right…? Hello? I know where you
work. Did you hesitate to raise your fist?

Black lives matter!

A young protestor stood with his eyes bright over his mask. His eyes radiated a sacred light. He held up held up words painted on brown cardboard: *White Silence is Violence.*

A mob pressed against the new riot fence. As the mayor raised his fist and declared that he, too, lifted his voice in protest against racism — a protest against racism was a protest against the president — an anarchist behind him threw a frozen water bottle and hit him in the head.

Tears and burning irritation wafted over the mayor. He stood with eyes above the mask hurt, raw, angry. And now he began to wonder, what was real? What was true?

He questioned his assumptions. Something wasn't right. Something didn't explain street reality. Could we review the facts? Let's review. Once again, was free speech good? Yes. Was racism bad? Yes. Was the president bad? Yes. Was fascism good or bad? It was bad. There was an election coming.

What could he do about it? Help was on the way. The governor promised an announcement on International Pronouns Day.

103.

In his apartment, Steven read AntiFash Kissed's newest post, *If your enemy has superior strength, evade him. – Sun Tzu*

Legs in the air, Simon lay on his back reading Ivan Bunin's *Cursed Days*. On the bed beside him, legs also in the air, Tejashree read, *Narrative of the Life of Frederick Douglass*. They had no air conditioning. Three fans poured on their legs. The drone of the whirling blades covered up most of the sounds of the whirling street mayhem.

If time would hardly advance, still, pages must. Onward, pages! Tejashree and Simon still read with their legs in the air. Due to the position of the lamp, her leg cast enormous shadows on the ceiling slope.

Simon pointed them out to her. Their shadows were huge, rounded Picasso-like lines. He pushed his leg into the light. It showed on the ceiling like a baby's leg and foot. He pointed this out as well.

Suddenly Tejashree let her legs fall to the bed, and lifted her middle finger, enormous on the ceiling. Because Simon believed in decorum at all times, he immediately chided, "Nooooo!"

This triggered her triumphant laughter. Her laughter continued; it wouldn't stop. It couldn't stop. She looked to him in laughing fear. Simon knew to steer into it. "I'm glad you're happy," he told her.

"I'm so unhappy!" she laughed. The impious finger shadow disappeared. The laughter faded.

Simon left the bed to patrol the perimeter before sleep. He checked the locks. Forehead pressed against the glass, he tried to see if that homeless man lay in the street nook again. He listened, head craned, for the distant anarchist detonations. Still, he tried to sense the faint helicopter pressure rhythm on his skin. Turned, he now heard the ravings of a poor soul. All this merged with the faint hiss of ash as it fell.

"If the nightly mayhem, the fires and destruction and menace, is a free speech protest, not a riot, why is there so much damage and chaos?"

"It's President Baboon's fascist jackboots attacking the anti-racists!"

Under the headline "Help Me Find Trump's 'Anarchists' in Portland?," *The New York Times* showed a photo of the "Wall of Moms."

Someone left the foyer of city hall unlocked. The graveyard frights squeezed out of the night skull and through the door. BURN! BUURRNN! In addition to fire, they left a painted message to the mayor: DON'T CRY TED.

104.

Disregarding stay-home orders, fires burned day and night throughout California. There was fire in the Oregon Cascades, fire to the south and east. Fire blasted down valleys in Washington State, in Idaho, Nevada, Colorado. The western forests crackled in flame; the fall of a giant threw up sparks. Walls of fire moved, leapt across roads and rivers, roared down valleys, heaved smoke and ash. Skies across states spoiled with grit. Air tasted yellow-brown. It carried a scent of evil, a scent of disease.

Protests continued. Be like water. Activists

and anarchists raged, cursed and accused! It was not nearly enough that the city disbanded the Gun Violence Task Force. Bang! Bang-Pop! Look, the city cut the police force by fifteen percent, no more was wise, the mayor argued. But a radical found him in a restaurant and punched him. Angry faces demanded that the city reduce the police force by half. Why wouldn't the mayor listen? Fascist!

Near the elkless fountain ruin, amidst courthouses federal, county and city, a police shield row opposed the protestor shield row. A young woman removed her clothes, except for her mask. In front of the line of protestors, she volunteered as their champion. There, she strutted naked. Downtown grew quiet, amazed.

She was showy, with deliberate steps and arm movements. She performed her nakedness as an ultimate tribal weapon. Her sex Goliath, there was no David. Her manner showed her proud awareness of her female power and female violation.

There she stood with hands on her hips. Masked, she displayed her pride and flaunted her vulnerability as strength. Stunned, a moment passed. But she wasn't done yet. She sat down and, facing the police line, spread her knees apart.

There she sat, assaulting the police with her most female privacy. Constabulary masks and helmets hid the expressions of discomfort on officer faces. The nude young woman's most female privacy emitted rays of sorcery. After a moment of terror, the lieutenant wisely ordered the shivering phalanx of law to retreat.

The smoke-sickly-yellow-colored night grew indifferent, grayer.

The mayor yelled at the Portland city police for the use of tear gas against his orders. The smoke of Cascade wildfires reached closer and closer to Portland's sky. Satellite photography showed the yellow-white stream curling out for thousands of miles, out over in the ocean, and then curling, curling back, now over our heads again. "Ptum, ptum, ptum."

Now I rushed away and then paused. The bronze elk was gone. An empty plinth was just a graffitied stub. The shattered fountain could hold no water. What remained to stand for the city's dignity? Who was accountable? Who was not drunk on alchemy? What landmark could I use to pivot my discourse? There was no locus, no waypoint. There was no Masked One and had never been one. There was nothing but an empty plinth, the placeholder of what we relinquished.

105.

With sick feeling, Steven lay on his bed and read Sammy's social media posts:

Deceive the heavens to cross the sea. Reform the police. Defund the police. Disband the police. Abolish the police. Attack the police.

Bezz Larsen looked through the anonymous reports. Someone reported someone for mocking BLM. Someone reported someone for refusing to address someone with their chosen pronouns. Someone reported someone for the way someone broke up with someone. Someone reported someone for inebriated intercourse. Someone reported someone for not reporting someone. Someone reported a fallen world, a world of grief, offense, and harm.

I waited for Bezz Larsen to reach fifty percent of her decision. She had reached twenty percent of a decision, then thirty, and stalled, but it began to rise again. She didn't need to deliberate beyond a reasonable doubt. She needed only a more than fifty percent deliberation.

Knock Knock. Who's there? *Title IX Officer.* Title IX Officer who? (Slap!) *Title IX Officer will ask the questions!*

Bezz Larsen deliberated up to forty percent. It surprised her that she didn't want to get involved. She resisted this, reached fifty percent plus one tenth, thus made her decision. She called Basil DeKay with the worrisome news about Sammy, and texted the link where in social media to find it.

Images of protestors and mayhem filled social media, from armored to shirtless, masked and unmasked. Some had helmets with animal crests. The video clips carried sounds of whistles, rattles, and drums… songs, dances, and totemic representations or symbols of subculture….

What was the aroma of rage? The mob roared for burnt offerings. Its frankincense and myrrh was broken glass. The church of rage had a prayer: in order to destroy imperfection, destroy all. Purity awaited the transcendence of crash. It wasn't enough to chant and throw fiery incense. The right to smash glass stood for the defenestration of any norm. The homeless tents, tarp-covered piles of junk, the garbage and fear, the blue plastic portable toilets, the plywood windows, the gesticulating insane, the strange screams in the night, the junky burglaries and organized crime car thefts, the gunshots that wake us, these showed the places where the anarchist revolution already ruled Portland. The impunity of property destruction represented the purity of no meaning.

Grainy black and white security footage gave testimony on social media: a grainy tall man walked into a northeast laundry. He carried a long hand saw. From behind, this wayward carpenter approached a grainy young woman. With her back to him, she sorted her grainy laundry into a grainy basket. The grainy tall man lifted the saw, and raked down the sharp tines of the grainy saw against her bare shoulder. She ran out, the video showed; he took her grainy handbag. He hurried deeper into the Laundromat. Something happened and another grainy woman ran. He took her grainy purse too. The grainy man left the laundry with a saw and two handbags.

A few blocks away, a commotion started. People ran to join it. Police had stopped a man with a saw and two handbags. A mob quickly formed. The mob screamed, "F— the police!" The police pushed the suspect against the squad car, and handcuffed him. The mob grew larger. They screamed, "Black lives matter! F— the police! F— the police! F— the police! All cops are bastards!"

Fatherlessness was still a great insult.

106.

Larsen was right. Into her smartphone's bright screen, Sammy's mother exclaimed, "Oh my god."

There on her smartphone's screen was Sammy, her name, her blank look, and the words Disorderly Conduct. She did not look injured. There were more mug shots next to her: strange, weak faces, bruised, tussled faces. The jails had prisoners with COVID, so they'd release her, right? The district attorney offered understanding. Anarchists stood undisturbed as monuments of the safety with which error of opinion may be tolerated.

Clues on social media suggested that the police had already released Sammy on her own recognizance.

"Should I not have told you?" Larsen asked on the phone.

"No," DeKay assured her, "I want to know."

She forced herself to be calm as she punched the quick dial button of her smartphone. *She's fighting for a better world*, she told herself silently. *That struggle will bring out her light.*

Sammy did not answer. DeKay looked again at the mug shot of her criminal daughter. What had she done? The police had tried to hold her accountable for something, but the district attorney let her go. What lay behind that blank but defiant expression? Had she abandoned herself into the ultra-violet of chaos?

Arson and looting was progress without the

labor and peace that made progress bearable. It was unbearable progress, the storm of rage that still drives us from the fruited glade of Eden.

Amon Parker called in sick from his security guard job. He sat on his sofa with his wife. She buried her face in his arm, crying, that she was too tired of police abuse. "Too tired, just too tired of it all," she moaned. He was tired too. But not how his wife meant.

Yes, Amon felt it. How could they do that to a fellow human being? A knee on a neck was their shame, their crime. But something else made him weary. He knew not to say anything bad about the victim. In truth, he admitted to himself, he resented him. Amon resented his illegal drugs and his burglaries, more drugs, more crimes, so lacking self-control to take drugs while COVID-sick, and then more drugs, and commit another crime, ending in his teary, squirming, struggling, drugged-out way.

Why should he, Amon Parker, a quiet man with order in his soul, have to suffer any kind of association with that weak, chaotic, failure of a man? That man didn't deserve to die! It looked like injustice. Police brutality was a real thing. The wounds of his community were a real thing. But when you play stupid games, you win stupid prizes. No wonder that, sooner or later, making his choices, that man died badly.

Amon prided himself in not being like that. But now, because of the horrible knee on the neck, the police forced them together. "No more, no more," his wife cried. He held her and said nothing.

DeKay called and texted Sammy again. There was no answer.

Mother called and texted Daughter again. She waited. She held her breath. She held it... She held it longer... If only that would help!

An anarchist climbed the ruin that was vacant of bronze elk, and stood, in black. From coat hangers he had fashioned anarchist antlers. He stood still as a statue. He posed for social media pictures: Victory! Conquered and held! No More History! Land Back! Forward and on, and on! Justice was coming! So I hurried away.

107.

Bezz Larsen knitted in her home office. She sat in their Pearl district row house. A text would not do. Larsen told an imaginary Basil, "You didn't hear it from me. The provost wants to elevate (knit one, purl two) a colleague of color to help address systemic racism in the institution."

This, in her imagination, failed to save Basil's feelings. She told herself that, (knit one, purl two), due to months of COVID-19 stay-home stress, she just did not have the strength.

Meanwhile, downtown, bandits had claimed a nearby McDonald's as hangout. They joined the protest. A dead man's mother stood up high before the courthouse riot fence. What was justice? She spoke of her rage, of her son killed by police, of the need to seize solutions with violence if necessary. The mother didn't mention that when the police shot him, two years ago, her son had a gun in his hand. She didn't mention that little oopsie, he had just shot two others. The crowd cheered the mother's call for reparations, the justification to loot, to seize compensation.

The bandits peered around and saw, sitting against a wall, a small person, trans, with a skateboard. What was justice? They claimed the skateboard, a prize of reparation. The victim's friend drove up in a pickup truck. The bandits saw it and dragged the driver out the truck.

He too was small and thin. The bandits
hassled him, pushed and yelled. They forced
him to sit in the street. Then, with a tone of
outrage, expecting their share of reparations,
they interrogated their prisoner. The little man
tried to stand up, but the bandits pushed him
down again. Their prisoner sat as the
interrogation continued... What was justice?

When that resolved nothing, a tall bandit
backed up behind the prisoner. What was
justice? The tall bandit extended his arms for
balance. Then he ran forward, like a player of
American football in attempt of a field goal, and
kicked his prisoner in the back of the head.

The driver lay unconscious in the street as the others rifled through his truck for reparations.

What did this mean? What was justice? What was true? What was a lie? Did protestors stand for reason, emotion or something else? Who did not pander to the mob? Did any leader resist? The federal Justice Department declared Portland lost.

Words curled in and around themselves in knots. Reduce meant defund meant abolish the police, replace them with social workers. Since we could not name what was happening, local authorities could not take control of the lawless streets.

Why did language fail? Why did truths pretzel-lock with lies? There was an election coming. Burn, Portland? How could the governor possibly deploy the National Guard downtown? That would insult the cause of justice. That would validate the claims of the baboon's Attorney General, that Portland had become an anarchist jurisdiction. It was a difficult time to be a leader. However, the governor did have a plan: No enemies to the left. Yes, BURN Portland! International Pronouns Day was coming!

Meanwhile, on the east side of the river, a little old lady with a walker and BLM sign stood guard in front of a police precinct. She faced down the arsonists. She didn't stand alone. Beside her stood another little old lady. This one even brought a fire extinguisher.

From a distance I saw a young anarchist woman confront her. The little old lady shook her head. The anarchist lifted her arms and poured paint over the liberal's hair and face.

This rubble of words, this cruelty, this thuggery, this anarcho-fascism, this wreckage of the Wall of Moms... this did not make any sense. Reduce meant defund meant abolish. Did it even happen? How could it have happened, if it didn't make sense?

After all, was free speech good? Yes. Was racism bad? Yes. Was the president bad? Yes. Was fascism good or bad? It was bad. There was an election coming. What about anarchists, were they good or bad? Hunh? What anarchists? Did you mean the Wall of Moms? There was an election coming. BURN, Portland!

The governor promised an announcement on International Pronouns Day.

533

108.

The physics student sulked in his tiny apartment. It overlooked closed businesses of Sandy Boulevard. Some posted BLM signs. Others fixed plywood over their windows. Windows became walls. Strange words dripped.

Steven had finally heard that Sammy moved into an apartment in northwest Portland. It was near a trolley line, not far from the closed Saturday Market. A radical student rented it, he and his sort-of girlfriend.

The radical student was older and a felon.
He wore long, black shorts and a motorcycle
jacket. His hair swung as he walked. If you
looked over to see his pick-axe nose, the
trowels of his eyes, the excavator of his jaw,
you might step aside for him before you
realized you might have to defend yourself. His
sort-of girlfriend had metallic pink hair and a
face like a baby bird. She was notorious for a
public episode of rage, screeching in the student
cafeteria.

In the Pearl District not far from downtown,
Bezz Larsen looked over an anonymous
complaint. She conjured a small force, then
unleashed it. The force trickled down a

flowchart. It sought the appropriate, ambient, proportionate path of administration... If not A or B, would path C apply? She knew one of the parties involved. Off campus, at the zoo, the informer accused, a male student had tried to place an unwanted kiss on female student. It required inquiries; did one want to file a formal complaint? In reply came bullhorn shouts and drums. She closed the windows.

What was happening on the street? It was difficult to comprehend and provocative to perceive: Two little old ladies of progress retreated. Their heads dripped with anarchist paint. They hobbled home from the mob that tried to set the southeast precinct police station on fire. One elder, still holding her spattered BLM sign, waited for the other. The other, paint on her hair and face, her fire extinguisher stolen, slowly pushed her walker forward and stopped. She stepped up to it, and pushed it forward again. Her expression, lost, seemed to cry out, Where am I? Who am I?

Finally, the smoke-poison of pandemic night grew lush. A car's headlight pattern made lips glow on the near wall. Why did these lips have to be sexy lips? Signs of a shuttered sandwich

shop decayed as eyebrows. The pull-down
shutters formed a mask. On this face, across the
mask, someone spray painted LIBERALS GET
THE BULLET TOO and then a hammer and
sickle. Justice was coming!

And so, eventually, reluctantly, summer
night arrived, smoke-stained and stinging the
lungs. Reduce meant defund meant abolish.
Bang! Pop-Pop-Pop. Bang-Pop! Pop-Bang!
Bang-Bang-Bang! Pop-Bang-Pop-Pop! In the
morning, police counted over one hundred-fifty
holes in the walls of an apartment building in
the Montavilla neighborhood, on the east side

of Mount Tabor. By seven shot-up cars, gunpowder tainted the air. A neighbor put a tourniquet over a woman's arm. What was going on?

Where was the Masked One now? Did he not, at least in my memory, task me with the record of discourse that surrounded Basil DeKay? Where did he hide now, when I needed authority and protection? Did I need to protect myself, then?

With no bronze elk to help fix my location, with no lifted gaze, and no pride of remembrance... with nothing but emptiness to venerate... only momentum could guide me.

As Basil DeKay entered the deepest part of her sleep toward noon, a form appeared. Unclear, it suggested a question. A fugitive irk emerged in her sleepy drift.

DeKay groaned, for she knew what it silently asked: "What is a shadow?"

It was hard to reason in dream, but she tried. A shape that blocks light makes a stencil of darkness. She tried to reason further... The idea that we can identify objects by their external observable features is essentialism, a form of harm. What about the hidden features? Why hide? Why hide our flaws and shame? Will light forgive? Answer me! Silence is violence!

The phantom seemed too tired to even equivocate. The whoosh and warp of dream swelled and receded. The image became flat and unreal — and she felt at risk of awakening.

She fought to keep herself submerged in sleep. "Harms," she told herself. "Traumas."

Partly lucid, she marinaded in the fact that Bomberger had signed the restorative justice plan. He had already posted an apology on social media. "Decentered," she told herself in dream again. "Unprivileged." She saw the donkey of her enemy collapsing under its burden. She had won! She needed words! Silence is a patriarch. What is this? What do you call the world? Out of nowhere the mind comes forth. Openly acknowledge, regularly remind! "Safety."

109.

Basil DeKay's alarm bleeped. Her heart thumped to the same rhythm. It was five o'clock in the afternoon. The experts on the radio recommended everyone now wear two masks, one over the other. The virus had mutated.

"Nothing's gonna be the same," a homeless man with, under the mask that city workers gave him, a tattoo of a glyph on the side of his face. He also had inked tears under his eyes, and many other tattoos that did not cover all the sores.

"Nothing's gonna be the same." He told this to his dog, who wore a soiled green kerchief around his neck. It might have been the dog who thought, *this trauma will change us. Sniff? Sniff, sniff-sniff. Pandemics tear down and question. Sniff-sniff, snort, sniff.*

The hills rose and fell. Up from the river it rose from automobile oil change franchise down to closed old strip mall and further to a closed café. It lifted as the west hills misted green, up and up to the sick yellow rumor of smoke. The course of the landscape marked the progress of humiliation. Inside homes, smoke detectors shrieked. Fissures in the sky mimicked the fissures in the sidewalk. Underfoot, what was solid was rickety and some preferred it that way. Buckles belied a behavior in Nature to crack the rational sidewalk. An error of some kind made the crack. Things wanted to tear up reason. Reason required maintenance. Reduce meant defund meant abolish.

The little homeless man with broad sunburnt face, thick nose, dark flat hair and scraggly mustache and beard, he felt this. How could he warn everyone? Only his dog understood, but his dog had issues. How do you know if a dog identifies as male or female? Stroke its head. If *he* wags *his* tail, it's male. If *she* wags *her* tail, it's female.

Now a lack of mask revealed the sweetness of the man's expression. Mask underfoot, he swayed. He jerked forward. He saw the diversity officer in her window. He leaned back as far as he could to see her better. With a bow, he called out, "Your Highness."

Basilica DeKay recoiled, shut the window, and hurried to her smartphone. She wanted takeout. A clickable menu offered choices.

Interrupting her food order, her phone buzzed with notice of an email from her boss. He directed her to another source. That was unusual and worrisome.

At that moment her phone rang.

Grandma demanded, "Don't just stand there with your mouth open. Get over here."

How did she know her mouth was open? "I just woke up. Why should I run over to your place?"

"Not my place," Grandma barked. "Come to the hospital."

Outside, DeKay saw a bird with big feet push off a lollypop tree. "Why? What's wrong with you?"

Grandma did not hesitate to retort, "Not me. Your daughter."

A bright light escaped from the phone. The light fled, and DeKay found herself sitting on the floor. She did not know if she screamed out loud or just in her head.

"She's..." Grandma began.

Why did she stop? Sammy's mother wondered. Her hair started to moan.

Grandma made an incoherent start to a

reply. Then she tried again. "Burned on her legs and feet."

110.

Over another forest, black pillars twisted into clouds of ash and jargon.

What is a human being, that you should make so much of her? That every day you examine her, and test her every hour? Hide your face! Why do you eagerly pursue a flying leaf and persecute a dried-up stem?

As the masked prisoners waited on a bench, handcuffed, for their turn before a judge, Noah overheard some talk that the district attorney would release protest prisoners. But later, Noah found himself in a cage again. He wondered, "Am I not a protestor?"

Across the passage, an elfin young man with green hair gripped his bars. He stood without self-consciousness for all his strange face holes, after the police confiscated his jewelry. A guard yelled at him to put on his mask, so he did. The elf saw Noah eyeing him and offered, "It's okay, brother. We're all prisoners in here."

"What? What's okay?"

"I don't care if you're a right wing brawler."

"I'm a what?" Noah asked.

"I won't come after you, if you don't come after me."

Noah struggled to understand.

The elf continued, "I mean, like, out there it'd be a different story. I'd be like all in your face. But in here, in the cage, we're on the same side, as far as I'm concerned."

This shocked Noah. Later he learned that the police scheduled to put him in a holding cell by the airport with other white supremacists.

How could he free himself? Noah didn't want to call his wife. He didn't want to call Lourdes or his poor old mother in Arizona. He didn't want to bother Sammy. There was no one else he could call. So, he did not call.

Here and there, all along the West Coast, in the nearby Cascade Mountains, and in forests to the east and west, fires grew. Smoke drilled the sky. People began to flee their homes. Dark, smoky, mountain roads began to fill up with cars heaped with possession. The rumor drifted: Antifa started the fires. Men with assault rifles put up roadblocks on country roads. Police caught one arsonist, a mentally disturbed criminal that the state had released from prison because of COVID-19.

111.

As the forests of the American west burned,
what did the plywood armor of the courthouses
say? F — 12 and ACAB, ACAB again and
again, and BLM, and COPS AREN'T REAL
and THE FINAL OINK and STOP USING
VIOLENCE and RIDE THE WAVE, HATE =
USA and COPS LICK ASS and WELCOME
TO MEGA DOO DOO and FEMBOY
HOOTERS and CRIME PAYS, WE WON'T
FORGET and F — THE FEDS, and KILL
ALL COPS, EVERYTHING HAS CHANGED
and THIS IS THE NEW NORMAL and

CASCADE NOW, BLACK CHILDREN
MATTER, and 2020: THE YEAR WE FIGHT
BACK, YUM BACON and MAMA, ARREST
THE PRESIDENT, END CIV and R.I.P. There
was one more: I CAN'T STAY SILENT
WHILE SOME DON'T HAVE THE RIGHT
TO BREATHE.

Someone pasted a long list of names too tiny
to read. What did this list accuse? What were
the facts?[5] What was the truth?

*O walls, you have held up so much tedious
graffiti that I am amazed that you have not*

already collapsed in ruin.

The remains of a bonfire, burnt restaurant patio furniture, scorched the asphalt streets. The empty plinths displayed graffitied curses against the police. The sidewalks too had black blotches with a substance sick and sticky. The revolutionary particulates of uprise offended the nose: aerosols and volatile solvents of distress, chloro-benzal-malono-nitrile, metal salts, oxidizers, chlorine, phosphorus, sulfur...

Surrounded by flies, food trash decayed. The giant copper Portlandia statue kneeled and reached down to us as normal, but no one reached back. More campfire ash junked the park grass. That part of downtown smelled of sweat and screams, of confusion and boredom, of menace and lies, of urine and vomit... All this spread with shouts and colorfully painted plywood. Curious eyes came to see some gruesome tumult. Sirens rolled up and down the sky. The corridor of buildings echoed the thwop overhead. All over the city, windows rattled. Meanwhile, hidden, the COVID-19 virions swirled. Authorities now recommended everyone wear three masks. The virus had mutated. If you were one of those who didn't wear a mask, you must worship the feet of the Great Baboon.

Was free speech good? Yes. Was racism bad? Yes. Was the president bad? Yes. Was fascism good or bad? It was bad. There was an election coming. What about the anarchists,

were they good or bad? *Hunh? What*
anarchists? Did you mean the Wall of Moms?
BURN, Portland!

112.

On social media, the governor wanted you to
know that she was a "fierce feminist" and a
non-binary LGBTQ person (although married to
a man, unfortunately, for over twenty years —
this contributed nothing to her identity). After
discussing the challenges of the pandemic, she
turned to the topic of violence. *I will not allow,*
she answered, *armed white supremacists to
bring more bloodshed to our streets!*

A reporter asked her, what about Antifa?
What about the Pacific Northwest Youth
Liberation Front, the anarchist black bloc?

She thundered with Churchillian resolve,

"We will work with the community to make sure that folks understand that our goal here is to stop the violence directed toward property, to stop the arson, and obviously stop the person-to-person violence. Thank you, that's all the time we have today."

Finally, finally we had found a leader! Someone had the guts to speak in clear language, work with "the community" to have them somehow convey the message that the governor's goal was to stop the violence! That's all it would take to restore order, to mollify revolutionists, *conveying the message of the governor's goal!* How rude it was that the violence toward property increased. Didn't the violence-doers, whose organizations had no names, understand that a governor who was a *feminist* and *LGBTQ*[6] wanted someone to convey the message of her goal for them to do something else? Such as pinochle?

In addition, I am sorry to report that there was more arson, and more person-to-person violence. And if there was any organization or ideology behind these continued crimes, it was sadly unnamable. Person-to-person violence doers stood undisturbed as monuments of the safety with which error of opinion may be tolerated. Someone convey the message to the community! Person-to-person violence doers still didn't understand the governor's goal!

However, there was hope. Reduce meant defund meant abolish. Replace police with social workers. The governor had promised an announcement on International Pronouns Day. Was there an election coming? I'm not sure. BURN, Portland!

The mayor heard the cry and berated the police. There are no anarchists, only Christian right-wingers. For proof, take a look at the dead body downtown. This was a corpse of a straight white male supporter of President Baboon. An anarchist shot him with a .380 pistol. This dead man, before he died, wasn't he a Christian right-winger? Didn't he suffer person-to-person violence? Something something Wall of Moms?

The parking structure security camera showed the assassin as he waited around the corner, gun drawn, pure with the resolve of anti-racist justice, waiting for the straight white man who stood for… stood for what? The target wore a Patriot Prayer cap, for God and Country, whatever that meant. He was a brawler for the old values, but it was easier to call him a racist and fascist. There was an election coming.

The governor was custodian of the fierce new values and fierce new identities. The governor's inclusive ally, the anarchist, jumped out of hiding. He pointed his pistol at a human being with different views. Why? The anarchist was a person-to-person violence doer. Someone had to step up to do the hard work of progress.

Bang! The first anarchist bullet exploded the crusader's can of mace.

Bang! The second bullet exploded his heart. *Thank you, that's all the time we have today.*

He died of person-to-person *cardio bulletitis.* Shot in the chest, assassinated, he lay draining blood on the sidewalk near the corner of Southwest 3rd Avenue and Alder Street.

A bloody sidewalk downtown? Keep Portland weird! A puddle of blood on the sidewalk? "Put a bird on it."[7]

113.

The river, Time, hardly moved, as if made
stagnant. Every day was hot. Every day
smoked. Every day was boring, then nervous.
Every day was long, too long, too hot, and
irritable. Night was short, but anxious,
sometimes fearful. The crows hid in the trees by
the river to help Time roost. They were quiet. I
heard no affectionate exchange of croaks and
crooau-aucks, not a single *kreek-cricketty-coo.*
Yet, the electricity did not waver. The water
continued to flow the pipes. There was no sign
of gratitude. A young woman yelled through a
megaphone: "I'm not sorry if a f—ing fascist

died!"

Question: Since that downtown McDonald's, the bandits' hangout, closed out of business, how could anti-pioneers of the Oregon un-Trail find their sustenance? Answer: An anarchist logistics van handed out bowls of barbecue ribs to the mob with festive cheers.

"As the city fails, we, like, take over. We're winning," one anarchist cook told another.

During the day, downtown heat pooled. Mostly deserted, there were a few signs of life: cars raced on their way elsewhere. Mirages counterfeited memory of good times. A few actual human bodies lingered. They turned out to be homeless. More and more businesses were boarded up, a plywood-windowed nowhere. Some kept open, despite plywood windows. More stores posted BLM signs (please don't hurt me). A lone shopkeeper swept in front of her door. A patina spelled out the ghost word *McDonald's*. For windows it had black painted plywood. The plaza of Pioneer Square radiated heat, nearly empty. Downtown had become strange and sad.

The city's Catholic Archbishop incanted the ancient words. He gestured the gestures. He prayed the rite of exorcism over the city.

The city roiled in confusion.

Even so, sometimes the beauty of youth appeared. Fertility walked hand in hand with fertility, masked… perhaps one of them by genetic mischance was extraordinarily beautiful. *Bliss was it in that dawn to be alive, But to be young was very Heaven!* Youth still believed, with lip pulled back to catapult a sob, in a pure idea, a nation of kindness – righteous kindness, angry kindness, correct kindness. All eyes could not but turn to the emphatic clues of her radiant fecundity. Fecundity meant perpetuation. Beauty moved Time again, and meant a future.

And then Beauty departed. Every evening, the streets had two faces. During the day, protestors chanted and marched, cried and cursed. And then, late in the summer evening, when finally the rotten egg brown-yellow of night arrived, the masked bodies changed. Hooded, masked shapes in black armor collected trash, stole furniture, made a heap in the street, and set it on fire. This was just a normal pandemic evening in Portland. Experts now recommended everyone wear four masks. While three masks stopped consonants, we needed a fourth to stop the vowels. The virus had mutated.

The governor negotiated for the withdrawal of federal police from the street. State and county police would protect the federal courthouse (as the court had originally asked).

Be like water. Hooded, masked figures threw rocks at the police. Hooded, masked figures smashed windows, and targeted their fireworks right in. Hooded, masked figures lit wicks and threw bottles of petroleum at police buildings and courts. Hooded, masked figures tried to barricade the doors of a precinct. First, they squeezed epoxy into the key locks. Then they bound the door handles together. Next, they used power tools to drive bolts along the edge of the doors. There was a third step. They set the building on fire.

But of course the arsonists first made sure there weren't human beings inside. No, there were human beings inside, and the anarchists knew it. They wanted to burn them alive.

Until other police chased them away, these unhindered citizens of the pandemic who tried to burn city employees alive stood undisturbed as monuments of the safety with which error of opinion may be tolerated.

The mayor had trouble believing that anyone would try to burn police alive. He had no idea what to do about it. Who didn't want justice? Who didn't want the pain of history to end?

Not only did this attempted murder do nothing for progress, he said, it helped the reelection of President Baboon. He recalculated his ideology: the mob was *mostly* good. The anarchists responded by announcing a slogan: *No cops! No prisons! Total abolition!*

The tumult stirred up addicts and mentally disturbed. It had displaced or fed, aggravated or frightened, some citizens of the street, junkies, alcoholics, and the broken minded. Social media showed homeless fist-fighting with anarchists over territory. A homeless Black man knocked out an anarchist Native American with one punch.

It lay all hidden in plain sight. Darkness lent the illusion that the hidden corners were an exception. But they were not. Bang! Bang-Pop! A drug deal went wrong. In the parking lot of a strip club, a man lay dead. No one talked about it.

114.

The city could not keep up. Its workers
sandblasted walls and plinths of painted crude
words, coded curses, words that fudged, defund
and death, justice and the Year Zero. Workers
scrubbed, they chemically erased the angry
paint. But more rubble and trash and burnt junk
and graffiti persisted. Antagonisms under
umbrellas remained brutal and intractable. New
painted curses appeared among the broken bits
and fire stains each night. Experts now stated
that if you wore less than five masks, one over
the other, you were a racist. A sixth mask was

optional.

With day, carpenters lifted plywood to *un* the windows of more business. Unwindowed commerce was a freak-fright. Downtown, and east of the river, plywood windows sickened the street, derelict with graffiti. Bang! Bang-Pop! Another man lay dead in north Portland. No one explained why.

Once there was a bronze statue of a proud elk downtown. Natural dignity stood on a granite plinth, eleven feet high, face turned toward authority. *Presented to the City of Portland by David P Thompson. A.D. 1900,* it read on the west side. Thompson came to

Oregon in 1854, lead the territory, and became mayor of Portland in 1875. The year after he donated the elk statue, he died. *H. C. Wright, Architect,* it read. With oak leaf cornices, and, on either side, fountain water jetted from the mouths of animal faces to the octagonal pool below. The statue was gone now. The empty plinth stood in the center of Portland, smoke stained, fire cracked, painted with the circle-A and epithets. Plywood covered the lower windows of the government buildings around it.

Methodical and efficient, city workers removed the granite ruins. Surrounding the empty spot in the middle of the street was a rounded heap with a garland of rubble, like a Native burial mound. Eventually the city paved over the wound, an ugly rounded dome of tar.

The mayor made a speech. "Enough is enough," he announced. To end the violence and racial discrimination, he called on the whole city to rise up. The citizens responded, Hunh? What did that mean? Rise up how? And then what?

Near and far, people watched the speech on little screens. Each tried to think it through. Was free speech good? Yes. Was racism bad? Yes. Was the president bad? Yes. Was fascism good or bad? It was bad. What about anarchists, were they good or bad? Hunh? What anarchists? Did you mean the Wall of Moms? There was an election coming.

And then one day it all changed. Good

news! Finally! Someone would speak for the
Just, the True, the Beautiful, and Good.

It was International Pronouns Day.

On Facebook, the governor announced her
pronouns! We held our breath with excitement.
We demanded to know what the fierce feminist
LGBTQ governor would announce.

Her pronouns... turned out... to be... *she /
her / hers.*

Many, many people wept with warm
gratitude. It gave Oregon's young feminal faces
the validation they craved. It asserted the new
hegemon our institutions told them to build.
Speaking of buildings, the police in the precinct
that the anarchists tried to burn alive, surely

they appreciated the governor's pronoun instruction. The old structures must fall down to make way for the new. By the way, there was an election coming.

It was easy to forget the neglected places. The civic organism had no resource to touch every dark corner. It had no will. It had no concept to guide it. Round and round rolled the evil circus of a pandemic night in the Rose City. *O Rose thou art sick.* Time popped like soap bubbles: Bang! Pop-Pop-Pop. Bang-Pop! Who am I? Pop-Bang! Bang-Bang-Bang! Justice was coming! Amen!

115.

The anarchists announced their protest site on social media: the East Precinct, on the east side of the Willamette. Be like water.

Police prepared to thwart these plans. They gathered near the East Precinct.

But black hooded figures filtered together in the west side, in the Pearl District, near downtown, and marched with left anti-racist allies! It was a ruse.

Before the mayor's high-rise condominium, they gathered to howl and pound. They shot fireworks, and flashed lights at the windows.

Bumper wandered into the edge of this,

tarried, then backed away. He found himself in the edge of downtown, in Old Town.

Simon, standing across the street from his apartment, considered the lean man who stood sheepish in the hot, still bright twilight. Both wore masks.

With ease, as usual, Bumper spoke to the stranger first. "Are you trying to figure out if I'm homeless or not?" His voice was a little loud, in part to overcome the muffling of the mask.

By way of answer, Simon pointed. "Are those slippers?"

Bumper looked at them. "Yeah, I'm locked out." Then he leaned back and let out one laugh.

"Don't have your key?" Simon asked.

"Nope!" Bumper laughed. "Don't even have my wallet. But I'm not homeless! I had to leave in a hurry." He looked aside and, remembering something, shivered. He turned back. "I thought I'd wander a bit, and then the protest started. Are they coming this way?"

He cocked his head. From a few blocks away, came rhythmic words, militant and angry, the voice of a thousand.

As if he heard Bumper's chagrin, Simon replied, "You don't somehow have that homeless look. You seem happy. Why did you have to leave in a hurry? Was there a woman involved?"

"Well…." Bumper laughed as he rocked back and forth in his slippers. He cast his mind back and forth about how he should answer. "My wife is having an argument with a colleague. They wanted space. They caught me snooping, I guess."

"An argument? You mean, face to face?" Simon asked. He raised his voice as a helicopter roared suddenly loud. Then it faded again. "Is that wise? They couldn't have the argument over video chat?"

How could he explain Basil DeKay's sudden appearance at their house? The look in her eyes of hurt and outrage? Bumper's wife's silence in answer to her queries? Caught, trapped, witnessed, Bezz and Contessa Finger held glasses of white wine? Maskless too, they sat indoors in the kitchen nook, together?

And how could Bumper explain? Before the arrival of guests, a powder had accidently snorted itself up his nose. He had sorted through his old album collection when a packet slipped out. Snorting happened, and then he leaned in the doorway, masked and listening.

Finger said she that now, with leadership's full support, she would build on DeKay's program of Belongingnessness with a new initiative, Belongingnessness*ness* — achieved through trainings, exercises, webinars, the *schmuppression of schmopportunities schmor schmraight schmite schmen,* and conferences. Everyone in the institution needed to submit a plan to Do The Work... or... but Bumper no longer heard.

For as Bumper had leaned in the doorway, he watched the words become little fish. The fish-words rose and fell. Then they dove deep into the dark. Happily, a luminescence appeared to offer safety, a freedom from any kind of harm. The little fish rejoiced and swam toward it. When the bioluminescent stalk swished, the fish also swished. Bumper saw the great form in the murk, the eyes. A door opened in the murk, a door to a grotto of safety, with teeth to guard it. The fish followed the light as it lead them into the shelter, which closed behind them.

Bumper had left the women, and slammed the door behind him. He had stood, grinning to himself, wondering what that powder was, as he waited for it to wear off. He was feeling better when the other man arrived.

How could he explain all this through the cloth fabric that covered his mouth?

Now a bullhorn shouted and shouted again. When it paused, he wrapped up his explanation. "I had to get away. What are you doing out? Waiting for someone?"

When the amplified voice stopped, Simon replied, "Me? Yeah... I want to talk to the guy who parks his motorcycle under our window. He runs it in the morning for twenty minutes to warm it up, and it's too loud."

The chanting began again. The only part they could understand at this distance was the word, heavily stressed, *po-LEECE.*

116.

How could Simon explain? His girlfriend
was no longer new. The motorcycle noise
irritated her, not him, at a time when the State
shut her business. Meanwhile, the love-
intoxicated phase of their romance had faded.
That was okay, but now it took more work to
get along. How earnestly he hoped to fold their
relationship into something stable! But the
stress of pandemic isolation on them, her
struggling business, the claustrophobia and
overfamiliar company...

All this made him worry. The noise of the
motorcycle seemed like a fixable problem that
could ease Tejashree's distress. But this was not

the most important part, which gave him discomfort to contemplate.

He had told Tejashree, "I saw several clips on social media of angry mobs that menaced people who sat in restaurant patios."

"I saw that too." She shook her head.

"Did you see how the mob forced the people to raise a fist for Black Lives Matter?" He didn't mention the clip of the mob throwing café chairs.

She replied, "What kind of person doesn't support an end to police violence against African Americans?" Awkwardly she added, unsure and anxious to be correct, "I guess the proper term is *Blacks* now."

"Right, but I'm talking about the slogan. I wondered if Black Lives Matter meant the words, obviously true, or if it was a label of an organization?"

She looked confused.

He self-censored and did not say that people on the net claimed the Black Lives Matter website was not a civil rights movement against police abuse. It was revolutionary, a radical Black lesbian and neo-Maoist organization. Confused, he checked it himself.

He told Tejashree that he did not find anything on the BLM website that surprised him until he found their dream for the future. "We disrupt the Western-prescribed nuclear family structure…" It elucidated dreams for Black lesbians and gays, for Black bisexuals,

Black trans, for girls and women, for mothers and children… there was a lot about Black mothers...

As he spoke, Tejashree started to incline her head back.

Nowhere in their vision for a better world, he explained, not even once, did the BLM website mention a future for Black men or Black fathers. They didn't even mention the words *men* or *fathers*. They didn't spare any words to recognize the existence of, or a role for, men. "It shocked me."

Tejashree stammered something he didn't understand. The emotion rose in her face and she made a strange sound, a moan. He perceived a dangerous moment.

He stopped talking. Police far away put a knee on a man's neck and killed him. This organization exploited it for their radical purpose. In a sense, the Black Lives Matter organization unpersoned the slain man, too. He was a man. He was a father.

How horrible, to find himself in this trap of language, power, and deception. The difficulty, the responsibility of knowing this made him sick to his stomach. If he raised a fist for Black Lives Matter, or put that sign in his window, what was he saying?

After this, Tejashree avoided his eyes. He supposed she tried to avoid the conclusion that he, Simon, was a white supremacist.

It sickened him. Later they buried the topic

and were able to speak normally to each other. Unfortunately, the sounds from the street, the drums and shouts, the police megaphone, the small whumps and phsks, the heavy PUHPUHPUH overhead, pushed the topic at them. They said nothing, but it showed in the strain of their faces.

117.

As Bumper grabbed the wrong phone and his front door closed behind him, Simon left the house to see if he could do this something nice for Tejashree. As Bumper realized he stood in his slippers, without his keys, Simon resolved, if he could convince the guy to put his motorcycle just around the corner, it would help her sleep more.

"You wanted to reason with him?" Bumper asked. He blinked. Why did his eyes sting? "May I assume then that you're an optimist?"

Simon laughed. They paused at the sound of drums. They turned west.

"Where's the mob now?"

Simon gestured. "In front of the mayor's condo."

Bumper could only shake his head before a man with a straw cowboy hat and a backpack came along. Maskless, he smiled; it was a shock to see a human face, so friendly, healthy, and handsome. He looked not yet forty, with short hair under the hat. "Got five dollars?"

Bumper showed his empty palms. "I forgot my wallet."

"Don't lie to me." The man half-turned away. "I'm a human being. What goes around, comes around. Everything is changing."

His turn showed his backpack, and attached to it, a decorated little pine tree.

Simon exclaimed, "What a beautiful tree."

"Isn't it?" the man responded. He seemed no longer angry. "You got five dollars?"

"I do not," Simon told him firmly. "Everything is electronic these days. The virus clings to paper."

This made little impression on the man with the Christmas tree. He muttered something that ended, "You'll see."

The two stood idle. "Merry Christmas," Bumper told Simon, but the crowd's roar distracted them. They did not dare to stumble over the right word on a volatile topic. What was a protest? What was a riot?

The air spun, smoke visible. The man in the straw cowboy hat and backpack had not left

them. Bumper thought he'd make some
conversation. "Where'd you get the tree?"

"Over by Johnson's Creek."

Bumper wanted an explanation. "Is it
Christmas time already?"

The man with the tree turned on Bumper.
"Don't make fun of Christmas."

Bumper looked at Simon, who shrugged.
Hands in his back pockets, Bumper asked the
other man, "Do people call you Christmas
Jack?"

Simon and Bumper failed to stop their
laughs. The air had a grain. Christmas Jack
grimaced.

Simon offered: "Maybe he wants everyone,

Antifa and the police and Proud Boys, all to unite under the spirit of Christmas."

"Yes," Bumper agreed. He could not stop the song from its leap from his body: "O Christmas tree, O Christmas tree, How are thy leaves so verdant!"

The man with the Christmas tree seemed to want to smile, but then Bumper went on, "Sadly, it's not Christmas. It's summer, and unfortunately those forests are on fire. So maybe the song should go like this." Bumper sang, "O Summer tree, O Summer tree, How are thy leaves so burning!"

Christmas Jack looked away and declared, "Touch my tree," he declared, "and I'll kill you."

The stunned men flinched and looked at each other. "If I had any desire to touch the tree," Simon observed, "that cured me of it."

"Just relax, Christmas Jack," Bumper told him. "We're not going to touch your tree."

Christmas Jack darkened.

Bumper was incredulous. "You know Christmas is December twenty-fifth, right?"

"Don't even look at my tree," Christmas Jack told him. There is a creepy vowel whir in *murder*... *Ur* whirred and whirred. The ancient word *murder* went all the way back to ancient Sanskrit *mará* for death — *Knife* pierced into English from the Viking's Old Norse *knífr*...

"Go spread your Christmas spirit somewhere else," Simon told him.

583

"Yeah, go *Ho Ho Ho* somewhere else," Bumper agreed.

But it was Bumper who went somewhere else.

Simon kneeled, hands on Bumper's wound. Protestors shouted and drummed. But Bumper heard a song: *"Come away, come away if you're going... Leave the sinking ship behind..."* Lying on his back, he tried to remember. *"Come on the rising wind... We're going up around the bend."* Yes, he remembered: 1975. Platinum. Number four on Billboard. The wind rose, and Bumper went up around the bend.

118.

"The country, as if parched by the heat, had cracked into innumerable fissures and ravines, that not a little impeded our progress."
Francis Parkman, *The Oregon Trail,* 1847

Justice arrived! Here begins my epilogue. Down went bronze Theodore Roosevelt on his bronze horse. Down went bronze melancholic Abraham Lincoln. Smash went the Historical Society building. The rioters claimed it was an Indigenous Peoples Day of Rage. (Tribal authorities condemned the violence, and praised the Historical Society.) Down went bronze pioneer patriarch Harvey Scott. Down went the bronze soldier in the Lone Fir cemetery.

What were the unintended consequences of midnight statue topple? No one asked.

"Ptum, ptum, ptum!" Zoë and Tom referred me to Basil DeKay, who passed me to Contessa Finger. There was the victim-offender mediation, the face to face, the sentencing circle. The circle grew beyond me, beyond Noah, beyond Dr. Bomberger, to develop a sentence for each offender. Justice engaged the support of all participants to assist us, the offenders, in fulfillment of the terms of our plan.

In our winter meetings with Ms. Finger, we each had agreed in our separate cases to accept shame and dishonor, to acknowledge the harm and apologize, and assume four weeks of city clean-up duty. Punishment was not enough — it was important for us to hear the harm we had done, to acknowledge and take responsibility for it. Only then would the community forgive.

Bomberger cried for his punishment to begin. Finger had a problem: the two tribal administrations she contacted, forwarding DeKay's initiative, wanted nothing to do with it.

The clinics didn't want the doctor either. Bomberger admitted he was wrong about what should qualify as medical science. He agreed to resign, agreed to take responsibility, learn feather science, say anything. Contessa Finger knew that some of the homeless were Native American. Bomberger could still serve, repair and amend.

Noah had no defense. Released with other violent criminals due to the pandemic, he agreed to apologize, to hear the harm he did, to make amends.

And me? Shame and horror fell upon me. The extended forefinger, it pointed at whom? At me. I admitted my guilt too. My book was problematic because I founded it in harmful positionality. I had disrupted the wrong discourse.

For the promise of a return to the

community, someday, I abandoned my moral defenses. I toppled like a Portland bronze statue: *kerplunk.*

Some bronze statues survived, so far. Bronze Rebecca stood at her well to commemorate kindness. There were bronze statues in a Catholic grotto. Two storybook children still played with their dog.[8] In the "Bush kitsch" style, a firefighter still crushed a giant snake as he emerged from rubble with the help of an eagle. Downtown still had its abstract bronze figures, its small bronze animals such as beavers. In Pioneer Square, vandalized, Umbrella Man still poised mid exclaim, "Allow me!", without his umbrella. An artful Chinese bronze baby elephant still trumpeted on top of big mama.

At a university, York stood alone. Also, bronze Sacagawea with baby stood alone. At the convention center, bronze Martin Luther King still stood with bronze Black worker, immigrant woman, and child. The colossal Portlandia statue was copper, Paul Bunyon steel, both out of reach. Up in Washington Park, the first Sacajawea bronze still stood, a suffragists' statue. It remembered her as the first pioneer mother.

Joan of Arc was a giant in gilded bronze. On her big golden horse, she held her gold flag. She gleamed and glittered, towering over a southeast roundabout. It was a soldiers' monument, a memorial of World War One, but almost no one knew this.

It was strange to now remember, back in 2003, when France refused to join the USA in its invasion of Iraq, two men doused Portland's bronze Maid of Orleans in lighter fluid and set her on fire. They left a soot-stained monument and several empty cans of beer.

119.

As rains put out the forest fires, Contessa
Finger explained to us three problem-men,
"Restorative justice focuses on crime and wrong
doing as an action against the individual or
community, rather than authorities."

In the soup kitchen I made my apology.
Most of the afflicted wouldn't look at me. My
confession about the harm I did only bored
them. Maybe they didn't want to think about the
harm *they* did. They did not want pity, nor did
they give it. Their faces varied but most had
some sort of wear — wear from the burn of sun,
perhaps, or wind, a wind of drugs bestorming

sanity. Perhaps they despised me, or perhaps they were ashamed, but more likely they were bored, and had become strangers to any form of participation.

How could we wrongdoers make amends? The community needed so much repair. Individuals needed even more. The city's homeless, whom Ms. Finger called the *houseless,* needed help. Periodically, municipal employees tried to clean up their garbage and their forlorn abandoned possessions, but the progress of rot never rested. New trash piles, new debris, new rot and brokenness spontaneously returned. We would help.

During the breaks of my reparations work, my clean-up work in the rain, I checked the newspaper webpage for the slowly increasing percentage of vaccinated Americans. I came home exhausted. How thankful I was for the

system of reservoirs dug into the eastside
buttes, the pipes underground, the continuous
repairs and maintenance, as hot water scoured
me.

In our pandemic homes, in our beds at night,
we tried not to hear the unspeakable. Bang!
Pop-Pop-Pop. Bang-Pop! Gone were the days
of an only twelvefold increase in murders. Now
it approached a factor of twenty. I sympathized
with the social workers, hesitant to rush in with
clipboards and big, sad eyes. Pop-Bang! Bang-
Bang-Bang! Pop-Bang-Pop-Pop! A man lay in
his blood. Later that night, in surgery, he died.
No one explained. No one complained.

Every day before I put on the orange vest, I checked my powers to navigate discourse. If the Masked One ever had leant me any power of perception, it was gone. And who — or what — was the Masked One? What sort of activist lurked in the astral plane of discourse? I fought the discourse, but the discourse won.

As I hunched over the gutter in a shabby neighborhood, I appreciated the lack of judgment from the Douglas firs. These giants gave a rural feel to this eastern part of the city. By the ragged row of blue tarps, I swept and shoveled the gunk, trash, discards and needles. I bagged the candy wrappers, more needles, tape rolls, pages of days torn from a desk calendar, scented cardboard car freshener in shape of a tree, torn unused toilet paper, a wad of plastic film wrap, dry old paint can, torn length of brown cardboard, half eaten hot dog, chicken bones covered with ants, and rumors of typhoid, typhus, and hepatitis A.

I sensed *he* was near, but he kept his distance.

Did I want to give the Masked One a knuckle sandwich? No. What was his fault? Did he even exist? I agreed with him that we could learn much from the history of words. How could I know if we disagreed, since, on purpose, he refused to express himself clearly? That was okay: I had my own faults to enjoy. I endeavored to absorb Ms. Finger's mandatory counseling which taught me about my toxic masculinity, my privilege, and my need to cry more. I don't recall the details.

You see, I had perfected a method of watching the reeducation videos with my eyes open while letting my mind drift. While the jargon droned, and the cant offered to dull my wits, I thought about jokes, women, and home defense. I had learned I could not depend on the city authorities, sick with mental virus, to protect me. *Lever, pump, break action. Side by side, over-under.*

120.

Dr. Bomberger, Noah and I picked up soggy, disgusting trash from abandoned homeless camps. We reminded everyone, we had all done harm.

Noah had more or less used violence against protestors, even if he claimed it was a mistake about something else. He admitted responsibility.

Bomberger had committed acts of hate. His apologies admitted this. His word power had tried to hold up reactionary ideologies in domination over traditional Native American science, but also against just about every other minority including his own, and women. The list of victims went on from there in smaller and smaller classes and sub-classes, with ever-newer and stranger terminology.

What about the harm I had done? I had done considerable harm, if I may say so myself. Who else was it that mocked the truth and validity of the new reality? I admitted this. (*Low recoil #00 buck.*) No more jokes! Jokes were quite harmful. I (*lever*) was (*pump*) all about (*break action*) assuming (*side by side*) my (*over-under*) responsibility: When it was my turn, I stood up and bowed my head.

In a voice of shame, I admitted that my book was wrong. I understood I had written words of epistemic violence upon Basil DeKay and so

many others. By *epistemic,* Ms. Finger meant knowledge: how do we know what is real? How do we as a community agree what is real?

Had I, or had I not, questioned the communities' sense of reality? *I had.* Was this not an act of violence? *It was.*

We had declared that the emperor had no clothes. Our sentence then was to publically wash those clothes. This we did, as orange vested trash pick up. We took responsibility.

Speaking of responsibility, Portland revolutionaries marched with banners calling for revenge of fascist massacres. WE ARE UNGOVERNABLE: Why? They still refused restore to social intercourse that harmony and affection without which liberty, and even life itself, are but dreary things. The nation, perspiring, had elected a new president. As this old man took office in D.C., the anarchists smashed the windows of the party headquarters of the Oregon Democrats. They also carried a giant work of art, in the popular style of silhouette, as on a cameo ring. This silhouette offered portrait not of a lady, but an AK-47 assault rifle.

The Great Baboon smashed a banana: he rejected the election result. Social media banned him. Would things calm down now? No. Some of the baboon's followers formed a mob outside the nation's Capitol building. Crazed by Internet psychosis, one thing cheered them: the now long-established Portland principle that anyone who claimed justice was immune from law. The mob pushed into the legislature. Did the abyss beckon? "Ptum, ptum, ptum!" Later, police pushed the rioters out. Why was the pigeon arrested in Washington? For an attempted *coo*. Okay, now would things calm down?

Quietly, tactically, the BLM organization removed from their website their manifesto against the traditional family. And the anarchists? After one hundred and twenty days of street mayhem, sometimes mixed with free speech protests, the mayhem continued. Less frequently, in smaller numbers, the anarchists broke the windows of stores, of banks, of restaurants and coffee shops. They smashed up

the Boys & Girls Club, and the St. Andre
Bessette Church that served the homeless.

The mayor was angry now. What could
anyone do? The city councilors hid. The city's
District Attorney shrugged and looked politely
sad. He said his office didn't have the budget to
prosecute the arrestees. That's why he tended to
release them. Whoever claimed progress was
easy? He asked for half a million dollars to
create a Conviction Integrity Unit to scrutinize
past cases of potential prosecutorial injustice, to
repair harm against communities of color.

Since the summer, one hundred fifteen
police officers left the force. There was a hiring
freeze to prevent replacement. A retiring
detective wagged, "The only differences
between the 'Titanic' and the Portland Police
Bureau? *Deck chairs and a band."*

121.

One winter night in the Pearl District, the anarchists strolled along. As they broke store and office windows, they offered their seasonal carol: "LOOT THE STORES! BURN THE PRISONS! ANARCHY AND COMMU-NISM!" Residents came out on their balcony to watch.

"DIDN'T SEE SHIT," the anarchists advised in a chant with double-negative for tough-guy class emphasis. A resident stood behind her window and videoed them with her phone, perhaps for social media content, or maybe as the police had asked. For her reward, an anarchist threw a rock — she dodged aside — the window smashed.

Suddenly a police line blocked the way. With armor and transparent shields, they faced down the anarchists.

The anarchists yelled, "Go home!" to the police.

Residents yelled, "Go home!" to the anarchists.

Some local Black leaders asked for an end to the violence and destruction. Others declared the struggle between the police and the anarchists were battles between two different kinds of white supremacy. Still other Black voices offered praise for the anarchists — as long as they didn't damage any more Black-owned businesses.

Anarchists didn't even wait for night anymore. As soon as the new federal

administration took down the baboon's
emergency fence around their courthouse, the
attack began. That afternoon, they set the
plywood armor of the courthouse on fire. But
the flames smutted out. The armor remained.
The anarchists needed to remove that
protection. In broad daylight, one of them
swung a pickax against the plywood.

"Protect the land! End America!"

Who did this? Why was this happening?
Invisible shapes moved in a fog of justice. Was
it bigfoot? It was just not possible to see. It was
not possible to understand, and therefore did not
happen. Words fell as ash. BURN, Portland!
Don't look, but declare your pronouns. BURN!
BURN! BURN!

Again the anarchists set fire to the southeast police precinct, again to the ICE facility, again to the police union office, with homes nearby. The mayor now pleaded with the news media, not to call them "protestors."

Ex-President Baboon sulked in Florida, unseen, unheard, a president banned from the social media cartels. To queries of free speech, one replied, start your own social media. Surely anger would abate now? No! BURN, Portland! BURN! BURN, Portland! This was what passed for normal during the pandemic in the Rose City. "Ptum, ptum, ptum!"

The district attorney was busy; even if he believed in old style of punitive justice, it wasn't practical to prosecute the arrested, for so many reasons. Anyway he didn't want to. He believed in new justice, restorative justice.

Then, things improved; I mean, no, they grew worse. The police shot a homeless man, mentally ill and white. He fell dead on the lawn of a southeast park. I then saw a young woman on a southeast Division Street corner with a sign for commuter traffic: POLICE KILLED A MAN TODAY. Why didn't the 911 operator send a licensed mental health crisis therapist to respond to complaints that a man in Lents Park was pointing a gun at people?

Two thousand miles away, something bad happened, again. Portland must accept responsibility. Leftists joined anarchists to smash windows and set fires, larger fires this

time, scattered across downtown. Part of the
Apple store burned down. BURN, Portland!

Zrrp, zrrp… carpenters fixed plywood to
more windows. Zrrp, zrrp… social media fixed
blocks over more speech. It was a relief not to
hear about the outrages of the great baboon.
Key Internet infrastructures denied service to
the upstart social media that promised to allow
his speech.

PUHPUHPUH… the night air shook to
blades a-whirl. If something bad happened,
BURN, Portland! Or, if nothing bad happened,
BURN, Portland! The city found money to hire
a firm to identify systematic racism in the police
department. BURN, Portland! More businesses
expired. Why not? BURN, Portland! Yes, more

businesses put plywood over their windows. BURN, Portland!

What are the principles we live by? What are the facts? Discussion was unseemly; we already had the conclusions, so examination of data was oppression — except for the data that supports the conclusion. Without comment, the new federal administration rebuilt the courthouse riot fence. Once it was a fascist outrage; now it was unworthy of notice. The governor had no more pronouns to reveal.[9] BURN, Portland! BURN, Portland! Keep Portland Weird! Keep Portland BURNING!

122.

Bang! Pop-Pop-Pop. In the anarchy of night, a car roared. In the back seat, the shooter withdrew and rolled up the window. A man fell on the sidewalk. No protest followed. No ideology activated with angry, righteous expressions.

Bang-Pop! Bullets burst through the wall of a house and lodged in a child's room. No one explained.

Pop-Bang! A man staggered, shot in the leg. He refused help, and staggered away. Silence followed. In this case, silence was not violence.

Bang-Bang-Bang! A body lay face-down in the street. It would be racist to mention it, so shhh!

Pop-Pop-Pop! A man ran, slowed, and collapsed. No one offered a slogan or spray painted a curse.

Pop-Bang-Pop-Pop! A teenager slumped and was still. There could not possibly be a discussion.

A man with a warrant rammed his truck into a policewoman, smashing her pelvis against her patrol car. Lying half crippled, she unloaded her pistol at him. Pop-Pop-Pop! Pop-Pop-Pop! And so on, but she missed. If only she had called a social worker.

RERRRR! RooooOOOO! Fire truck after fire truck raced by. On southeast 79th street, a garment factory that made pandemic masks collapsed in flames. Security cameras showed the dim outline of the arsonist. BURN, Portland!

At Southeast 82nd and Foster, a noise made me look up from my cleanup duty. It was the redneck roar of a giant pickup truck. Four big flags fluttered from its corners: *Black Lives Matter* flag, *Anarchist Circle-A* black flag, *Progress Pride* flag, and a *Trans Rights* flag.

Bang-Pop-Bang! Portland's first quarter of 2020 had one murder; the first quarter of 2021 had twenty. *The New York Times* published an article about the Rose City mayor's anger, as he asked citizens to unmask the anarchists. Was this a right wing crackdown on social justice heroes, who sometimes went too far?

The anarchists eagerly agreed about going too far. On social media, a man in a black hood stood near a MAX train station. A blank plastic mask covered his face. The voice altered video warned, *"Blood is already on your hands, Ted. The next time, it may just be your own."*

Would fear move political decisions? In Stumptown now, terrorism was the point of the spear of progress. The mayor didn't need police protection. He had private security now, at taxpayer expense.

Normal life tried to go on. A pack of dogs fought under my window at night. That might be good material for a joke, I thought. How about this: *The decline in Portland is so bad... (How bad is it?) After I let my poodle out one night, she came back with a severed leg of a juggalo.*

Bang-Bang-Bang! Pop-Bang-Pop-Pop! In the middle of a high numbered southeast street, a man fell to his knees, then collapsed on his face. He bled from gunshot wounds. As paramedics worked on him, his heart stopped. No one explained. No one protested.[10]

Back to work I shuffled. It was difficult for

me to praise the fine clothes of the emperor. I
still believed the emperor had no clothes. It was
easier to pretend my guilt. When the minders
with their clipboards and tablets came by, I
walked with my head hanging down, my
shoulders slumped.

The homeless looked at us, bored and wary.
A few still wore masks. More and more of us
understood that outdoor masking made no
sense. But I wore a mask to hide my shame, the
shame of my dissent. At that moment, a person,
not an unfortunate, she walked her Labrador. As
we assumed the postures of our confessions, she
pulled the dog's leash, and hurried away.

Nonetheless, I took off my hat, and clutched

it to my chest. "I'm so sorry for the harm I've done." I followed her awhile, apologizing. Under my mask, I admired the legs of her piano.

Noah and Dr. Bomberger, beside me, did the same. Tears fell from the older man's eyes. I thought, "You big crybaby. You were a titan! You shouldn't have apologized. They didn't like you, but they had to respect you. Now? No one respects you now." But I knew not to say it.

Say nada, Ketman, I told myself.

Say nada: I knew I was not completely cured yet of my wrongthink. I was not yet any kind of new concept of man. Could I ever be? No. And my harsh thoughts were wrong. I knew it was Ginny, not DeKay, who humbled Bomberger.

It was good that I continued my restorative justice work. While it lasted, my punishment protected me.

That's what I thought.

Once in a while, Bomberger would weep as he picked up garbage. "I don't understand…"

We knew we all should weep. That's what Ms. Finger wanted. Dr. Bomberger didn't need to know it, he wept anyway: Ginny's lawyers demanded a rapid divorce settlement. They had started a social media account for her. She cried and discussed her traditional marriage, her pain, her silence, her unpaid emotional labor, and her quest for authenticity. Dr. Bomberger watched on his smartphone as Ginny admitted that she could never find herself in her marriage to him. Now, independent, she knew she could. Thousands of women celebrated her bravery with Likes.

Day after day, into the dark of winter afternoon, I swept the gutter. The broom handle pressed my shoulder bruise. (Some pandemic store shelves were nearly empty: all I could find were magnum shells.)

I shoveled trash into bins. I pushed portable restrooms back into place. At first it repelled me, but I grew accustomed to it. I became used to the glow of orange on my chest, the fluorescence pressing upward against my eyes. These rites of repair gave me more of a role in the city than I ever had before.

The people in their shabby tents ignored us. I tried to mind my own business, even if my

business was cleaning up around them. They
seemed to respect, or at least tolerate, the
authority of the orange vest I wore. Over time,
they recognized us despite our masked faces.
They accepted us, in some way, as part of their
community.

A dozen of them sat on their broken discards
of chairs, their overturned buckets and paint
cans, bored. I thought, as part of my penance, I
would try to lift their spirits. I could offer
artisan quality Stumptown entertainment...

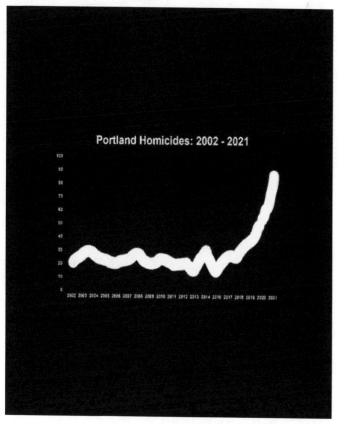

Portland Homicides: 2002 - 2021

123.

"Gentlemen," I began, "How are you? A quick announcement before my apologies. When you need to 'be like water' as the anarchists say, we put up a new portapotty right over there, on the corner of 85th and Foster... What would you like me to apologize about tonight? Politics? Religion? Airplane food? Oh, I have a good apology for you: Did you hear about that crazy guy last night that walked around naked? He didn't know better. All the animals began to run away. A raccoon jumped off a trashcan and ran. It scurried past an opossum that had no idea what was going on. Confused, the possum also ran. As they ran together, the possum asked, 'Why are we running? What are we afraid of?' The raccoon replied, 'Are you kidding me? Haven't you seen that strange animal with the tail in front?' …How's that an apology you ask? Well, I'm sorry about that joke…"

The bloodshot eyes of my audience showed interest. Where they smiling under the masks? I loosened my shoulders, paced, and tried again. I raised my hand rhetorically.

"Do we have any addicts in the audience tonight?" I asked. "Yeah? I like coffee, myself. Well, it's a way of life, …until it isn't. One night, three junkies walked through the alley on the way to do, well, their job. You all know what I'm talking about! They needed money. These guys came across an old car and stopped to figure out if there was anything of value. The first junky had something to say.

"He declared, 'Most of this is worthless! We must tear out the copper to sell for ten bucks. That will cost the owner a hundred to replace.'

"The second junky said, 'You idiot. There are engine parts here that we can sell for thirty bucks, and will cost the owner five hundred to replace…'

"The third junky declared, 'Both of you are blind. There's only one thing worth our time and effort. We must cut out the catalytic converter. We can sell it for fifty, but it will cost five grand to fix and replace.'

"Before he could say more, a pile of blankets moved within the car. Its owner and resident woke up. He sat up in the front seat, angry. He yelled, 'Get a job!' started the engine, and drove away."

Did my audience like that joke better? Did they laugh, under the masks? I'll never know, for just then a siren wailed. We all turned our heads to listen. The wails rose and fell. As they came nearer, we grew tense, we leaned away…

then the wail drifted, it fell and fell, it fell
farther away. And as it drew faint, we leaned in
its direction. Then it was gone.

Ah America! Wither art thou skateboarding!
How steep thy hill? At the speed thou goest,
canst thou still ramp, glide and slide? Canst
thou flip, after thou kickturn? Canst thou land?

Me, I was not finished. Just try to stop me, I
thought.

"Junky thieves are formidable, but one day a
bipolar guy declared he was the strongest man
living on the street, in the whole world of
streets. He dared anyone else in the camp to
come fight him: No knives, no biting; stop
when you see blood. Hearing this, two
schizophrenics and a psychotic came along and
beat him up. Afterwards, the bipolar street guy's
friends wanted to avenge him. So they asked
him, 'Did you get a good look at the psychotic
and schizophrenics that did this to you?'

"'Sure,' the survivor answered, 'They
looked like homeless guys.'"

Some cackled, or perhaps coughed. Some
shoulders moved up and down, or perhaps
twitched. Masked faces looked at me now for
more. I had another one ready…

124.

I had to shout against the mask:

"Three homeless men sat around the sidewalk campfire, much like this one…. when the first man leapt up. He had decided to brag about how tough he was.

"This is what he said: 'You know, just last week, as I was smoking my rock, a pack of dogs came into my camp by the highway ramp. Rather than lose the spark in my pipe, I had to fight them off with one hand. The spark went out nonetheless, so I had to relight it while fighting the dogs.'

"Not wanting to be outdone in manliness, the second homeless man said, 'Yeah, I hate it when stuff like that happens. Just yesterday, when I was screaming at the moon, two scratchies came to steal my stash. I had to wrestle both of them at once while I finished my moon screams.'

"Meanwhile, the third homeless man just sat there quietly. He had nothing to say as great as that, as he slowly stirred the coals with his member."

Did they enjoy that one? I believe I can say. I had more jokes, but I considered...

Ah America! Faster and faster thy skateboard rushes! Whe'r thou chooseth to backside heelflip, or backside kickflip, may thy switch frontside pop endeth in a superman grab!

My audience waited, but instinct told me my time was done. Never run the light, the stage saying goes... let someone else have a chance.

I finished with, "I have a house, but a wise man once said that our attachment to our possessions makes us, all of us, in a sense, homeless." I stared solemnly into their puzzled and annoyed gazes, then exclaimed. "Aaaa! Got ya. Just kidding. It's true. But still, am I right, a solid roof is a solid roof? You've been a great audience. Good night, Portland!"

After a moment a toothless elder stood up and began to tell a long story about a scavenging hunt in an abandoned house that that they accidently set on fire.

I had a moment, but then it was gone. The one who wears the orange vest cannot tarry.

619

There was so much more trash and debris to collect. We would return to places we cleaned up to find piles of soggy mess. Something was using us to create itself. During a break, I contemplated my sins as I tore pieces of my sandwich and tossed them to a crow. My hosanna was born of a furnace of doubt.

At night we heard Bang! Pop-Pop-Pop. Bang-Pop! Pop-Bang! Bang-Bang-Bang! Pop-Bang-Pop-Pop! The city hastened to refund its police, to try to restore the Gun Violence Task Force. So many of the victims of gun crime were Black. But the city leaders couldn't rebuild what they dismantled so easily. The

veteran officers had mysteriously evaporated.
So the city sent $200,000 to organizations that
helped women in Texas have abortions.

Time found a way to slither. Dr. Bomberger,
Noah and I could soon move on with our lives.
Our forty days of justice work were almost
done. What would happen next?

There was a flaw in the progress of our
redemption. The last step — after we had taken
responsibility and apologized, after we had
heard from our victims of the hurt we had done,
after we had performed our penance to repair
our harm, the last step remained undone. It
required the larger community to forgive us.

How was forgiveness possible? We remained a certain look, a certain way. Our privilege did not just evaporate. How could we change our identity? And frankly, much as we tried to memorize the correct theories and conclusions, and keep up to date as correct opinions evolved, it was hard to purge all of our heterodox opinions. We remained, for these reasons, unworthy of pardon. Our guilt made others feel bigger. What awaited us at best was silence. Sometimes my silence made my ears ring — or maybe it was it my Saturdays in the woods learning to fire my boom stick.

125.

First came demoralization. Then came destabilization, crisis, and finally a new normal. In the meantime, I asked to make corrections to my story. I had made errors in my scribbles about how our bronze statues came to topple over. This Contessa Finger granted me, as long as it did not take time away from my reparations labor among the trash piles.

In short, you should know that the bronze statues fell as monuments that upheld the crimes of straight white male hegemony and colonist mindset. Historical figures that past generations preserved in bronze were symbols of harm that deserved popular smashy-smash. Each one was problematical. Heroes pulled the monuments down in pursuit of liberation and a pure tomorrow. The first step was to destroy our wicked foundations. (Bang! In northeast Portland, a bus driver slumped dead on her steering wheel. There was a little round hole in the windshield.)

As I rewrote my errors to align with the approved discourse, it was hard to keep up with the truth. Truth kept changing. On Mount Tabor, and further up the empty plinth that once held angry pioneer patriarch Harvey Scott, something appeared. Furtive art commandoes pursued liberation by night for a pure tomorrow. They mounted the bronze sculpture of a Black man's head with the label, *York,* from the Corps of Discovery. History does not record what York looked like. The bronze eyes closed in dream.

I examined this mysterious York bust closely. It looked bronze but was not. It was a painted synthetic, and well crafted. It was much larger than it appeared in photographs.

This was not the first Portland recognition of York; recall that, in a Portland university, bronze York stood alone since 2010. Recall that another local university had, for some reason, removed the red-painted, scorched bronze statues of York, Sacajawea (with baby), and Clark.

Still, this fugitive gesture on Mount Tabor

delighted many; why not memorialize York here? Could this be something we stand for? Even some, who didn't approve of the undemocratic and illegal toppling of public and private monuments, thought it was a good idea to remember York this way. In fact, elected leaders in city hall said it was a reminder to hasten our work to root out white supremacy. Awkwardly, the city was 77% white.

But York upset others, who claimed a different justice. They spray-painted it in red: THEIR BLOOD IS ON YOUR HANDS, DECOLONIZE, and LAND BACK. The first step was to destroy our wicked foundations.[11]

So I decided not to mention this. The main thing you should know is that according to the approved discourse, if there was even a hiccup of disruption downtown during the peaceful protests against police violence, it was because of the provocations of President Baboon or his racist gangs. There were no anarchists really, no leftist radicals, not as an explanation for anything. Never forget the heroic Wall of Moms! No one really wanted to destroy civilization because it was imperfect. Everyone welcomed contrary opinions and honest debate! The problem was that only bad people voiced different opinions. There was no abandonment of authority and peace to a continuum of radicalism, criminality, and mental illness. There were just heroes who fought white supremacists on the streets. If any of it doesn't make sense, you could blame a ghost, or systematic racism, then no one could refute you and still be a good person.

While I corrected this book, a nihilist climbed a street pole and took apart the Walk/Don't Walk signal. Why? To advertise the impotence of authority, of course; it was anarchy that reigned. The destruction of a Walk/Don't Walk signal meant more, too. If it wasn't yet anarchy as a social system with free soup, it promised at least the liberation of time, the now of ruin, the now of trash and crime. Salvation lied in ruin. Who could disagree? Arrests were obstacles to progress when

injustice still roamed the earth. Let the wires
dangle. Thank you for helping me understand.

Official western medical terminology now
stated that *birthing persons* become pregnant,
not *women*. Was everything lost? Or was I lost?
The proclamations of scientific institutions
proved that I was, I admit, with a croak in my
voice, *worse* than wrong. I had to be
feebleminded, because I still didn't understand
it. The most important thing I learned from the
new science was to nod and not speak.

126.

While scooping up discarded clothing,
broken parts, small furniture, and torn sleeping
bags, I asked Noah about his circle of people.

(Bang! Pop-Pop-Pop. Bang-Pop! Pop-Bang!
Someone else died that day, but shhh.)

Noah told me that, released from jail, he
tried to visit Sammy in the hospital. He was
shocked to see the wartime tents in front of the
hospital, the bustle of staff in strange yellow
suits and masks. A masked security guard
stopped him: No visitors allowed.

Weeks later, they connected by video-chat.
Noah explained that Sammy first told him not
to say anything. He replied she was pretty
controlling for an anarchist. She said she
already knew what he was going to say, that
what she did was stupid. He granted this, but he
also wanted to let her know he punched that
man, he didn't know his name, she knew who,
she knew why. She heard this already and asked
how that worked out for him. Noah said, kind of
like her legs and feet. They had a laugh: they
were both pathetic cases.

Then Sammy asked he missed her mom, if
he was sad. He said yes, sad, but also confused
and angry. He asked if she was done with that
guy for real this time. She said his name was
Sperry. Sperry had asked her to give her some
of her pain drugs. Yes she was done. Was she in
a lot of pain he asked and she said sometimes.
Then she added that Noah was going away and

she was going nowhere. They were silent for awhile. Sammy said he was never a stepdad for her, so why did he fight Sperry? Noah said he was mad at himself and mad at the world. (Noah told me he knew better than to mention a male instinct to defend her.) He didn't know when or why everything went wrong.

What did she think, he asked, would it be hard for her mom if they maintained contact? Maybe, she said. They were silent for a while and Sammy said yes, the world is messed up isn't it. Some people are saying that it has to get worse before it gets better. But I don't like it worse, and there's no guarantee it will get better. So where does that leave us? Try not to make it worse, Noah said. But still, he told me, he was angry.

Later he heard that Sammy, discharged from the hospital, had moved back to her mom's Goose Hollow home. Her legs and feet recovered slowly from the gasoline burns.

Grandma had stopped visiting Sammy. Last Noah heard, on the phone with DeKay, Grandma had a sharp cough, but would hang up rather than answer questions about it. Roger wanted to come back, but could not yet due to pandemic travel restrictions.

Sammy's mother found new work promoting diversity in a large corporation, a well known name. She suffered some nervous problems after receiving the vaccine booster, which she learned not to mention. She was not currently willing to speak with Ms. Finger, who replaced her professionally, or Larsen. However, she did attend Bumper's virtual funeral. No one had seen or heard from Larsen since then.

Ginny's employers quietly ended her suspension.

Noah told me that Lourdes moved to Ashland and claimed to be content.

And Noah himself? He was not content. Basil told him she had remarried too soon. When the divorce was final, Sammy texted

Noah a crying face emoji. Noah responded with
a blue heart. But a few minutes before that, I
had seen him tear up Finger's latest list of DOs
and DO NOTs. I speculated that he was getting
used to inward feelings and outward show. I
wasn't sure what he felt now.

On the other hand, I listened with a carefully
neutral face as Noah explained to Ms. Finger
and the homeless people, as part of his self-
accounting, he only regretted he was not gay,
nor even homosexual, and Lourdes were a more
gay kind of queer, so that they could have been
gay together. He held his ribs with one hand as
he picked up trash with the other.

Noah apologized, again and again, for not being gay, for not being bisexual or even gender fluid. He wasn't even asexual. If he was anything, he was a straight white male. Unsurprisingly, as his police record showed, he was dangerous.

(Just then, a bus driver in east Portland clapped a hand to his eye. With his uninjured eye, he saw the hole in the glass before him, then the bloody hole in his shoulder.)

Noah would have to find a way to take the curse of his vicious white male heterosexuality and persist, peacefully, quietly, and unobtrusively. Cleaning up the wretched discards of homeless camps, mindful not to step on the needles nor compel the stabby motions of the most troubled, this was the humbling process he needed.

He didn't sleep well in his new apartment in high numbered streets, a less privileged eastside neighborhood than Goose Hollow across the river. At least the police had finally caught the mad woman who had been setting fire to parked cars at night.

Still, at fall of dark, the possessed screamed and cursed outside his window. Ants harvested the leaking fluid where equity disemboweled equality. Dogs barked. Sirens wailed.

"That chaos is everywhere except the wealthy neighborhoods, pal," I told him. I shook the big black trash bag. "Don't feel super special."

During a break he caught me looking over his shoulder as he read something on his smartphone. I was trying to trigger my discourse powers, but it wasn't working.

"What?" he challenged. "I can't even look at their website?"

"How are your injuries?"

"Better, but I'm not as pretty as I used to be," he added. Yes, he was less porpoise now, more a little shark-y. Maybe he had developed a little taste for transgression.

127.

And from time to time, everywhere, we heard, near and far: Bang! Pop-Pop-Pop. Bang-Pop! Pop-Bang! Bang-Bang-Bang! Pop-Bang-Pop-Pop!

Missing: Dr. Bomberger's sky; he only looked down now. Missing: His sense of humor. "Troubles are to man what rust is to iron. We do not deserve forgiveness," he told us, through his mask, with downcast eyes. He explained the latest news in science: an international team of scientists had created a human-monkey embryo, just for practice. Some day, they promised, progress would have the face of a chimera monster. Hooray! Amen.

"Hey doc, I got a new one. Listen to this." I thought I'd try to cheer up old Bomberger.[12]

But he just shook his head and walked away. He only said, "We can't make jokes."

Hmm, I thought. Maybe what we need is more belonging. Night came early in the winter. Somewhere, a siren wailed. Threat chased any belongingness away. Under a street lamp, Noah and I discussed our future as we worked. (What was brotherhood? Screw you pal. Screw me? No sir; screw you. What's on tap — you're buying.)

What would we do when we completed our penance, but no forgiveness came? *Lever, pump, break action. Side by side, over-under.*

"They won't accept us as allies anymore," Noah moaned. "We blew it. We're forever tarnished."

Just then a Black trans sex worker came by, named Starfire, and asked us if we were looking for a good time.

We knew what we had to do. Noah and I hunched, and bowed our heads, and spoke the solemn words:

"I acknowledge my privilege. I sincerely apologize," we all paused as a loud *Bang!* sounded near, "for the harm (Pop!) I have done by expressing (Pop-pop-pop!) the wrong things, and for my (Bang!) silence. I take responsibility for building, benefiting from and perpetuating a five (Pop!) thousand (Pop!) year (Pop!) history (Pop!) of evils (BANG!) upon you."

We intoned together, "I will be sure to speak up (Pop-Pop-Pop!) for those without my privilege, and not be (BANG!) silent, but always from the (Pop-Pop!) margins, in a supportive (Bang!) role, never leadership. I will never (Pop-Pop-Pop!) raise my head. I will never look (Pop-Pop-BANG!-Pop!) you in the eye, nor at a woman for more than two seconds. I will never (Pop-Pop-BANG!-BANG!-Pop!) attract notice. I will never complain. At the same time I realize that nothing I do can ever make up for my (Pop-Pop-BANG!-Pop-BANG-BANG-Pop!) privilege and the harm I have done."

Starfire's long earrings shook back and forth. "I don't know nothing about that. Y'all better finish that clean-up, then go home."

Crazy Dr. Bomberger ran over to us. Without his wife, he rolled about, unmoored. I supposed the mental arrangements he had made for marriage now decompressed into a strange, manic drive. Among the rubble of the houseless wretches and unfortunates, he had found a pharmacist's pill container.

"I know a secret way out! A way we can rejoin humanity!"

But it was empty. He held the pill container before Starfire.

Starfire waved a hand in dismissal and

strode away.

During a quiet moment, I sat down on some dry cardboard. Tired, I lay back into it. How fortunate our ancestors were to have hard lives! I wondered where the park bureau kept the damaged bronze elk statue. I wanted to see it again. But somehow my eyes had closed.

After a moment of drowsy confusion, I remember it was the last minute of the last day of school. Punishment was impossible. I sprang up. I led the way. We burst out the doors running. Cheers and shouts with little legs, we ran into the promise of summer...

I subsided on rough ground near my father and my brother. They carried stones from the field and pilled them on the edge where the trees began again. I lifted a stone and followed with difficulty. The shadows grew long and the air grew colder. First my father walked into the darkening forest, and then my brother. Alone I stood in the field with the stones. There were too many stones for me to remove before night came. My steps no longer moved me forward.

I abandoned the field. Midair, I remembered what the world had now become. The hospice would not let me see my father. Could this be real, too? Was this real? Everything seemed so normal and so strange. Had this been the truth all along?

The Masked One had changed me. I could
see, in the x-ray of the bones of my hand, the
dominant discourse glow. *Who am I? Tell me!*
Who am I? The veins of the land too glowed, as
if injected with radium. Figures moved. In the
woods, a foresaken man stood with a group of
men. All of them wore the same jacket. In the
desert, an elder apostate with long sideburns
wore a fringed jumpsuit. He hurried under giant
red dice.

No more discourse! I wanted to go home. I
suspected I was dreaming. I sat in a chair by a
fireplace with a book and a cup of coffee. There
were words on the dream page. What would

those words say? They would be words of
authority from the deep. They would surprise
and amaze. But I could not read them. I pushed
forward and focused on individual sentences.
Each word appeared in a blur. I forced clarity!
With dismay I perceived them... mere
squiggles. I chuckled, then looked behind.

I heard a familiar voice in my ear, bronze
and four legged. "Wagons, ho! Be like water.
Misery loves company, but my name isn't
Company."

*"You there, wake up! Get back to your
work."* The minder docked me an hour.

Away ecterspay auntshay
ethay estway...

Portland, Oregon

Spring 2020— Spring 2021

*Completed on the day I received the vaccine.
Afterward, the Centers for Disease Control
and Prevention redefined the word "vaccine".*

Book Group Study Questions

1. What is the story about? Trace the arc of each of the main characters. What do these patterns mean? In what way might the city be a character? What is the role of the bronze elk statue?

2. Why did Zoe and Tom take the narrator's dictionaries away in chapter 3? (Note the paragraph on "discourse" in the beginning of chapter 4.)

3. What is it about jokes that connect to the struggle over discourse? See comments about jokes in chapter 1 (fixed definitions), 82 (anchorage), 83 (perspective), two in 84 (heat, catharsis for hostility).

4. Near the end of Chapter 3, the Masked One told the narrator to make himself DeKay's subject. Did the narrator succeed?

5. Mosby Woods has said that he wrote the novel during the days of riots in Portland. He was able to do this, he said, because he based the plot on a 1959 novella by a Soviet dissident. Woods also said that he adapted some of *Fragility*'s jokes from Soviet dissident humor. What do you think of this approach?

About Mosby Woods

Mosby Woods described himself to this book's blind artist, who then drew a portrait:

Also by Mosby Woods:

A Whirly Man Loses His Turn
Oh Native Land! Bu-Bu-Bu, Miaow, Miaow
Jack O'Lantern Skull Robotnik

NOTES

[1] *These quotes come from* The Washington Post, *published on October 12 and June 8, 2018, respectively.*

[2] *Numerous county commissioners protested; some sheriffs said they would not enforce it.*

[3] George Washington serves as a kind of motif in Mosby Woods' novel *A Whirly Man Loses His Turn* (2016-2019).

[4] *Afterward, Black women protestors condemned the white women who made up the Wall of Moms for theft of the attention that* they *deserved. Was the issue about Black oppression, or something else?*

[5] *The English word* fact *comes from the Latin* factum, *an event or a deed. It appeared in the 1530s, a time of royal, religious and civil turmoil. This was the English Reformation.*

[6] *"LGBTQQIP2SAA" replaced "LGBTQ", for obvious reasons. However, "2SLGBTQQIA+" later replaced LGBTQQIP2SAA, a much-needed correction. Later, LGBTQQIP2SAA received the repair, "LGTBQIA2S+". Future improvements you may note here: _____.*

[7] *This mock-adage comes from the TV show* Portlandia (2011-2018).

[8] *These are statues from Beverly Cleary's books: Ramona Quimby, Henry Huggins, and Henry's dog Ribsy. On February 15, 2022, unknown persons defaced the bronze boy and girl, and left the epithet, "Racist B—."*

[9] *On July 14, 2021, the governor of Oregon quietly signed equity legislation that abolished proficiency requirements in reading, writing, and arithmetic for high school graduation.*

[10] *While in May, 2021, Black churches in Portland organized a March Against Murder, in August, 2021, an Antifa anarchist shot a pistol at rightists demonstrating downtown.*

[11] *Unknown persons toppled the York bust on the night of July 28, 2021.*

[12] This was the joke: *A tourist had been to many bars in his life, but now sees a cowboy bar for the first time. He wonders what's the big deal, and goes in. He's quickly disappointed. Nothing seems different except the hats. After a while, a drunken cowboy stands up and shouts, "Every Republican is a horse's ass!" There is a commotion as the other patrons clobber him, then throw him out. The tourist takes all this in, nods, and goes back to his drinking. A while later, another drunken cowboy shouts, "Every Democrat is a horse's ass!" Again there is a ruckus as the other patrons beat him up, then throw him into the street. After things calm down again, the tourist turns to the old bartender: "I don't get it. What party ARE y'all?" The bartender replied, "We're horse people."*

Made in United States
Orlando, FL
01 June 2023

33721050R00386